VOWS FULFILLED

DUBOIS-ARAZI FAMILY NOVELS
BOOK THREE

UNOMA NWANKWOR

KEVSTEL PUBLICATIONS

I'm thankful to God from Whom the gift comes.

To Kevin, Fumnanya & Ugo
To my beloved mother, Amama
I miss you like crazy, and I love you. Always & forever.

ACKNOWLEDGMENTS

To my Lord and Savior Jesus Christ. I thank you for paying the ultimate price that I may have life and for your grace which I do not deserve. Thank You for the gift of writing and I humbly pray I continue to be a vessel in this journey.

To my dad and mother in-law, *Daalu.* Thank you for your constant prayers and words of life, courage, and hope upon me.

To my readers, author friends. Special shout out to my sister writer friend, Rhonda McKnight... thank you, thank you. Sometimes support doesn't always come from the people or places you expect but trust in God and He will send the right people to you.

NOTE FROM THE AUTHOR

Hey there!

We're headed back to my first FICTIONAL town, Tweede Kans Cove. This town, although fictional, borders the real city it was mirrored after: Ifrane. The cultures and traditions are based on facts although a little loose. There's enough given in the book that will ground you. However, I highly suggest you go here to read about the town.

When we were first in Tweedes, we learned about Yasmine and Kojo in A Promise Fulfilled. Then Mustafa and Zaina in Destiny Fulfilled. Now we get to read about the baby of the DuBois-Arazi pack; Salma DuBois-Arazi

As usual, most of the languages, Arabic (which is never capitalized), French, and Yoruba can be contextually deduced. However, all translations are in the glossary.

Without further delay...enjoy!

Unoma

PRAISE FOR UNOMA NWANKWOR

"Whew! Unoma's characters were so real. They were honest, flawed, vulnerable, stubborn and saved by grace. I love when Unoma uses Africa as the backdrop for her romantic settings. Her spiritual message was clear: God's mercy and grace. Look out the Jamieson men, the Danjuma Brothers have arrived!!!" ~ **Pat Simmons, Award-winning author of the Guilty Series.**

"I love how Unoma Nwankwor weaves the distinctive, spicy flavor of West Africa into her novels. I feel right at home with the food, pidgin English, quirky expressions, and cultural norms. I'm also enjoying watching her grow as an author. **~Sherri L. Lewis, Bestselling Author and Missionary**

Nwankwor adds more depth with the cultural nuances that could be a roadblock or a gateway to understanding. She expertly intertwines all these elements, including faith lessons, to make a tightly woven story for a reader's enjoyment. ~ **USA Today Review of An Unexpected Blessing.**

"Unoma's writing reads effortlessly. There is the perfect infusion of faith and international flavor. Readers are quickly swept up on a romantic literary adventure. **The Christmas Ultimatum** is a great read for anytime of the year" ~ **Norma Jarrett Essence Best Selling author of Sunday Bruch**

"**When You Let Go** is a true testament of the power of God within ourselves and our marriage. Although we are tested every day, it is up to us to lean on our faith to get through those difficult times and offer forgiveness to those who may have hurt us in the process. Amara and Ejike's faith was tested throughout this novel but once they learned to put God at the forefront of their household, they were able to weather the storm." ~ **Diva's Literary World**

PROLOGUE

Grandma Olly's Birthday Party
(Destiny Fulfilled)

Salma's skin prickled and the hairs at the back of her neck stood. She let out a low breath. An irritated one, but low all the same. After all these years, she knew exactly who had just entered her space.

Yasmine's question confirmed it. "Isn't that Qasim?" her sister asked. "I didn't know he came with Qadir."

Salma's heartbeat accelerated as she cautiously turned. She watched the man who had caused her so much pain search for her with his eyes. Qasim Adesina stood in the distance with his older brother, Qadir.

Annoyed though she was, Salma couldn't deny the fact that God had taken extra time on that man. Before his eyes locked with hers, she did a slow sweep of his body. His six-foot, three-inch frame was clad in a burgundy, traditional dashiki set with metallic gold embroidery. The color contrasted perfectly with his dark skin. The beautiful skin that made her stomach do backflips from the memory of its feel against hers.

Blinking away the thoughts of years ago, Salma continued her inspection. His body was still the beauty of flesh she remembered. Each muscle looked chiseled to perfection, a clear indication that the gym was still one of his favorite spots. Qasim ran his tongue briefly over his full lips and she let out a breath. At that moment, his dark eyes held hers and his legs moved towards her. Not wanting her sister to be privy to how much this man irked her nerves, Salma began to walk towards the house.

"It's time to present Grandma with her gift. Let's go," Salma ordered.

She was a few feet from her destination when Qasim blocked her path. She knew that if she did or said what she really wanted to, they would end up causing a scene. Qasim was the most laid-back man she knew, but he was still a man, Black and African.

His presence consumed the air around her. She found it difficult to breathe. He still had that power and she hated it.

"Hello, my Star," he said.

Salma raised a brow and shook her head. The nickname he had given her years ago still had the power to make her weak in the knees. But she wasn't going to let him distract her from the matter at hand. "Why did you come?"

He shrugged. "Your brother invited me."

She shook her head. "This isn't a good idea."

His brow rose. "Why not? So you can keep seeing Hamza Alami?"

Salma's eyes bugged and anger surged through her veins. *How did he know about him?*

Qasim placed both hands in his pockets and leaned against her ear. When his lips met her ear lobe and pulled gently, she shuddered.

"Time's up. Time to come home."

Infuriated, Salma bumped his arm and walked off. *I wish I could wipe that stupid grin off his face.*

A few minutes later, Salma stormed into the study of her grandparents' home. She paced in front of the oak table where, as a kid, she always sat next to her grandfather, eating cookies while she waited for him to read her a story. It was the same place she came to as an adult to feel his spirit and now, to get herself together. She turned to the sound of the door creaking and saw her sister, Yasmine, standing in the doorway.

"Are you okay?" Yasmine asked.

Salma didn't want to make this a big deal, so she did what she had done since that infuriating man turned her life upside down.

"I'm fine, Yas, I just needed a minute."

Yasmine walked closer. "Are you su—"

"I am. I needed a minute. I got it." Salma took Yasmine's hand and ushered her to the door. "Now let's go give Grandma her gift."

She could feel the doubt radiating off her sister, but kept walking anyway. Qasim was not a topic that was open for discussion – not today, not ever...again.

CHAPTER 1

*S*everal months later...

Salma stifled a gag as the omelet she ate earlier threatened to make an unwelcome appearance. The faint odor of rubbing alcohol and bleach mixed with too much disinfectant tied her stomach in knots. But not nearly as tightly as the reason she was sitting in the doctor's office—which was something she never wanted to do. Yet here she was, waiting to be seen at a specialist's clinic in Rabat, Morocco's capital.

"God is my refuge and strength, a present help in times of trouble. Therefore, I will not be afraid." She murmured Psalm 46:1, then turned to her sister. "Yas..." Salma whispered under her breath.

In a flash, her big sister, Yasmine, was there beside her. Two days ago, Salma had called her in distress. Without hesitation, Yasmine left her own family in Accra and quickly came to the rescue. Even though Salma usually resisted Yasmine's maternal presence, today she welcomed it. Ever since they were orphaned at a young age, one thing had stayed the same – Salma relying on Yasmine for strength.

Yasmine furrowed her brows. "What's wrong? Does anything hurt?"

"No, I feel fine," she said, her voice shaky as tears streamed down her cheeks.

Yasmine cocked her head to the side and raised an eyebrow. "Sally, if you don't wipe your face, I'm calling the whole family. You act like you've been given a death sentence."

Salma sighed and wiped away the tears on her face. Although she knew Yasmine was only trying to bring her out of her funk, her sister also knew how she felt about threats.

Salma rolled her eyes. She detested that stupid nickname her family insisted on calling her. "Don't you—"

"There goes my feisty baby sister..." Yasmine's phone buzzed interrupting Salma's response.

A quick glance at the phone told her it was her brother-in-law, Kojo Sarbah. When Salma called for her to meet her in Rabat, Yasmine asked no questions. Despite having two older kids and a nine-month-old baby at home, she hopped on a flight. However, Salma didn't want any unnecessary drama for her sister, so she allowed her to tell her husband it was a health emergency. Unlike their older brother, Mustafa, and her twin Omar, who would've insisted on tagging along immediately, Kojo gave them a two-day deadline. If they didn't provide an update within that time frame, he would tell the whole family what was happening.

As Yasmine reassured Kojo that she was fine and that they were waiting on the doctor, there was a knock on the door. Yasmine said her goodbyes and took her seat on the chair in the corner.

"Ms. DuBois-Arazi, I have the results and it confirms what I told you when you arrived earlier," Dr. Sanjay said.

The older man put up some films against the illuminated light and walked over to her on the examination table.

"But Doctor, I can feel it." She lifted her hand and touched the mass on the side of her left breast.

"And I don't doubt that, but it's not cancerous. Here...raise your arm," he instructed.

Salma's lips moved in silent prayer as the man felt around the lump she felt a week ago. The one that stopped her in her tracks and made everything at that moment seem inconsequential. The one that made her do an inventory of her life and not find everything as she had envisioned. The one she thought God was using to get her attention.

She had rushed to her doctor in Tweede Kans Cove, her heart pounding with fear. Without waiting for him to conduct whatever tests he wanted to conduct, she frantically booked an appointment in Rabat with a breast cancer surgeon, then called her sister.

"The accident you had a few years ago—"

"Two years ago. My ribs have since healed, and I've been fine." After an accident returning from Marrakech two years ago, she'd suffered broken ribs, but hadn't had problems after they healed.

While asking about details of the accident, Dr. Sanjay continued to feel around the area where she noticed the small lump. Salma furrowed her brows. There was nothing special about the accident. She was on her way back from a warehouse to check out some supplies when she was rammed by another car at the light.

"Well, body trauma can affect the lymphatic system and that is what this feels like. A swelling in the node due to some form of bodily trauma," the doctor said.

Salma's eyes darted toward Yasmine. The hope she had in her eyes was something Salma wanted to feel for herself, but in her case, something always went wrong, so she needed to be sure.

"Are you sure?" Salma asked, studying the doctor's body language.

If there was even a sliver of doubt in his eyes, she'd book a trip to New York for another opinion. Nothing was going to catch her off guard if she had anything to do with it. Ignoring her question, the doctor went over to a drawer, pulled out a syringe and tore the packet. Next, he felt around the small mass. She winced as he rubbed the area with a cold alcohol swab.

"You're going to feel a little pinch. One, two, three…"

Salma closed her eyes as the needle went in. She didn't open them until she felt the foreign object leave her body.

"Look," the doctor said.

Salma stared at the yellowish liquid in the syringe.

"See, it isn't breast cancer. It's a buildup of lymphatic fluid that was caused by a blockage. Feel it."

From her peripheral, Salma noticed her sister walking closer. Salma touched around the area and her eyes pooled with tears when she couldn't feel anything. Over the last several days, she had played every possible scenario of how she would live her life if she was indeed diagnosed with cancer. Going down the rabbit hole of Google, she knew that being thirty-five years old didn't exempt her from the often fatal disease.

"It's not there, Yas. Touch, it's not there." Salma pulled Yasmine closer, and the doctor stepped back a little bit.

Yasmine felt the area she had prayed over this morning and pulled Salma in for a hug. "Thank you, Jesus. Thank you."

"From what you tell me, you seem to be stressed. I know you said you have a big event coming up, but…take some time to relax, breathe, and enjoy what's around you. Isn't there something you enjoy doing apart from work?" Dr. Sanjay asked.

Salma pondered the doctor's question. As the director of guest services and activities for her family's resort, her days were packed. Maintaining top notch service and ensuring customers had the ultimate experience when they stayed at Grand Amour Luxury Resort and Spa was her goal and took priority over most things. However, if she was being honest, she limited her play time because everything she loved was shared with one man.

Qasim Adesina.

For four years, she'd borne her soul to him. So yes, there was something she enjoyed doing apart from work. But those were things she hadn't done since the man she did them with tore them apart. Or she pushed him out of her life. Either way, he was no longer there. Despite Qasim's warnings that her time was running out, she hadn't seen or heard from him in months. They had known each other for nine long years, but for the past five of them, they'd been stuck on a wheel that never stopped spinning. But now, all she wanted to do was get off.

~

*L*ater that night, Salma laid her head on Yasmine's lap as they curled up on the oversized sofa in their hotel suite. Her eyes were focused on the television in front of them. No matter how much Yasmine tried to update her on the series they were watching, her mind wouldn't settle down. Despite the physical distance between the sisters, they still tried to maintain some of the traditions they were used to. One of them being watching a television series together, currently *Good Girls* on Netflix.

Salma enjoyed the feel of Yasmine's fingers in her hair. Her sister tucked her black, shoulder-length tresses behind her ear as she fussed at the anti-hero of the show.

"Do you ever miss her?" Salma asked. The events of the last several days made her ponder on things she'd since relegated to the back of her mind.

"Who? Mama?" Yasmine asked, picking up the remote to pause the program.

"Yes..."

"I guess sometimes. I miss the way she used to take us to the market, the stories she told as she washed our hair—"

Salma sat up. "Do you remember those baskets she weaved and the sfenj she rewarded us with..." the doughnut-like fritters used to be their favorite snack as kids. "...when we remained absolutely quiet so as not to rattle *that* man."

That man was their father, Ahmed Arazi. He shattered their lives when he killed their mother in Salma's sixth year of life. His actions resulted in him dying in incarceration, and she and her three siblings becoming orphans. It wasn't until their grandparents—whom they didn't even know existed—rescued them from the orphanage that their situation improved.

"I do miss her. We all do, I guess." Yasmine shrugged. "It took me a while to come to terms with how that trauma has impacted my life, so I try not to think about it too much and appreciate the good things in my life." She turned her gaze to Salma. "What's wrong? You're usually the one who has everything under control."

Salma gingerly tucked her legs underneath her and turned to face her sister, the corners of her mouth barely lifting in a sad smile. Through years of effort, she had created a strong exterior of sass and confidence, shielding herself from any situation that might make her appear vulnerable. Her mother, Bella DuBois, the woman she despised, was the reason she was this way. Her whole life, she had forgone anything that would remotely have her in a weak position, all because she was determined never to be as weak as the woman who gave birth to her.

"I try, Yas. I really try to replace my bad memories with good ones, but I dislike her. The more time that passes, the less I miss her, but my dislike for her doesn't seem to fade." Salma shook her head. "I love her on some level, but I really don't like her. In fact, I resent her, and I don't want to feel this way."

"You sound like Musa—"

"No, our brother blamed himself for not protecting mama from our father. I don't blame myself. I blame nobody...but her. She was an adult. She should've taken us out of that situation." Salma stood and began to pace the length of the hotel living room. "Do you remember Evans?"

Yasmine squinted, trying to remember. "Your high school boyfriend?"

"He broke up with me because I didn't cry enough when I

caught him with another girl." She folded her arms across her chest. Turning her gaze to her sister who had a perplexed look on her face, Salma shook her head. "What about Sanders? The college boyfriend...he broke up with me because I—quote—was too masculine. He wanted someone soft spoken..."

"Sally, none of those men deserved you. They—"

"Oh, I know that, but did they lie though? Who wants a woman who makes them feel emasculated? Who wants a woman who seems unbothered when her man cheats...I mean."

Yasmine jolted from the sofa. "Stop this right now! There's nothing wrong with you. You don't have cancer; you're still breathing and living. What happened is in the past. You can take charge of your life again; trust me I know. But what you're not going to do is make it seem as though something is wrong with you! Stop."

Salma fell into her sister's arms. She hated this feeling and had worked so hard to ensure she never came across as weak. "Sometimes, I get tired of being strong."

"Then don't be. Be open and God will send someone to you."

"He already did and because of her, I fumbled that too."

"Who? 'Sim?"

Salma stepped back at the mention of Qasim's nickname. Her eyes bugged at her sister's words.

Yasmine laughed and dragged her back to the sofa.

"What, you think I'm stupid? I knew when you guys claimed to be friends that there was something more. You were so smitten when you talked about him until you just stopped. After you remained tight lipped, I assumed you guys called whatever you were doing off. Besides, you were off limits. He's Omar's friend and Mustafa and Qadir have business together."

Salma looked at her sister. Guilt crept up her spine. Everything her sister said was true except for one minor detail.

Yasmine was right though. It was never too late to start over. Her clean bill of health made that more obvious than before. To do that, she needed to come clean.

"Yas, I need to tell you something."

Salma began to tell her sister how she lost the one person she knew was her **one** because of the issues she had over her deceased mother.

~

Ignoring the buzzing phone in one hand and steadying her shaken mint tea in the other, Salma clung to the laptop under her arm. Reaching the back elevator which led to the executive offices of Grand Amour Spa & Resorts, she used her elbow to press the up button. Yasmine's third call could wait a few more minutes until she got to her second-floor office. Having only finished her first meeting of the day, Salma had a few more to go and didn't have time to go home for a change of clothes if her white on white ensemble got stained with spilled tea.

Riding up in the elevator, she made a mental note to visit her grandmother when she got off work. It was either that or she was sure the matriarch of the DuBois-Arazi clan would make good on her threat and show up at her door. One week had passed since she got back from Rabat and two weeks since the initial doctor's visit in Tweedes that made her decide to distance herself from her family.

With Mustafa as CEO and Chairman of the resort and Omar as Food and Beverage Director, they both had out of town engagements, so she was able to move around without worrying about running into them in person. The main challenge was avoiding contact with her grandmother.

Setting her stuff down, she powered on her laptop and picked up her phone just as it began to ring again.

"It's Monday, Yas. I'm working," she said.

"And that's why I'm calling. I thought you were supposed to be relaxing?"

"I have work to do." Salma had a long list of items she needed to attend to. It was early May and in eight months, the end of the year frenzy would roll around. Christmas was the busiest time of the year for the resort. For the past five years, she and her team had organized and put on a different theme for each year.

"Why do you think you can harass me into doing what I don't want, but I can't do the same to you?"

Salma laughed. "I got it like that."

She picked up her tea, took a sip and peered at the screen. Her sister was in her little son, Enam's nursery, tidying up. Motherhood had always looked good on her, even after she was widowed. But now that she had reunited and married the love of her life, creating a blended family, Yasmine was glowing, and Salma loved it. Her stepson, Kwame and her daughter, Anisa seemed to give her an additional purpose. There was a time when all she did was coast through life.

"Where is my little munchkin?" Salma asked.

"With his dad downstairs. The other kids are in school. I took the day off to tidy up around here and get my house in order."

Salma frowned. "Where is your cleaning crew?"

Grand Amour had four locations across Africa, from the western to eastern and southern coasts, with their headquarters located in Tweede Kans Cove in the north of the continent. As General Manager and Director of Operations for the resort, Yasmine was just as busy as Salma was. She moved to the Ghana location once she got engaged. KJ, as the family called him, was an award-winning music producer and owner of New Sound Records. Formerly a member of the now retired neo soul gospel group, 891 Crew, the world knew him as 'Keyz.' Although she still visited Tweede Kans Cove often, Salma missed her not being next door to her. At work and at home. The DuBois-Arazi siblings all had villas that were close to each other and a few miles away from the resort.

"They'll be here tomorrow, but it doesn't mean the place has to look like a pigsty." With a basket under her arms, Yasmine stood to face the camera. "Are you sure you're okay, Sally? I've never seen you act as shaken up as I did last week."

Salma thought about it for a minute. Was she okay? She should be, but there was now a nagging feeling she had every morning when she woke up. Sometimes, she felt empty, unfulfilled, like she was missing a part of her. Whatever it was, she wanted it to pass so she could go back to being the Salma she was used to being.

"I'm fine. I promise."

"Are you going to tell Musa and Omar about what happened?"

"No, why should I? Nothing came of it."

"True...I know you told me not to stress it, but you know I can't act like you didn't drop a bombshell last week. Have you talked to Qasim? When are you going to tell Musa and Omar?"

One thing her sister was good at was staying out of people's business. Salma loved her for it, however, once you invited her into your business, it was hard to get her out until the matter was resolved.

Salma sighed. "Not yet. I promise I will. Can we drop it?"

"Sally, I don't want this to blow up in your face."

"And it won't. Qasim isn't worried about me, and I have this big thing I'm working on. I need to give it all my attention."

"From what I saw during grandma's birthday, that's far from true, but this needs to be resolved for you. Starting over...remember?"

After reassuring Yasmine again that she was going to handle it, Salma shifted them to other topics before her sister took the hint and landed back on business.

"Fair. So how is the Guest Excel Program coming along?"

"I thought you were taking the day off?" Salma smirked.

Yasmine waved her off.

Salma was glad Yasmine agreed to steer the conversation in a different direction and began talking about the Guest Excel Program that both departments would work on. The program was mainly created by Salma, as part of a mandatory training for all who worked with guests, but Operations had an important role to play as well, so Salma and Yasmine decided that both teams should cooperate on this project.

Several minutes later, after the sisters threw a few more ideas around, they shifted the conversation to the family. They tried to decipher who the woman was that was taking up Omar's time. They knew she had family in Tweede Kans Cove, but weren't quite sure of their relationship status. She seemed to pop up then disappear just as fast. Then they moved on to Mustafa, particularly empathizing with how nervous he was now that Zaina, his wife, was pregnant. Something about Zaina announcing her pregnancy turned him into mush. He hated them pointing that out.

"I mean he's still grumpy, but that baby is doing something to him." Salma laughed.

"Wait until it's your turn."

"And that's my cue to get ready for my next meeting."

Salma's hand instinctively moved to her stomach as she thought of her past and future. She wasn't against love or family, but was apprehensive about getting hurt again. The man she had loved had broken her heart and set a seemingly impossible standard for others. That made her angrier at the man who turned her life upside down.

"I'll let you go because if KJ yells my name one more time, we're fighting." Yasmine yelled back, telling her husband she was on the phone. "I know you don't wanna talk about it again...but tell Omar what happened between you and 'Sim."

Salma scoffed. It was easy for Yasmine to say, but she wasn't ready for the war that would ensue between the Dubois-Arazis and the Adesinas once everything was out in the open. Things were never supposed to be this way. Now, for the second time in not so many weeks, she really was ready to get off the merry-go-round she was on. Holding everything in over the years had been a hassle. However, letting it out might just prove to be worse. After a promise to call her sister over the weekend, Salma hung up the phone. As she set it down, it buzzed again.

Hamza: Good morning beautiful, I trust you had a pleasant night. Are we still on for tomorrow night?

Salma read the text over and over. Out of all the men she'd gone out with through the years, Hamza Alami, owner of Harmony Winery, was the one who could possibly compete with Qasim. Since love triangles weren't her thing, she needed to contact Qasim. If he wasn't tired of their status quo, she was. After she mulled over the situation, she decided a delicious meal and fine wine wouldn't hurt. She smiled and replied.

Good morning, yes, I did. Of course, we are.

She swiveled her chair to face the huge window that gave her a serene view of the Atlas Mountains. Leaning back, she savored the rest of her tea. The view was the best feature of her office. The mountain would soon be capped with snow, but now its lush, dark green peaks provided a picturesque view that she'd never get tired of. Her fingers stroked the gold cross necklace her grandmother had given her years ago as the story of Moses and the burning bush floated through her mind.

"Remember God is never far away," her grandmother had said as she clasped the necklace around Salma's neck. "But if you need Him, you must call out to Him."

Knowing that and doing it were completely different things. For the umpteenth time in the last few weeks, Salma wondered if the unease that had been simmering inside her was God trying to get her attention. A sudden ding from her calendar jarred her back to the present. Dissecting whether this was her burning bush moment, or thinking about the person she knew deep down was responsible for the fire, would have to wait. Now, duty called. It was time for her next meeting.

CHAPTER 2

"If you clench your jaw any harder, you're going to crack a tooth."

Qasim Adesina closed the Instagram app and stuffed his phone into his pocket, ignoring his older brother, Qadir's burning gaze. He didn't want to listen to another lecture about how everything would be okay soon. He shouldn't even be in this situation in the first place. For five exhausting years, he'd given up parts of himself for his family. All he got in return was thank you for "sacrificing for the family."

"I know you don't want to hear—"

"*O tọ.* You're right. I don't."

Qadir made a low sound indicating his frustration. But before he could utter a word, his phone buzzed again, providing Qasim with the needed interruption. Qasim kept his eyes on the highway while their driver navigated the roads of Lagos Island. They sat in the back of a 2023, black-tinted, bulletproof Land Rover Range, trailing behind an equally bulletproof tinted Mercedes ESQ SUV with his parents, Chief and Chief (Mrs.) Adesina, inside. The convoy was completed by two other similar decked out SUVs with their security detail at both ends. Over the years, it had become normal for him to experience this level of security as an Adesina, yet two things remained: it was exhausting, and he was tired of it.

"You've been in a foul mood since Morocco. Mummy thinks you need a wife, daddy is worried and frankly, it's getting on my nerves," Qadir growled. "You know what you need to do, but since you refuse to do it, please can you not let whatever it is you saw on social media bother you while we are here."

It was Wednesday morning and currently, the brothers and their parents were heading to Helping Hearts, the million-dollar, state-of-the-art clinic owned by their father's doctor, Dr. Jabir Danjuma. However, the visual of Salma DuBois-Arazi with another man's arm snaked around her waist with his lips on her cheek wasn't a sight Qasim could put on the back burner until he felt like thinking about it again. But Qadir was right. He needed to get himself together.

His mother was starting to hint at him finding a woman. To her credit, she didn't hound any of her four sons about it. And as much as he resented the decisions of his father that messed up his life, he didn't want the man worrying about anything. The time when his dad had to have open heart surgery years ago was the scariest moment the Adesinas had ever had to endure. The possibility of the patriarch of the Adesina clan leaving this earth was a humbling experience for them all.

Recently, his father had been having heart palpitations and at his mother's insistence, the family had left their base in Ibadan, boarded their jet, and made the forty-minute flight to Lagos to see his doctor. The heart surgeon was the one who performed his father's surgery and had been responsible for his care ever since. Dr. Danjuma's reputation preceded him, so they were all comfortable with the surgery being performwed in Nigeria instead of London where the family had a second home.

Several minutes later, Qasim settled into a white chair in the doctor's office, looking around the room intently. His brother, Qadir, was on the other side of the room while their mother kept her hand clutched in their father's grip, providing a comforting presence their sons were used to seeing from her. Suddenly, the door creaked open and Dr. Danjuma stepped inside wearing a white coat and holding a clipboard. The doctor smiled at them all and Qasim felt himself relax slightly. After greeting them, the doctor turned to their father.

"Chief, you're fine," he said.

Qasim watched his mother's shoulders visibly relax as she let out a sigh. His father was the strongest man he knew, but even the great Qavi Adesina couldn't camouflage the relief and joy that danced in his eyes at the doctor's announcement.

"Your recovery continues to remain in line with expectations. Although I still recommend you remain as stress free as possible." Dr. Danjuma's eyes darted from Qasim to Qadir before returning to their father. "I trust Qadir and Qasim here are doing everything to ensure that you have limited contact with the business."

Qadir verbally affirmed the doctor's assumption while Qasim responded with a head nod. Over the years, the doctor had become quite familiar with all of them. Qasim and Qadir had even met the doctor's brothers a time or two. So, he was privy to how hard their father worked and what he and his brother had been doing to relieve him of a lot of his duties.

"They are. But Doc, I can't just sit idle. Sit around doing nothing," their father fussed.

All of them chuckled. Qasim shook his head. The problem wasn't that he wasn't allowed to work; the problem was that when they did allow him to do a few things, he ended up doing a lot.

"And I'm not saying you should. But I need you to take a step back from the busy. You're retired. Find some other hobbies that would occupy you. Leave the business to these guys."

Dr. Danjuma paused then looked over at Qadir, then his eyes landed on Qasim. "What happened to London?"

"Don't ask." Qasim shook his head, his eyes darting to his father.

His father grunted and his mother shook her head.

Earlier in the year, they all agreed as a family that his parents would spend more time in their London home. That didn't last three months before their father was itching to return home. Why his father couldn't be content with an extended vacation with their mother, Qasim would never understand. If he were given a chance to be with the woman he loved, he would do it in a heartbeat. Circumstances beyond his control kept him from Salma, but after seeing her in Tweede Kans Cove some months ago, he wasn't sure how much longer he could last. Especially after the picture he got this morning.

Qadir thought he was stalking Salma's page on Instagram, but that was far from it. He was sent the picture. Now that his father was given a clean bill of health, he needed to get back to Ibadan so he could dig deeper into what his lady was up to now.

Three hours later, Qasim reclined in the leather seat in his office and scanned the figures that stared back at him on the screen. As Chief Financial Officer of the family-owned farm, Ilẹ Oloro Farms, his days were never void of activity. Monday morning was when he liked to get an update from his assistant, Anita, about any financial abnormalities that he should be concerned about. But nothing about the week was going according to plan.

On Monday, he and Qadir, who was the Chief Executive Officer of the farm had an impromptu meeting at the state capital. One that ended up taking up most of the day. The day before, Tuesday, he had to attend a one-day convention in Abuja in place of one of his managers who couldn't make it at the last minute. If it weren't for the importance of the topics being covered, Qasim wouldn't have bothered. However, learning new ways to mitigate risks brought on by recent market fluctuations was one of his main focuses for the rest of the year. Implementing hedging instruments, diversifying product offerings, and establishing strategic partnerships would go a long way in minimizing the farm's exposure to market risks.

Ilẹ Oloro Farms was made up of eighty-two acres of farmland for crop cultivation, forty acres for livestock farming, twenty acres for value added processing facilities, eight acres which hosted affordable housing for low level staff while the offices sat on two acres of land. At a total of one hundred and fifty-two acres, the farm was the largest in West Africa. Having been in the family for four generations, it was the Adesina legacy.

A legacy Qasim had put his life on hold for.

"Sir, I know we gave the supplier an extension, but that has passed. What would you like me to do?"

Bringing his attention back to the matter at hand, Qasim idly stroked his low, well-manicured beard. "Call the supplier. There's no way they can keep hiking up the price of the fertilizer, but still be late on delivery. We have a business to run. Tell Samson I said one more delay and I'm breaking the contract," he said. "I've been more than generous; he needs to fix his supply chain issues before our next shipment, or be ready for my next move."

His next move was bound to cost the farm money, and someone was going to pay for it. Most of the people he did business with knew not to get on his bad side. Why Samson wanted to take a ride on the wild side was anyone's guess.

For the next several minutes, Qasim and Anita worked on strategies for suppliers that were proving to be problematic. Next, the finance manager joined them and provided information on the research he and his team had done on analyzing the factors responsible for the market fluctuations they had been noticing. The changing supply and demand dynamic, shift in global trade, and new technologies weren't things that would go away anytime soon. So, while the manager talked, Qasim ruminated about the steps he needed to discuss with Qadir and eventually implement. The continuous unsteadiness of the market had the potential to affect the bottom line of the farm if something wasn't done quickly.

~

*L*ater that evening, Qasim opened the door of his home. Not bothering to wait until Qadir entered, Qasim walked back through the living room of his six thousand square feet home and retook his position in front of the stove in his kitchen. He had left the office a few hours ago, made it to the gym, showered and was doing what helped relax his mind – cook. Turning the spiced shrimp in a bowl, he set the pan back on the fire as his brother walked into the kitchen and opened the refrigerator to help himself to a drink.

"If you've come over to eat, I'm all for it. But if you've come over here to lecture, I'm not in the mood," Qasim said, getting his warning out of the way while he drained the pasta.

"Well too bad. I'll eat and you'll listen to what I have to say."

Qasim grunted. His brother still carried around some guilt for the position Qasim found himself in. However, Qasim didn't need his guilt or remorse. He and his brother were once very close. So close that it had hurt that Qadir knew exactly what Qasim was walking into when it came to the family business but failed to inform him. Qadir decided to keep their father's secret rather than be real with him the way he'd done all his life. That hurt. But more than hurt, it cost him their relationship. He couldn't lay everything at Qadir's feet because once he found out, he still decided to go ahead with the plan. But he wouldn't have if he had known what was at stake.

That was five years ago and although their relationship was better, restored even, it still didn't help with the fact that they caused him to lose the one woman he knew for sure he couldn't live without. That was one of the reasons he hadn't let her go. Not completely. However, he knew that Salma would never come back to him unless he untangled himself from the web he had entered.

"Look, the deal with the TOB will end in six months. I don't know what you saw today, but sticking to the plan and waiting it out is the best way to go," Qadir said, sliding on the stool.

Qasim scoffed at his brother before returning to the stove. TOB was short for The Onyx Brotherhood. The Brotherhood was a secret, but not so secret society that operated in the western part of Africa. People knew about them, whispered about them, but no one ever came out claiming to know them, or have an alliance with them. Their members were in all major sectors of government and held huge significance and power. What started off as a group of men who wanted to protect the interests of small businesses against the monopolization of big companies had over the last thirty years turned into a cartel-like underground organization. Behind their legal front, they dabbled in smuggling, information brokering, vigilantism, and money laundering. They were the proverbial boogie man and the current thorn in Qasim's side.

Apart from the farm, the Adesina family owned a lot of other ventures, not only in Nigeria, but Africa as a whole and in Europe. From commercial and residential real estate, to owning shares in some of the top banks and companies in Africa, the family wouldn't hurt for money for many more generations to come. Money afforded them the finer things in life, including the ability to send their four sons to prestigious boarding schools and colleges in America and England.

Qasim and his brothers were no strangers to the farm as they worked on it every summer when they were back in Ibadan on holidays. After high school, all the boys earned their degrees. While Qadir always wanted to come back home to help run the farm, Qasif remained abroad, studying to become a pediatrician while Qamar focused on his career as a software developer. Qasim, however, decided on a different route. In college, he played soccer for his college team. At twenty-one, upon graduating with a degree in Business and Finance, he joined the U23 team of a club in the Major Soccer League. That stint only lasted six months because he was scouted and approached by Viva City Football Club in the United Kingdom. Qasim didn't think twice about leaving the States for Europe. He went on to become one of

Europe's most successful center midfielders and played for ten years until suffering a career-ending injury.

Qasim's depression over his injury was short lived when his father had a heart attack months later and needed surgery. With their father being out of commission, Qadir needed his help to run the farm. Their younger brothers had no intention of working for the family. Most days, the last born of the Adesina brothers hardly wanted to even be a part of the family. There was no doubt that Qasim would do whatever was necessary like working for the farm. However, if Qadir and their father had been straight with him and told him how deep the family's entanglement with TOB ran, maybe Qasim would have been better prepared to handle them.

"'Sim, are you serious?"

Qasim turned around and saw Qadir staring down at his phone. He took the device from him. Qasim's jaw clenched as he studied the second picture that had come through today.

"I'm going to kill this guy." Qasim placed his phone on the counter and turned back to the stove. He put the finishing touches on the shrimp scampi.

"I can't believe you still have Paul keeping tabs on Sally," Qadir said.

Not providing a response since he didn't have one, Qasim shrugged and plated their food. Of course, he had someone in Grand Amour on his payroll. What did his brother expect? His heart was there. She needed protection. He had no doubt that her brothers could protect her. But could they protect her from a threat only he and his family knew existed? Besides, Paul had nothing to worry about. He was getting a paycheck from the resort working in their security department and he was being paid heavily by Qasim.

After a few moments of eating, Qadir looked up from his plate. "If she finds out—"

"She won't."

"So, this is why you've been grumpy lately. Who's the guy?"

Qadir pointed at the phone that was now face down, referring to Hamza Alami.

"Someone Paul thinks deserves my attention since he keeps sending me pictures." He put the strands of twirled spaghetti in his mouth.

Over the years, Qasim knew of Salma's so-called dates. But he derived some satisfaction knowing those men were only around for a limited time—the longest being three dates. At six dates, Hamza was becoming too comfortable with what was his.

Qadir set his fork down and picked up his drink. "Bro, I see the look in your eyes. You need to wait this thing out. You can't go—"

"Save it, Q. I can and I will. I'm tired of waiting."

"But you promised her you'd be totally done with the Brotherhood."

"And we're almost there."

"Almost... but not there. Six more months."

"I know Star. For her to be this close to that man means she's beginning to care for him a little bit. Whatever I promised her is now out the window. I'd be a fool to sit by and allow another man to come in and take what's mine."

Star. Short for Starlight.

His thoughts drifted back to that night – the night he declared his love for her and gave her that name. They were standing beneath an inky sky with a million twinkling stars. At that moment, he realized she was the only illumination he needed. She was his guiding light.

"Okay I get it. But are you ready for her brothers? If you go to Tweedes stomping, you gotta tell them the truth." Qadir shook his head. "Something you should've done years ago. They're going to be livid."

Qasim waved him off. "I can handle them. They have every right to be angry, but no matter how they slice and dice it, Salma is mine."

"No one is arguing that fact. But she's their sister and Omar is your friend." A beat passed between them. "Imagine if one of your friends got with Shola behind our back."

"He'd be dead," Qasim said, without missing a beat.

Qadir laughed. "See how quickly that came out? You know that's hypocritical right?"

Shola Balogun was their cousin on their mother's side. She was as important to him as his female cousins on his father's side, the Kalus. But unlike his Kalu cousins, Shola lived with them since she was in primary school. She was currently in college in America. Shola was the baby sister they didn't have.

"I warned all my friends. Omar didn't say anything about her being off limits." Even though it was the truth, Qasim knew his rationalization was weak. Omar might not have said his twin was off limits, but Qasim knew he was bothered when he and Salma got together. He hunched his shoulders. "Be that as it may, it's too late now..."

"*Ti gba*. But are you prepared for the fallout? It will be easier if *your woman* is standing by your side."

Qasim thought about the implied meaning of his brother's words. Everything between him and Salma happened so fast. Before they had time to tell the families, it was over. The only reason his brother knew the depths of their relationship was they had come to physical blows when Qasim realized the reason his woman had been in danger was because Qadir failed to disclose how far and deep the reach of the Brotherhood was.

Qasim rubbed his hand across his head. "I know..."

"Since you won't back down, let me clear my calendar. I'll go to Tweedes with you," his brother said.

Qasim shook his head. "That's not necessary."

Qadir lowered his head for a moment, then looked up at him, his normal brown eyes darkening. Qasim already knew that whatever he was thinking about wasn't good. Qadir had a reputation for being sinister when it came to protecting the family. The brothers were all grown and could take care of themselves, but Qadir, forever the protector, took his role seriously.

"Hear me good... if either of them crosses the line with you, I will rain fire and brimstone on their doorstep. You and Sally might get caught in the crossfire, but nothing will stop my wrath." He finished off his drink. "And your security detail is going with you. Non-negotiable."

"You do know that you're not my father."

"*O fẹ sọ fun baba rẹ?* Because I can tell him, and we both know that will be a bigger headache."

Qasim smirked and picked up their dirty dishes, heading to the sink. As much as it annoyed him to admit it, Qadir was right. Chief Qavi Adesina did not play when it came to any of his sons. He also knew that there was no deterring his big brother, who in this case was the lesser of the two evils. Qasim had to be delicate in his approach because technically, he could've handled things differently with Omar. But whatever Salma wanted, in their case, secrecy, his job was to provide. For peace to reign, Qasim hoped the DuBois-Arazi brothers saw it that way. However, before he faced them, he had to come clean with his own family first.

CHAPTER 3

The constant buzzing of her phone jerked Salma awake, interrupting the nightmare that had plagued her for days. In this dream, her family surrounded her, wagging accusatory fingers at her and radiating heated rage. She knew it wasn't just a dream, but a premonition of the punishment she would face when they finally found out about the secret she'd hidden for so long. Groggily, she grabbed her cell phone and squinted at the screen. If it wasn't one of her siblings, the person would have to wait for a call back. Seeing who it was, Salma answered the Facetime call.

"Where have you been?"

"Good morning to you too, O." Salma yawned.

"Are you just waking up? Why is it so hard to reach you lately?"

Salma groaned as her twin brother fired off questions he didn't give her a chance to answer. Her eyes lifted to the timer; it was a little after ten.

"Always so rude…"

"Answer the phone when I call Sally. Don't make me worry." The seriousness in his voice was evident.

Salma let out a breath and apologized. The bond she shared

with Omar often scared her. Their therapist had even gone so far as to say they were codependent. They shared a womb, but according to her, they also shared trauma. Before their parents died, while Mustafa and Yasmine took on the role of protectors, as the youngest siblings, she and Omar relied on each other to stay as quiet as possible to avoid their abusive father's wrath. They did everything together, even ending up at New York University for their higher education.

"I'm at grandma's," Salma answered. "Will you be back in time for dinner?"

The week had been more demanding than anticipated, but Salma was able to escape her grandmother's lecture about her recent disappearances by promising to stay over Friday night with her and spend Saturday morning with her in the garden. As a family, they had dinner together on Saturday evenings. Omar was currently in Casablanca while Mustafa and Zaina had flown back in from Tanzania, her home country, the day before.

"Yeah, I'll be there, but you still haven't answered my question."

Feeling his despair, Salma retold the story of the last week to her brother about her health scare. When he remained silent, she sat up in the bed.

"O, say something."

"I can't believe you hid that from me. Me?" His voice shook.

The familiar sting of guilt crept up her spine. Omar was the one who grated her nerves like no other, but he was a part of her, the person she was closest to. They promised to never keep things from each other. However, in the last several days, the reality that she had broken that promise, not once but twice, made her feel terrible.

"I know, but this was what I was afraid of. I didn't want anyone worrying and obsessing. I was doing enough of that on my own."

"At least big Sis was there..."

"Yes." Salma chuckled. "You know she's the most levelheaded of us all—"

"Promise me, no matter how you think I will feel, don't keep things from me."

"Promise. There's something else I need to tell you when you get back." After her last date with Hamza, Salma realized she couldn't move forward unless she handled the past with Qasim. Hamza was too good of a gentleman to string along without coming clean about her situation.

Omar pushed her to tell him what was on her mind now. She insisted they talk face to face. Once he gave up his quest, they caught each other up on what'd been happening before he told her he had to leave for the airport. After saying their goodbyes, Salma hung up the phone and walked into the bathroom of her childhood room. She needed to find her grandmother. The woman always knew how to help her calm her troubled mind.

Several minutes later, Salma approached her grandmother who was in a secluded area of the backyard of DuBois Manoir. It was what they called the ten-bedroom, sprawling mansion that her grandmother and late grandfather lived in. Also, where Salma and her siblings had been brought to from the orphanage. Although big, huge in fact, the manoir always felt like home. Many nights, she and her siblings played games, did crafts, and watched movies with their grandparents. The domestic staff weren't stiff like most of the ones Salma saw in movies. Instead, they were all friendly and treated them with the same reverence they did their grandparents.

"*Bonjour, grand-mère*," Salma greeted in French.

With their mother being French and their father a full-blooded Moroccan, Salma and her siblings were fluent in Arabic and French. When they lived with their parents, they spoke Arabic, but when they moved to Tweedes, their grandparents taught them French.

"*Mon enfant, tu es en retard.*"

Salma apologized for her tardiness and walked over and

planted a kiss on her grandmother's cheek. Grandma Olly, as she was fondly called, wasn't actively gardening. Instead, she was seated under the covered shelter she had built in the middle of the garden. Greeted by a gentle breeze that carried with it the subtle fragrance of blooming flowers, Salma took in the soft, golden sunlight that bathed the scenic expanse of the estate. Birds chirped melodiously in the background, adding a harmonious soundtrack to their peaceful surroundings. She sat next to her grandmother as they observed the landscapers pull the weeds, add fertilizer, and fill up scanty areas with flowers. To the side of her grandmother's rocking chair was a stool that held her cold mint tea.

Salma broke the silence and asked the older woman if she had taken her medication. Last year, she had to have hip surgery and with her diabetes, Salma was always concerned. Grandma Olly always said she was fine, but Salma felt the need to look in her eyes when she said it. Her grandmother had a history of hiding things she knew her grandchildren would worry about. Especially Mustafa. He would turn everything on its head to make sure their grandmother was okay. After she felt satisfied with the response, Salma remained quiet, taking in the view, and trying to gather the words she had to say.

"Speak child. You know I always know when something is on your mind."

"I don't know what to do about Qasim," Salma blurted out.

Grandma Olly kept her focus on the garden, then asked. "Why are you ready to talk about him all of a sudden?" She lifted her tea. "When you came back from America with your tail between your legs, after the night of your confession, you refused to talk about him again."

That rainy night in her childhood bedroom was a night she wanted to forget.

"That's because there was nothing left to say. Then as time went by, there was no need to say anything." She shrugged. Her gaze lingered on the Atlas Mountains in the distance. "I was hurt, angry and grieving. Everything was so gray. Most importantly, I didn't want my brothers disappointed in me…"

"I guess seeing him at my birthday party triggered something."

"Not really…"

"Then what did? Until you tell yourself the truth, you'll keep circling in uncertainty."

In the next several minutes, Salma narrated an abbreviated version of what made her want to deal with the skeletons she had in her closet. Her health scare. After chastising her as Omar had done earlier, her grandmother ended by saying she understood why she kept it to herself.

She gestured to an area that didn't look quite as pristine compared to the rest of the garden. "Do you see that patch right there?"

Salma acknowledged it.

"When I first started planting this garden, no matter what I did, that part was determined to remain barren. I tilled it, put fertilizer in the soil, and tended to the flowers with much more care than I did the other areas. But still nothing. Then I had a professional in to diagnose the issue with that part of the land."

"What was it?"

"Deeper, underneath, there's a slab of limestone that prevented growth. No matter what I did, the roots didn't go deep enough, so the plants were never stable, unable to withstand the elements. However, digging up the slab wasn't something I was invested in, so I left it alone."

Salma knew there was a point to this story and needed her grandmother to get to it fast. "Grandma, if Qasim is the slab in this story, I was invested in him. You saw that."

Her grandmother was the only one she told of her relationship with Qasim. The older woman saw it for herself when she visited Salma and Omar in New York several years ago. The moment her grandmother spotted them together, she pulled

Salma aside and warned her to be careful with the situation—especially since Qasim was famous and friends with her brother.

Her grandmother faced her. "I did. But I also knew that although you were shiny at the top, your roots were not deep enough. Instead of digging up the slab, you pushed it deeper, pretending it didn't exist."

"But he lied to me. Just like *that* man did to—"

"Your mother is dead and gone, my child. I know of your wounds, but you alone are responsible for your healing. It's a journey, but if every time you get triggered, you stop moving forward or in your case, shut down, you'll never truly be able to heal your roots so they can be planted."

Her grandmother stood and so did Salma. She helped her down from the raised platform and helped her walk into the garden.

"I understand why you want to visit an unfinished past. Regrets are a terrible thing. But before you wake up giants, make sure you're truly ready for what that requires. You must be open to things not being so black and white. Open to accepting apologies and giving forgiveness, both of which have nothing to do with reconciliation."

Salma nodded.

"Also ask yourself why you got with him in the first place." She raised her finger to silence Salma's response. "Don't say because you love him. Love is action, that also entails a commitment to the future. If you don't see that for you and him, do what needs to be done."

Before this talk, Salma was prepared to come clean with her brothers. However, her grandmother was right. It would be foolish of her to stir up turmoil if she was uncertain of what kind of future she and Qasim were going to have. So, she had to call him first. If the outcome of that call wasn't too bad, that might lessen the impact of the chaos she knew would follow.

~

"*S*o even on vacation you couldn't resist?" Omar asked.

He reached for a piece of grilled chicken and placed it on his plate while Mustafa grunted in response. Everyone at the table guffawed, and Zaina gave her husband a pointed look. She had just recounted the story of catching Mustafa sneaking away to the bathroom during their vacation in Zanzibar to answer a business call. It had been quite a feat trying to convince him to take time off.

As the Chairman and Chief Executive Officer of Grand Amour, Mustafa's calendar was always packed. Zaina had confided in Salma that getting Mustafa to travel less was more of a challenge than she anticipated. After their nuptials, Zaina also traveled a lot setting up her new business, a sustainable interior design company. She was no longer a full-time, traveling environmental consultant for her former employer, but she did remain the consultant for the environmental team in all the Grand Amour locations. However, now settled in Tweede Kans Cove, Zaina felt the absence of her husband more than ever, but Salma reminded her that marriage wouldn't change him overnight. Besides, she knew who he was when they promised to have and to hold.

"It was one call," Mustafa defended himself.

"It should've been no call," Zaina sassed.

Mustafa leaned over and kissed her lips, silencing the remainder of her commentary.

Salma turned to her grandmother who was at the head of the table. The joy that radiated on her face always gave her a sense of peace. The talk they had earlier grounded her and gave her a lot to think about. It wouldn't be fair to anybody to rush into this situation blind. She needed to be sure of what she wanted.

"Apart from that, I hope you guys had a wonderful time," Salma said.

"Yes, we did. Come over to the house later and I'll show you this new purse I got for us."

Salma nodded. Us being she, Zaina, and Yasmine. The three of them had grown quite close. Well as close as can be considering the distance and everyone's schedule. After another few minutes of laughing at Mustafa's expense, the topic of conversation shifted to the town and what the council was doing to fight the impending arrival of some big conglomerate that wanted to buy land and build bigger companies. The scowl on Mustafa's face grew deeper as he talked with noticeable distaste about one of the companies he was actively fighting in court.

"They visit our small town, they like the appeal, but then they turn around and try to build their bigger buildings, stripping the town of what made it attractive in the first place," Mustafa said.

"But how do we stop that, dear? Once the township gives them permission, they can do whatever they want," Grandma Olly said.

"The fact that they can doesn't mean they should," Omar chimed in.

"Good thing Tweede Kans Cove doesn't operate like other cities. There has to be a town hall meeting of the residents and the request for acquisition had to be put up for a vote in the 'Expansion Law' that was put in place," Salma said. "The people trust us and know the impact we've had in the town over the years. There's no way they will vote for another resort to come in and threaten that."

Grand Amour didn't have a monopoly on the hospitality business in Tweede Kans Cove. There were other hotels in their town. However, those other hotels and Grand Amour had a good working arrangement. The fact that this new company, wanting to buy land, didn't even deem it fit to look for land further away from Grand Amour was already an indication that they weren't only coming to take a piece of the pie, they wanted the whole pie to themselves.

They wouldn't allow that to happen. Although their grandmother strictly prohibited business from being discussed at dinner, she allowed them to discuss this freely. Salma watched the lines of worry take over her forehead and was thrilled when her phone rang. Yasmine, Kojo and the kids appeared on the screen. Their grandmother's eyes lit up as she talked to her great-grandchildren and fawned over the fact that Zaina would soon be adding to the growing number.

While Omar was desperately trying to make their grandmother understand that she shouldn't look to him for children, Salma's hand went to her stomach. She leaned back as her mind traveled to the time of forbidden love that held so much promise. A time when she thought she'd finally be able to do what her mother couldn't do.

Protect her child at all costs.

But even that she'd failed to do.

It was another memory she had pushed to the back of her mind. In all her efforts to be everything her mother wasn't, Salma was now faced with the fact that the apple really didn't fall too far from the tree.

CHAPTER 4

When Qasim left his office, he had every intention of heading home to brood over the information his private investigator, Rah, had given him. Instead, he found himself asking Daniel, his driver, to make a detour to his parents' home. It was either now or be summoned in the morning. He knew that with the mood he was in, some blameless piece of furniture would bear the brunt of his frustration. Recalling the contents of the manila envelope that had been handed to him earlier, his blood bubbled up in rage, causing the heat from his anger to burn in his chest.

Over the past couple of months, he had been dealing with mysterious issues that he'd normally leave to the Operations Manager, but when they became frequent and affected the bottom line, Qasim got involved. Their crops had been stuck at the dock for over a week. Their highly skilled workers were being poached and Brownfield Farms, a midsized farm, suddenly had the money to hire lobbyists and regulators targeting government policies that would place them at a disadvantage. The last act that drove Qasim over the edge was his finding out that the market was intentionally being manipulated.

It was impossible for Brownfield to keep cutting prices, offering discounts, and other marketing gimmicks without running out of money. Qasim and Qadir had been suspicious that the Brotherhood was involved in these sudden moves, but they lacked proof. Fortunately, Qasim's private investigator provided him with the necessary evidence. Seyi Bashir, one of Alhaji Ranti's top aides at TOB's acquisition department, was seen in photographs with the suspected parties. This was all they needed to know who was behind it.

For the past five years, despite his faith and beliefs, he had done whatever the Brotherhood asked of him. This meant walking the morally ambiguous line of honoring agreements his father and grandfather put in place while also upholding his values. Unfortunately, he had to do deals that weren't always ethical, but provided necessary help to their community. But just like stray cats couldn't resist a bowl of milk, so too, the Brotherhood could not leave things alone.

Two months ago, Qasim had made it exceedingly clear that the last agreement linking the farm to their money laundering activities was coming to an end. His father and brother agreed to his plan but insisted the ten percent profit margin they currently received from TOB be replaced. It was a huge feat, but he was currently working on it with a tourism project. But then Brownfield started becoming a problem. Thanks to some provisions set when Qasim's grandfather joined the Brotherhood, coupled with his father's heart attack, the family was able to cut ties with the organization, but were still held responsible for any previously set contracts. For fifteen years, amongst other things, the farm served as a front for cleaning the Brotherhood's money – something Qasim had no knowledge of until he attempted to shut down those offshore accounts five years ago.

He pulled up to his parents' house. After an electronic sweep under the car, security opened the gates for his driver to enter and drive up the winding road that led to the Adesina mansion. Once the truck was parked in its designated space, Qasim got out of the vehicle. He had just stepped onto the porch when the door opened and one of his parents' drivers came barreling through.

"Ah, *Oga* Qasim, Sorry sir," he said, bowing his head. "Good evening." He opened the door wider and stepped to the side so Qasim could pass through.

"Where are you rushing to Collins?"

"Madam forget something for her car. I want to collect it."

Qasim nodded and headed inside. "Where is she?"

"Kitchen, sir."

Glancing at his watch, he smiled. *Of course.* One thing about Remi Adesina, she ran her home like a well-executed game plan. Unlike most of his friends, his parents didn't study abroad. Instead, they graduated from one of the top universities in Nigeria, Obafemi Awolowo University. After graduation, his mother went to nursing school while his father joined his grandfather in managing the farm.

Qadir was born in Nigeria, but by the time their mother was pregnant with Qasim, their father had enough money for her to give birth to Qasim and his younger brothers abroad.

His mother was bustling around the kitchen, preparing dinner. No matter how much money they had or the domestic help she employed, his mother still believed that no other woman should cook her husband's meal, or they might take him from her.

"Felicia, refill this salt container. How many times will I tell you not to allow it to finish? Dorothy, is the table set? I hope you used the new china. Qasim should be here soon."

"What are you over here fussing about, *Iya mi*," Qasim entered the kitchen and walked over to his mother. Prostrating, he greeted. "*E̩ kú ìrọ̀lẹ́*, ma." He stood then pulled her into a hug.

"*Kú ìrọ̀lẹ́, omo mi*," she said.

The familiar scent of her perfume engulfed him. She was in her late sixties, and her dark skin still maintained its glow. Her twisted salt and pepper hair was wrapped in a scarf matching the flowing boubou she had on. Pulling back, she studied him. Lifting her hands, she cupped his cheeks. Qasim bent a little so she wouldn't have to strain so much.

"What's wrong, my son? How was work?"

Qasim's eyes darted around the kitchen, taking in the evidence of the catfish stew, white rice, and fried plantains they were about to have for dinner. His mother was very perceptive. She swore she could feel when something was wrong with her boys. Be that as it may, there was no way he was sharing what was on his mind with her.

He kissed her forehead. "I'm starving, that's all."

"Hmm." She narrowed her eyes at him. "I know that's not it. But since I have a God that is ever faithful, I'll take whatever worries you to Him."

"My prayer warrior. You do that."

"Hmmm, I shouldn't be the only one praying on your behalf. You were the one I counted on."

"*Iya mi*, what are you talking about?"

"That beautiful young lady I saw you with in London. I had hope. Qadir has been engaged for God knows how long. Your younger brothers act like I'm speaking in another language anytime I speak of a woman."

Qasim was stunned at the direction this conversation was going in. One thing he had always admired about his mother was that she wasn't the cliché African mother. She'd never hounded them about marriage before. She did meet Salma one summer when he had failed to time her arrival properly and it ended up coinciding with his mother's.

As for Qadir, that arrangement was for business purposes. A deal between families. His brother maintained his own life and that was entirely his story to tell.

"Where is this coming from?"

"I'm getting old, *omo mi*. I want grandchildren." She sighed. "You are almost forty, your brother is—"

"Madam, everything is set." Felicia, one of the domestic staff barged in. "Oh, sorry ma, I didn't know *Oga* Qasim was here."

Grateful for the interruption, Qasim moved closer to the kitchen door. *Almost forty? I wonder why thirty-eight can't just be thirty-eight.*

"So, you didn't hear our voice?" his mother shouted, taking out her frustration on the staff.

"Sorry, ma." Felicia genuflected, with one knee close to the ground, and the other bent.

His mother waved her off and Felicia left the way she came.

Qasim smirked at his mother. "You know she didn't do anything to you..."

His mother sighed. He knew her well. She felt bad but not enough to apologize. Instead, she'd find one expensive gift to give her.

"I'm just tired of tying *gele* for everyone else's children's wedding. I thought if I let you boys be, that you will find your way on your own. I should have arranged—"

"No, you shouldn't have. You see how that worked out with Q?" Qasim drew her close. "Pray hard. God might answer your prayer soon."

"Are you serious?"

The gleam in her eye was almost comical, but Qasim held his composure. Funny though it may be, the hope in her eyes threatened his rational thought process. If he couldn't appeal to Salma's heart to come back with him, he'd have to kidnap her. The thought of his woman hoisted up on his shoulders as he carried her to the jet had another smirk creeping onto his lips.

Dismissing the thought, he answered his mother, "Nothing is impossible with God. But in the meantime, where's your husband?"

"Your father and brother are in the study. I told them no business talk, and that goes for you too."

Qasim acknowledged her request as he headed out of the

kitchen. His mother was oblivious to the "other" side of the business and that wasn't going to change anytime soon. Turning the corner, then descending the stairs, Qasim sauntered down the hall to his father's study.

"I don't care what you say. I have worked too hard and long for you and your brother to come in and run my empire to the ground," his father snapped.

"Nothing is being run into the ground. And last I checked, you're not supposed... who is feeding you this information?" Qadir quipped.

Qasim entered the room to find his brother standing by the bar while his father was upright in his favorite recliner. Right after his operation several years ago, his father stepped down from his active role as CEO of Ilẹ Oloro Farms, but maintained an honorary position as chairman emeritus. He was supposed to act in an advisory capacity only. But his former assistant, Kasai, was still plugged in and ran things by him, although he had been warned several times not to.

"It's that fathead Kasai. I see he no longer wants his job, so I'll gladly relieve him of it in the morning." Qasim walked over to his father and prostrated.

"*Ẹ kú ìrọ̀lẹ́*, sir."

After his father patted him on the back, acknowledging his greeting, Qasim stood and took a seat in the chair between his brother and father. "I'm letting you know, your wife will kick your behind if she hears you snapping and raising your voice over business." He turned to Qadir, "And you will collect a stray bullet for being an enabler."

Qadir raised his hands in surrender while their father scoffed. Their father's goal had always been to make sure his sons were equipped with every tool available to them to make their lives better than his was. Coming face to face with his mortality made him an open book. He shared with Qasim and Qadir how their grandfather, who worked for Nigerian Customs for a while, was almost evicted with his two small children and wife. At the port one day, he was approached by someone who turned out to be from the Brotherhood. All their grandfather had to do was look the other way during one of his patrols to allow their smuggled contraband through. The compensation he received from doing their bidding helped what was then a small farm and created an allegiance to the underground organization. As they were now finding out, all money wasn't good money and evil always came with a price.

"Kasai keeps his job and that's final," his father said, his gaze darting between both his sons until he got their agreement. "We have been flying under the radar for years. Why are we suddenly getting all this media attention?" His eyes roamed the room.

"I wasn't sure at first, but I'm pretty certain your buddies are behind it," Qasim said.

"The Brotherhood?" Qadir asked, his brows furrowed. "I knew you were looking into it, but I swear, I thought you were about to tell me one new politician that was trying to vie for community support was behind it."

Qasim knew the reason his brother wasn't so worried was that if it was a politician, all they had to do was pay him a visit, ending with all parties coming to a mutually beneficial agreement.

"Nope, I had Rah do some digging and get this..." Qasim scooted forward in his chair. He ignored his father's scowl and told them about the texts and emails before sharing the picture. TOB was the one sponsoring all the moves Brownfield was making to bring heat to their doorstep.

"The poaching and recent high turnover?" his father asked. "We can't keep training people and losing them a month later to a farm that's not even a quarter of our size." He stood and walked behind the mahogany desk in the corner. He removed a cell phone from his top drawer. "This ends now. Let me call Bolaji."

Qasim and Qadir exchanged glances. Just as the family had a trained security team that handled their protection, they also had a team that wasn't as polished in their techniques. Bolaji was their leader. Old habits die hard, but Qasim and Qadir were doing everything possible to steer the business in the right direction.

Qadir was the first to speak. "Pops, hold on. I have already talked to HR about having a mandatory retention period after training."

Although Ilẹ Oloro Farm was what the family was known for, they owned many other businesses. Adesina Enterprises was the parent company and all staff, regardless of where they worked, started from training in the corporate office.

"And please for *Iya mi*'s sake, stay out of TOB's crossfire. We have it covered," Qasim said.

This was an intimidation tactic, so they'd crawl back asking for their protection, but TOB had the wrong Adesina. Qasim wasn't his father or grandfather, and he had a brother who stood lock in step with his every move. Who he was most afraid of was their mother, if she had to hear about her husband being pulled back into the business that "almost killed him before his time." Her words.

Their father's menacing scowl slowly dissipated, and he returned the phone to its place. Why he still had it was something Qasim didn't want to get into.

"Your grandfather and I worked hard. Toiled day and night to turn this farm into what it is today." His father walked from behind the desk back to the sitting area. "I see the improvements both of you have made since taking over." Raising his index finger, his frown returned in warning. "However, I'll do anything necessary to ensure the Adesina legacy does not crumble. Anything."

What his father had said wasn't entirely true, although that wasn't a fact Qasim was willing to argue. Of course, they worked hard, but years of working hard and yielding only a fraction of the profits they thought they were owed led them to enter lopsided contracts with the Brotherhood. The price of dining with the devil was the unholy alliance he and his brother were now left with untangling. After reassuring his father that everything would settle down soon, the three men headed down the short hallway and back up the stairs.

"I hope you haven't forgotten. We play against the Okolis this year in the Play for the Course," their father said, as they stepped into the living room.

"Pops, I'm good, but you know we might have to get Q some lessons." Qasim chuckled. The golfing event where each of the families that belonged to the exclusive golf club played for charity was always held in October. Just in time for the upcoming holidays.

"What are we talking about?"

Qasif came out of the kitchen with a bottle of water in his hand. He greeted their father, before dapping his brothers. Before anyone could give him an answer, Qamar came out of the kitchen with his arm draped around their mother's neck.

Qasim studied their youngest brother. As everyone was now used to, he avoided eye contact with their father while offering him a greeting devoid of warmth. His attitude toward their father was something he and Qasif tried to talk to Qamar about, but from the look of things, nothing was sinking in. Qadir didn't have patience for him at all, so their baby brother had him in the same category he had their father in.

"When did you get in?" their father asked, directing his question to Qamar. "I didn't know you were coming in."

"This evening. Mummy knew," he responded, walking over to the television.

Qamar's animosity was the reason he lived in L.A until about a few months ago when he relocated to Abuja with some of his fellow Silicon Valley startup buddies. Before his father could respond, Qadir stomped past Qasim who grabbed his arm, halting his mission. Qasim hated the shift in the atmosphere, but whatever Qadir was going to do would make it so much worse.

The painful look in their mother's eye was worthy of whatever Qadir had in mind, but Qasim wasn't up for separating any fights tonight. All he wanted to do was enjoy the evening with his family and head home. Their mother walked up to their dad and Qasif did what he did best, diffused the situation with a joke. He teased Qadir again about his poor golf game and then blurted out some silly random facts about the probability that Qadir's golf game wouldn't be any better this year than it was last year. They all laughed and Qadir hopelessly tried to defend himself. Qasif's ability to douse an inferno so effortlessly made him the great pediatrician he was.

Everyone's laughter ceased when their mother spoke. "*Ehen*, before I forget. Whoever's responsible for sending your aunty her hibiscus tea didn't do their job. She mentioned it when she and I spoke earlier. Qadir, please check on it."

Their father grunted and Qadir pulled out his phone to most likely text his assistant. The aunty their mother was referring to was their father's only sister, Bola Kalu. She lived in Enugu with her husband and had a love affair with the hibiscus tea they grew on the farm. Someone failed in their duty to ensure she never ran out and that person was going to be on the receiving end of Qadir's annoyance.

"I'll call Aunty B in the morning, she'll get it before the end of the day," Qadir announced after pocketing his phone.

"If Kalu can't buy the type of tea she likes then I wonder what —" their dad started.

Their mother swatted his shoulder. "Chief, leave that man alone."

Qasim and his brothers laughed. Their aunty was married into a very wealthy Igbo family from the east of Nigeria. She never wanted for anything, and their father knew that, but to him, no one was worthy of his sister. His real problem was that he had wanted her to marry his friend. Although he respected her husband, he always found a way to give the man a hard time.

"*Oya o*, let's eat. The table is set, and my protectors are all here," their mother announced dragging their father with her.

With each person's busy schedule, it was rare they were all

able to make every monthly meetup. But the brothers made a promise not to miss more than two consecutive meet ups. It made their mother happy and Remi Adesina's happiness was always the goal of the Adesina men. Qadir and Qasif followed their parents while Qasim hung back to talk to his youngest brother. Once Qamar got closer, Qasim lifted his hand and smacked the back of his head.

"Ouch, what was that for?"

Qamar was taller than them all, but that meant nothing as far as Qasim was concerned.

He narrowed his eyes at his brother. "I see you want to keep acting stupid."

"What? That man knows I don't mess with him like that."

"That's between you, him, and Jesus. But you can't come into his house and disrespect him."

"I greeted him, he asked me a question, I answered," he scoffed. "What else you want me to do?"

"A'ight keep playing dumb. Next time I'mma allow Q to kick your behind."

Qamar chuckled. "Yeah, good looking out. It would have been bad if I had to put big bro on his back because he's trying to defend his Pops."

Qasim laughed. "Okay, I see you have jokes, but seriously, you can't come into his house and disrespect him. Stay away completely if that's the energy you're bringing."

Qamar sighed. "What I can't figure out is why YOU are not mad. He literally—"

"I have been mad, but it's been addressed, and it's done. You need to find a way to do the same or it will keep eating at you." Qasim stopped at the archway to the formal dining area. "It's been years, so maybe you're happy with the way things are. But what you did back there can't happen again. Or the only time you'll see *Iya* is if you invite her to where you are. I'll make sure you are banned from this house." He tapped his shoulder. "This is your last warning."

Qasim heard his brother mumble something under his breath. Whatever it was, he really didn't care about. He'd issued his last warning and it was in Qamar's interest to abide. Qasim was about to bring his lady back to his home and there was no way he would have her enter a house divided.

CHAPTER 5

ednesday morning, the following week, Salma quickened her stride as she turned the corner, her Giuseppe's clacking against the tiled hallway floor. Her watch read five minutes before the training session was scheduled to begin. A smile tugged at her lips. The deal with Harmony Winery had been signed and now it was time to get her team up to speed, ready for the Grand Amour tourist package that highlighted the winery in a few months' time.

She had ten of her top customer experience managers attending the theoretical aspect of the training the team from Harmony was conducting at Grand Amour. According to the schedule, in about two months, the same team would go to the winery for the boots on the ground training. As with all her initiatives, Salma tried to ensure she was present for the major milestones.

As she entered the conference room, a wave of hushed anticipation filled the atmosphere. Her gaze was immediately drawn to the large screen mounted on the wall, displaying vibrant visuals that seemed to dance in tandem with the rhythmic hum of the projector. Her assistant rushed over to her, and Salma handed her the folder she'd brought along. As she made her way to take her preferred seat at the back of the room, she acknowledged the greetings of her employees. She was proud of the diverse mix of employees whose faces now reflected the blend of curiosity and attentive engagement she liked to see.

The scent of freshly brewed coffee wafted toward her as her assistant approached her. Salma took the cup, thanked her, and looked around. "The team from Harmony isn't here yet?" she asked. Nothing irritated her more in business than tardiness.

At that moment, her phone buzzed.

> Hamza: Good morning, running late, got caught in construction entering the town.

"I was told that they'd be five minutes late," Lia, her assistant said.

Salma lifted her gaze from her phone. "Huh?"

"The team conducting the training. They would be about five minutes late."

"Oh, okay, thank you."

Salma walked to her seat and powered up her iPad. She took a sip of her coffee and aimlessly scrolled through the resort's social media apps. It was the only mindless work she could think of doing right now that would take her mind off Hamza. It had been a little over a week since they went out to dinner last. That was also the night she told him about her complicated relationship status. She didn't go into details, but insisted she had to sort that out before she'd consider them moving forward. He had agreed to keep their relationship strictly professional. However, he sent her flowers twice after that and was tagging along with his team. Something that was completely unnecessary.

Her mind jetted to Qasim. She'd called his office some days ago and got his assistant. Nerves got the best of her because she hung up without saying anything. She'd rehearsed everything she wanted to say, but at that moment, she froze. Later in the evening, she was going to try again. The limbo she was in was no longer acceptable; he needed to let her go.

Glancing at the time at the bottom of the home screen, Salma shook her head. *It is entirely too early to have men I currently have nothing to do with flooding my mind.*

Salma continued her scrolling. The social media team reported to her sister. However, Salma liked to check in and ensure they were on task.

Moments later, Mr. Alami walked in, flanked by two men at his side. Salma stood and strolled toward them with her assistant in tow. Starting from his bald head, her eyes quickly took in the man that she had become quite familiar with over the last couple of months. The grey, double-breasted, pin-striped suit he wore over a white shirt was perfectly tailored to his medium frame. She and Hamza were the same height at five feet, eight inches. She'd probably give him another inch, but not more than that. That among other things was why she constantly found herself comparing him to Qasim. His six-foot, three-inch frame allowed him to tuck her under his arm comfortably.

"Ms. DuBois-Arazi, are you okay?" Hamza's hand on her arm brought her out of her brief daze.

Salma cleared her throat. All eyes were on her. "I apologize. You're welcome, gentlemen. Lia here will take you to your seats, show you where the beverages are, and in about..." she glanced at her watch "...ten minutes, we should get started."

Hamza gave her a concerned look which she ignored. One thing she respected about him initially was his ability to be strictly professional when it came time to handle business. He understood when she told him that her reputation was important to her. Even though her family owned the resort, she refused to let people think that any of her accomplishments were due to luck or privilege instead of hard work. Women were still viewed with a certain level of skepticism in African culture; her being a single woman was worse. She was determined that merit would always be tied to her name and not her gender.

Hamza and his team walked off with Lia while Salma walked to the front of the room. After giving her team a brief update on the adjusted agenda, she made her way back to her seat.

Minutes later, one of the men who introduced himself as Nigel, the winery's guest liaison, began to explain the history of the winery, the work they'd put into it since Hamza had inherited it from his grandfather, and the types of vineyards that had been established. He spoke about the quality of the grapes they were producing, and the meticulous care he took in ensuring they were of the highest caliber. He went on to give a high-level summary of the process of winemaking, from the aging of the grapes to the bottling of the finished product. In his experience, these were some of the questions tourists asked the most.

As the presentation went on, Salma could feel the interest of her team growing as engagement increased with the questions being asked and the overall discussion. By the end of the session, Salma stood to give the closing remarks while telling the staff that lunch was being catered in the resort's restaurant. As Lia ushered everyone out, Salma directed her gaze at Hamza who was on a call in the corner of the room. Their eyes locked in for a moment, then soon after, Hamza ended his call and approached her. Salma could feel a shiver run through her body as he came closer, his intense gaze making her heart beat faster.

"That went well don't you think?" Hamza asked, his voice low and husky.

"It did but I had no doubt. We've been working on this for about six months. Most of them know each other by now," she replied, trying to keep her voice steady.

Salma walked a few steps to where she'd been sitting to pick up her phone and iPad. The look in Hamza's eyes was unmistakable and she needed to get away from him. One thing she never did was lie to herself. She might twist the truth for others or keep her thoughts to herself, but she was too grown to lie. Weeks ago, she admitted that he had the potential to be more than a business partner. She was attracted to Hamza, plain and simple.

But...

There was a but... Her body might be free, but her heart wasn't. Five long years later and she still wasn't in possession of it. No matter how hard she'd tried. She'd told Hamza that last week, but his nearness meant she might not have been clear enough. He was a beautiful man that sent vibrations through her body, but nothing could happen. Salma turned away with a throat-clearing sound as they almost collided. They stood face to face, the tension between them palpable.

A smile tugged at the corners of Hamza's mouth. He leaned in close enough that she could feel his body heat radiating against her skin as he whispered in her ear. "I couldn't help but notice how stunning you look today."

Her cheeks flushed, a wave of anxiety swelling up in her. He took a few steps back, tilted his head sideways and arched an eyebrow.

"Umm... thank you," she stammered.

"Relax, Salma. I'm not going to bite...unless you want me to."

Salma took a deep breath and said firmly, "We've talked about this, Mr. Alami."

He smiled again, eyes crinkling up in the corners. "I see we're back to that?"

She swallowed hard. "What?"

His grin widened. "Formal titles..."

"Yes, when it seems like you didn't get the message." She glanced at her slim gold watch, took in a sharp breath of air, and set her jaw. With an appointment looming, she didn't have time to deal with people who had difficulty understanding how she felt. In two strides, she was at the door and about to reach for the handle to open it wider.

"My beautiful Salma, I did hear you. But then I thought about it, and I do not agree."

His words stopped her hand mid-reach and brought her icy gaze back to him. "What?"

"I think it is fear holding you back."

She clenched her jaw and closed her eyes briefly before turning slowly back toward him. "Oh really?"

He shrugged his broad shoulders. "Yes, you claim to have this thing you need to get settled, but—"

"Claim?" Despite her attempts to remain calm, heat rushed up her neck as anger began to simmer within her chest. "People say they want the truth, but when you give it to them, they find a way to make it be a lie to satisfy the story in their head." There was so much more she wanted to say, but this was still a place of business, and she had her next appointment getting closer with each passing second. Everything that had drawn her so strongly towards him before suddenly became lackluster in comparison to his present attitude.

He held out his hands in a sign of surrender. "I didn't mean to offend you. I'm pointing out that we work well together, and we get along great too—"

Shaking her head, Salma conceded despite herself. "We do and I'd like to continue...the work part that is. It was wrong of me to agree to go out with you in the first place."

"No, it wasn't. Whoever this man is, I'm sure I can give you everything he never could." In a swift motion, Hamza took her hand. "He was a fool to let you go."

"Wow, Star, that's one heck of a proposition."

Salma's breath caught in her throat as the familiar velvet timbre of *his* voice washed against her skin. She slowly turned to find Qasim leaning against the doorframe, a picture of nonchalance. But Salma knew him better than anyone. Although reflective sunglasses covered his eyes, from his tone, she knew he was a bubbling volcano ready to erupt at Hamza's slightest provocation. She'd seen the "other" Qasim Adesina in action and that wasn't a sight she ever wanted to see again. Taking a deep breath, she steeled herself and silently prayed for composure.

"Qasim, what are you doing here?" Salma asked, her tone cold.

He sauntered into the room with a smug grin plastered on his face. Salma could feel Hamza's eyes on her, but he was the least of her problems right now. *Devil you know and all.*

Even with the thick tension that now enveloped them, she took the time to give Qasim a once over. As she'd come to expect, he was immaculately dressed in a black suit with a light pink shirt which complemented his dark skin. He looked exactly the way he did when she saw him last—confident and annoyingly sexy.

"The man made you an offer." Qasim stopped by her side. "It's rude to keep him waiting."

His cologne mixed with his body wash wafted up her nose, threatening to throw her off kilter, but she fought against giving him the satisfaction. He knew how she felt about people ignoring her or trying to handle her and in the space of a few minutes, he had done both. As she opened her mouth to set him straight, her intended speech was halted by Hamza, stepping forward.

"And who are you?

Qasim's malicious laughter sprung her into action. She stepped in front of him. Immediately, she knew that was a mistake when Qasim put his hands on her waist, slightly lifting her and placing her behind him. "Don't do that again."

She lifted her brow.

He lowered his lips to her ear. "Never put yourself between me and another man," he answered her silent question.

She grimaced, and he turned back to Hamza.

"My apologies, the name is Adesina, aka *fool*."

Although Qasim introduced himself, he didn't offer a handshake and even a blind man could see that his stance was less than friendly.

Salma had had enough of the show. "Hamza, as tempting as that sounds—"

"Is it though?" Qasim asked.

Her brows furrowed. "Is what?"

"Is it tempting, Star?" The unspoken challenge was evident in his tone.

Salma shook her head. "Hamza, like I told you before...I'm not—"

"Salma, I have no idea who this guy is, but I know—"

"You didn't tell him?" Qasim taunted.

Salma turned to Qasim. "Stop it." She still had to work with Hamza. She wasn't ready to tarnish that relationship just because Qasim decided to pop up and stake his claim.

An ill-timed, yet valid claim.

"What? I'm not the one keeping the tru—"

"Qasim!"

"Salma!" He stared at her. "Tell him so he can cut his losses, or I will."

"I can't believe you're doing this here."

"I wouldn't have to if you wrapped this up. We have things to discuss," Qasim sneered, clearly irritated.

"Hamza, this is my..." She clung tightly to the word she knew would change everything. A word she only had a few months to relish in.

"Come on, Star, you can do it..." Qasim winked. His expression dared her not to take the plunge.

She rolled her eyes. "You're so full of it."

"Will someone tell me what's going on?" Hamza seethed. The darkness that crossed his face was almost tangible as his gaze darted between them.

"Your offer is a waste of time. My *wife* and I have things to sort out, but under no circumstances was she ever up for grabs."

"Your what?!" Hamza turned to her in disbelief, his voice trembling with rage "Salma?"

"Mrs. Adesina," Qasim corrected.

"Qasim, stop it or I swear..." She glared at Qasim, warning him not to say another word. He knew when to back down and this time was no different. He raised both hands in surrender as the truth hung heavy in the air.

"Hamza, look. I'm sorry, but this was what I was trying to tell you. I have things to sort out, so I'm not available—"

Hamza raised his hand, dismissing her. One thing she did know about him was that he was a very proud man. Without another word, he picked up his briefcase and walked out. She wasn't worried about him reneging on their deal because they had a binding contract. However, she never wanted bad energy with any of her business partners.

She turned to Qasim and rolled her eyes at him. Unfazed, he smirked at her and that was her cue to leave the conference room. As she made her way to her office, her mind raced trying to figure out what her estranged *husband* was doing here.

~

*S*alma strolled towards her villa, with Qasim a few steps behind. She could sense the intensity of his stare on her back. They were both in agreement that the office wasn't the place to talk. Earlier, he'd had made himself comfortable on the couch in her office as she gave Lia last-minute instructions. With Mustafa and Omar both out of town on business, and Zaina being in their Botswana location, Salma didn't have to worry about running into them. She couldn't explain something she was also clueless about.

She had planned to talk to Qasim, but that was over the phone. There was something different about the look in Qasim's eyes. Whatever he was here for, the one thing she was certain of was he wasn't going to leave Tweede Kans Cove until he got it.

Over the years, she had let go, but wasn't quite sure she forgave him. They were still in an awkward place that she had no clue how to navigate. Their issues were a wedge between them and the last she checked, nothing had changed.

Salma had furrowed her brow when two men pulled up in a sleek black SUV outside Grand Amour. Qasim opened the back door for her, and she hesitated, glancing at him skeptically. "Did you really have to bring them?"

"Yes, and you know why," he responded firmly.

"It's a small town. Nothing is going to happen here."

"Small towns equal unwanted gossip. Please don't fight me. Get in, I'm exhausted."

Salma scoffed and entered the car. "You wouldn't be so exhausted if you weren't beating your chest like King Kong back there."

He tipped his head back against the leather headrest and shut his eyes. "I had to. You were giving that man the illusion that he can have what's mine."

"I haven't been yours in years."

Qasim didn't respond for the rest of their ride to her villa. Now he stood in the center of her living room staring at the self-portrait that hung over her fireplace. Salma watched as Qasim's eyes roamed over the painting. He had always loved this image. It was an oil replica of a picture he took of her as they stargazed years ago. His eyes lingered on it sending a shiver down her spine.

"This is my favorite picture from that night," Qasim murmured, his voice low and husky.

Salma nodded, her throat tight. She knew why. The night he took that picture was the night he proposed. Although every time she entered her living room, she was reminded of the moment of joy that had her floating in the clouds and the subsequent pain of her rapid fall, she couldn't bring herself to get rid of the painting. It had also become a symbol of her strength and resilience.

Qasim turned to face her, his dark eyes burning into hers. "I've missed you, Salma," he said softly.

Salma's heart quickened in her chest, her body betraying her in a way that she had thought was long gone. She ignored the sentiment. In the past, she was all heart when dealing with Qasim and that had cost her dearly. Now she was going to take everything he said from a logical perspective. With that resolve, she asked, "'Sim, what are you doing here?"

"I told you I was coming to take you home."

"Home?" She sucked her teeth. "That was months ago."

"I had things to tidy up. Now I'm ready—"

Anger rippled through her. "You have some nerve. So just like that, I'm supposed to follow you to Nigeria?"

Qasim took a step closer, his hands in his pockets. "Years ago, like a thief in the night, you ran from me." He raised his index finger to silence her argument. "Although I hated it, after my anger faded, I understood it. I failed at the most important part of my job and that's protecting you. Because of that, I let you have your way." He shook his head. "But this space between us, I can't do it anymore."

"I have a life here." She folded her arms across her chest. "And what has changed? We can't just pick up where we left off...be the way we were."

"Our lives are with each other. And the goal isn't to be the way we were; the goal is to create a mosaic with the pieces we have left. I can't do that alone."

After a few moments of silence, Qasim turned and took a seat while she paced the length of the area. He made everything sound so easy. The situation she'd successfully pushed to the back of her mind would implode in her face in a few days. Salma shuddered at the vision of Saturday dinner turning into a disaster.

She had a few days to prepare for the disappointment she'd see in her family's eyes. A look that was bound to kill her. No matter how headstrong her family thought she was, their opinion mattered to her. But with Qasim, nothing else had mattered. Her impulsive decision five years ago had gone wrong so fast, and now she had to deal with it.

"Talk to me," Qasim said.

Salma halted her steps and faced him. The only person who knew she was married was Grandma Olly and recently Yasmine. Her brothers were going to hit the roof and she needed some time to prepare for that to happen.

"My brothers. My family, yours...you make it sound so simple, but it's more complicated than you're willing to admit."

"I never said it was going to be easy. I might lose one of my closest friends, but nothing or no one is going to stop me from getting my wife back...except my wife."

"That's what I don't want. You and O..."

Qasim stood and walked to her. He held her shoulders. "Look, I can handle your brothers. Truth be told, I'm more scared of you." He smirked.

"You made me this way..."

He chuckled. "You're supposed to use the hard girl stuff on outsiders, not me." A beat passed between them. "Anyways, I'll always give you whatever you want, but not telling your brothers about us was a mistake. I regret indulging you. However, it'll be fine. O and I might never be the same and I'm good with that as long as your relationship with him doesn't change."

Her eyes darted toward the clock on the wall. Every Wednesday, she spent some time at Beautiful Eyes. Her commitment to the town's orphanage was one Salma didn't take lightly. Although her stay at an orphanage was brief, she'd never forget how it felt to think no one in the world wanted you.

"I know you have the thing at Beautiful Eyes. I don't want to disturb that." Qasim walked up to her and cupped her face.

"How do—"

"I'm in the penthouse suite of the Palace Cove on the outskirts of the town. I need to handle some business then rest a bit. Have dinner with me?"

She had no plans for the evening other than to work on her knitting, a new hobby she picked up after her doctor's visit in Rabat. The hobbies she loved had become too painful to indulge in because of the man standing before her.

"Come on, Star, it can't be that bad that you won't share a meal with me?" he asked, his voice calm. Almost pleading.

Her hesitation didn't come from a lack of longing, but rather from the depths of her wounded heart that still bore the scars of their past. The air was pregnant with an unspoken tension. She had avoided talking about their situation for five years. Now it was time. Good or bad, they needed closure.

Salma nodded.

Qasim walked up to her and kissed her forehead. A bitter-sweet mix of familiarity and uncertainty coursed through her veins, stirring emotions she had thought were long buried. She watched him leave, feeling a combination of a sliver of hope and apprehension. Salma wondered if this dinner could be the first step towards healing their shattered bond, or if it would only reopen old wounds and tear them apart forever.

CHAPTER 6

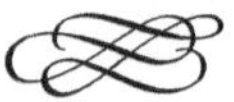

Qasim stepped out onto the balcony of his penthouse suite. Dressed and ready for dinner, he took in the majestic silhouette of the Atlas Mountains against the fading hues of the evening sky. He would've taken up residence in Grand Amour, but figured it was best to put a little space between him and the DuBois-Arazis.

After settling a few things in the office in Ibadan, and checking on his own private ventures, he had boarded the family jet with his two aides in tow. His late flight landed him in Marrakech from where he made the journey to Tweede Kans Cove.

The information Paul had provided him about the whereabouts of the DuBois-Arazi brothers proved handy. Taking Qadir's advice about it being easier to talk to Mustafa and Omar if he wasn't fighting alone, he headed to Salma's office the moment he got into town.

What he wasn't expecting to see was the Moroccan shooting his shot with his wife. Qasim had never been a jealous or possessive man. He considered himself mild-mannered when it came to other men admiring or approaching his wife. However, seeing Mr. Alami standing so close to Salma with a smug look on his face sent him over the edge. The bond Qasim and Salma shared was one of soulmates. They may have lost their way, but she owned him completely as he did her. That he could bet his life on. But he was still a man, and blamed himself for allowing another man to get too close to his wife.

A gentle breeze carried the scent of blooming wildflowers mixed with the distant aroma of Moroccan spices through the air. Qasim held a glass of amber liquid, its smooth warmth radiating through his fingertips. The taste of aged, non-alcoholic whiskey danced upon his tongue, its oak and vanilla flavor evoking memories of shared laughter and tender moments with Salma. She'd introduced him to the brand when she was fed up with him "drinking his pain away," when he was drowning in self-pity from his football injury. As he gazed into the vast expanse before him, Qasim raised his eyes towards the heavens, silently addressing God.

"Father," he began, his words carried away by the wind, "I stand here in awe of the beauty that surrounds me, yet my heart aches for my wife. I messed up thinking I could do everything without You. Show me the way to bring her back into my life, to mend the fractures that have torn us apart."

He recognized the mix of desperation and reverence in his voice. The vulnerability he had become comfortable with exposing resonated with the quiet stillness of the evening. In the silence of his thoughts, Qasim listened for a divine whisper, a sign that would illuminate his path forward.

In the months after Salma left him, he was in his own personal hell and set on a path that would've cost him his life in time. He felt betrayed and manipulated by his family. Salma, who was his best friend, wife, and lover had left him...he had no one. Qasim was on a path to go head-to-head with TOB. Nothing could stop him. They'd destroyed his life, so he was about to make theirs very uncomfortable. Qasim shuddered when he remembered the day.

Dressed in all black, his gun tucked behind his back, Qasim trotted down the stairs of his home. A home he'd built specifically for his new wife was now a prison that housed nothing but his rage. He'd been back in Ibadan full-time working with the farm for six months when his world was turned upside down. Now everyone involved was about to feel his wrath; he owed them all retribution. Retribution for all the pain he went through. The weight of vengeance rested heavily upon his shoulders, fueling his steps as he neared the bar in his home. He poured himself a drink and picked up his burner phone. He'd turned off his real phone and left it in his bedroom. It had been going off all evening. Qasim didn't want to speak to anyone. Not his parents and surely not Qadir. He'd arranged with the rival gang his dad used to exert his revenge. However, fate had a different plan in store. A text message came through the phone in his hand.

Oga 'Sim, fire on the mountain.

Qasim stared at the words that were code for their hideout being raided. As rage burned through him, he contemplated other ways to go about what he was trying to do. The best revenge was damaging the pockets TOB was trying so hard to protect. Qasim had found out the route for the container transporting TOB's goods worth ten million dollars. Redirect and disperse. That was his goal. However, it wasn't a one-man job. The inconvenient and unanticipated delay soon emerged as the catalyst for his change of heart.

That night he'd drowned himself in cognac; the delay of his mission burned him in the chest. He needed to strategize. One thing he couldn't get to drown in his pain was his mother's voice. For the past month that he'd been on his rampage, she'd pleaded for him to reconcile with his father and his brother. Images of her tears when he stopped attending dinners, going to the main house or when her gossip-mongering friends told her they saw him in the unscrupulous part of town, plagued his mind.

With his bottle in one hand, he stood from the couch and made his way up the stairs. In the depths of his mangled thoughts, the word "reconciliation" echoed, like a whisper from a forgotten voice.

"I'm...no...not trying to re...reconcile with anybody. The only woman I want won't talk to me," he slurred, climbing the stairs.

With Me.

The voice resonated with gentle assurance, a balm to his weary soul. One he didn't want to receive. The next day he'd woken up to a massive headache, but in his pain and grogginess, he remembered the stillness of the night. Then a week later, without rhyme or reason, Qasim woke up in a nightmare. The mangled bodies of his loved ones and farm hands were cast upon the farmland. Their families pointed accusatory fingers at him blaming him for not choosing a different course—one that would seek understanding and forgiveness rather than perpetuating a cycle of violence. He woke up in a cold sweat and he fell to his knees. The imaginary noose around his neck led him to cry out to the One his mother never stopped talking about.

Jesus.

The buzz of his cell phone jolted him back from his memory. Through the glass sliding door, he saw the device on the bed. Qasim walked back inside. He'd been raised in the church, so Jesus wasn't a stranger to him. When he was a freshman in college, he got saved. But as the years passed with him not attending church or reading the Bible, coupled with the fame and notoriety of being a professional soccer player, Qasim had strayed far.

"Hey 'Sif," Qasim answered his brother's Facetime call while taking note of the time.

"Check you out! Looking Casanova sharp. Sally won't know what hit her," Qasif joked.

Qasim smiled and shook his head. Salma hated that nickname. The only reason his brothers knew of the name was they'd heard him and Salma arguing one day, and he called her that to grate her nerves.

"Don't let her hear you calling her that."

"She'll be all right." He smiled. "Anyway, just checking in. You know it's like pulling teeth to get Q to share anything."

Qasim laughed. "Q will always be Q, but my business ain't to be broadcasted." The last contact he had with Qadir was when he left Salma's villa. There were no updates to give as nothing had really happened.

"Whatever. You announced your business over dinner. I'm just trying to find out how it's going 'cause the Sally I remember is going to rake you over the coals."

Qasif laughed at his expense. Since he'd be handling a lot of his meetings virtually, he'd given his family a very abbreviated version of what he was doing in Morocco. As far as they were concerned, he was going to get his girl. Qadir was the only one privy to his marital status. Marriage to an Adesina wasn't taken lightly. If his father knew he had a daughter-in-law, someone bearing the Adesina name, roaming around unguarded, he would've raised hell, making Qasim's plight worse. Qasim gave his younger brother the short version of what had happened since he landed in Tweedes earlier.

Their dinner reservation for the night was at the Atlas Oasis, a top tier restaurant on the outskirts of town. The location was to increase their chance of complete privacy. He sent a text to his driver while his brother spoke.

"Hmm, two things. I'd keep an eye on her dude an—"

"He's not her dude."

Qasif chuckled. "You know what I mean. The man offered her whatever she wanted—"

"That won't move her," he defended.

"I know that, you know that, but he doesn't. Neither does he know the weight you come with."

His brother's words played through his mind. Qasim hadn't given Hamza a second thought, but his brother might be right. Apart from knowing he was her husband, Hamza didn't know *who* he was.

Qasif continued with another chuckle, "I hope you have a life insurance policy for Paul. Because when Salma finds out..."

"Like I told Q, she won't."

After a few more jokes at his expense and Qasim threatening

to hang up the phone in Qasif's face, the conversation shifted to the rest of the family. Qamar had gone back to Abuja, while Qasif was preparing for his annual community health fair. His brother's clinic was now a few years old, and the community looked forward to the free event every year.

This year, the event faced an unexpected hurdle of stigmatization. Qasim clenched his jaw. This was the result of the recent negative media coverage the farm had been receiving. Another result of the Brotherhood flexing its muscles as the ties that bound them were on the verge of breaking. After Qasim provided Qadir with all the evidence he had gathered, his brother promised to handle the problem. With what Qasif just told him, Qasim wondered if he should've taken Qadir's advice and waited until their ties were completely severed before coming for his woman.

*

Under a starlit sky, Qasim studied Salma. They were seated atop the beautifully adorned rooftop terrace. Soft candlelight flickered, casting a warm, intimate glow upon her face. She looked breathtakingly beautiful in her flowing ivory dress, her shoulder-length, black hair cascading down in loose waves. Salma set her fork down and lifted her head. Tucking her hair behind her ear, she lifted the globe of Stella Rose and placed it close to her lips.

"You're staring." She took a sip.

"I'm admiring God's creation."

"There you go..." Salma set her glass down, placed her forearms on the table and leaned forward.

Against his will, his eyes went to her cleavage. When he picked her up a few hours ago, his breath caught in his throat when his eyes roamed her body. Her olive skin glowed against the ivory ensemble. The way her dress slithered and coiled enticingly across her breasts, hips, and thighs, stopping just after her knees was nothing short of exquisite. The hour-long drive to the restaurant was relatively quiet. They engaged in small talk which as a couple, they never liked.

When he asked about her afternoon at Beautiful Eyes, she became more relaxed. Volunteering at the orphanage was something she took very seriously. Over their dinner of a fragrant lamb tagine, seasonal vegetables, and a side of couscous, they'd discussed their families. Through Omar, Qasim knew some of what was going on with the DuBois-Arazis, but as a man, Omar wasn't as animated as Salma in his delivery.

As the flavors of the slow cooked meat exploded against his tongue, Qasim digested the story of how Yasmine's husband turned the waiting room of the hospital into a war zone when their son was being born. After taking Yasmine to the back, the nurse promised to come get him. That turned into a thirty-minute wait with no update that triggered something in the guy. Qasim didn't blame Kojo; ten minutes would have been too long for him.

Although Salma was acquainted with members of his family, she had only met them once. She was okay with everyone except his dad. His unannounced entry into their New York apartment, flanked by his security detail definitely had something to do with it.

"You're stalling, baby. I'm still waiting for the answer to my question."

The corner of her lips rose slightly. "What question?"

"I want you back home where you belong. With me, I–"

"You know that's not possible."

"Why?"

"I told you I have a life here. My job, family – they are..."

He took a deep breath before speaking in a low, measured tone. "Your family existed when we got married and the plan was never for you to live here, and I live in Nigeria. What has changed?"

She averted her gaze and sighed. "Are you kidding? A lot has changed. You turned out to be a whole different person from the one I married."

"Don't say that. I never presented myself as anything other than who I was." He clenched his jaw. "Let's be real, I've always been me. The Brotherhood doesn't change that. Granted, they were a part of my family, but I was unaware of how deep the ties were until after I took the CFO position. After we got married." He wiped the corners of his lips with the napkin and threw it down on the table. "Because of you, I tried my best to untangle myself from them. You ma—"

"Are you saying it's my fault those thugs grabbed me? My fault they held me for hours because they wanted to send you a message. My fault that–"

"Don't put words in my mouth. Nothing is your fault, but you made it so hard for me to talk to you when I did find out. So, I tried to handle things on my own. That's what ruffled their feathers."

Qasim's chest tightened as his mind went back to that time in his life he desperately wanted to forget. He had been out of the league for nine months and had been wallowing in despair in his London apartment. Salma helped him get through that. At that time, their years-long friendship had turned into a secret love affair. When his father became ill, Qadir asked him to put his degree to use and work for the farm. He had been working for three months when he and Salma got married on a whim in Paris. Around that time, he found several dummy accounts through which the farm helped the Brotherhood launder money. His brother and his father kept that from him. When Qasim tried to forcefully shut it down, the Brotherhood went after Salma.

Salma crossed her arms and stared at him. "You should've trusted me," she said quietly.

"I trusted what you showed me," he muttered.

"And what was that?" she asked, her voice barely above a whisper.

"That you'd run. And that's exactly what happened."

"You let me," she whispered.

"What was I supposed to do? You were not listening to anything I said for days. Then when you finally did and I thought things were okay, I woke up and you were gone."

Salma lowered her head. "I had to…"

"Why?"

Qasim waited for the answer to the question he had wondered about for years. Why did she give the illusion that they were fine, but still ended up leaving? He was about to ask her again when she looked up from her phone that just buzzed.

"We have to go." She placed the white napkin on the table, scrambling for her purse.

Qasim was out of his seat and by her side at the speed of lightning. "What's wrong?"

She looked at him with wide eyes, her hands trembling as she sent out a text. Qasim dropped some money on the table and called his driver to pull around in front. As they walked out of the door, he could hear part of her conversation with Omar. Their grandmother was being transported to the hospital. Qasim knew how much the elderly woman meant to Salma and her siblings. The lavish birthday party to celebrate her eightieth year on earth was a testament to that. He got Salma into the car and buckled her seat belt before entering and securing his own. The car began to move as Salma got off the phone.

Salma turned to him; her eyes glossed over. "Grandma Olly fell in the tub. We need to—"

"Already on the way. I'm so sorry, baby, she'll be fine." He squeezed her hand.

Qasim stared transfixed as Salma undid her seatbelt and shuffled over to him. Without words, he knew her expectation and opened his arms for her to crawl in his lap. Her frame curled into a ball against him. His arms went around her, gathering her closer, while her scent of jasmine and a woodsy note from her perfume wafted up his nose.

Her body trembled as she nestled her head on his shoulder.

His breathing synced with hers in a gentle melodic dance. Salma placed her lips gingerly on his neck and a warmth spread throughout him. To the ordinary person, the move would seem sexual, but he knew Salma better than anyone. She was scared and needed comfort and connection. He tightened his arms around her to quelch the fear radiating from her. Whatever his wife needed, he provided. He'd failed before; that wasn't an option again.

CHAPTER 7

No, I didn't tell Yas. Pls, don't travel. Musa will kill me.

Zay: Neither he nor O will be able to get there in time. I don't want you alone.

Neither will you, pregnant lady, and I'm not alone.

Zaina sent a smiley and googly eye emoji. Salma sighed then dropped her phone on the kitchen island. She picked up the boiling water and poured it over the lemon tea bag. She added a little bit of honey just the way her grandmother liked it before picking up the buzzing phone. Sighing, she read her sister-in-law's messages.

Zay: You finally gave Hamza a real chance?

Zay: Silence huh? I thought we were past this.

Zay: Okay, I'll mind my business.

You should mind your business…but it's not Hamza.

Salma walked back over to dispose of the trash when her phone began to ring. Rolling her eyes, she answered.

"Spill it…"

"Good evening to you, Mrs. DuBois-Arazi. You know this is the opposite of minding your business."

Zaina fake whined. "Come on, I'm bored. Your brother and I are in different time zones, I don't want to wake him. Your niece or nephew is restless, so I'm awake."

"Do I look like entertainment?" Salma chuckled. "And you know that whiny voice only works on Musa."

Laughing was a sound she was happy she could make after the events of earlier this evening. Contrary to what the house manager said when she called, her grandmother didn't fall to the floor, she missed her step coming out of her shower, but was able to use the handle to break her fall, causing her to sprain her wrist. They had been asking her to let go of the DuBois Manoir when she started getting older. However, she refused because according to her, it housed the memories no other house could give. When her brothers got back, Salma was going to ask them to convince her to at least let them restructure the home so that her bedroom would be downstairs instead.

"It was worth a try," Zaina said.

Salma contemplated whether she should tell Zaina. She wasn't sure if she could keep her secret. Quite frankly, she had never put her to the test.

Before she went to dinner with Qasim, she had talked to Yasmine. That talk totally changed the way she thought that dinner would go. She had been so annoyed with Qasim for so long that she didn't think she would be able to sit with him over a meal.

"Qasim is here," Salma confessed. *The whole family will know soon anyway.*

"What?! How? When?"

"Hmm, I'm pretty sure he used a plane and early this morning."

Salma rolled her eyes at Zaina's laughter. After he made his surprise appearance at their grandmother's birthday party, Yasmine had inquired about the tension between them. While she did, Zaina was there. Over the past couple of months, it had been a running joke between Zaina and her sister that they'd found the one person who Salma was afraid of.

Afraid, no. But Qasim had access to the deepest parts of her. Her fears, pain, goals, passions, and scars. He saw her so wholly that she'd submitted completely to his leadership, until she felt he was no longer worthy. However, the knowledge of his unworthiness didn't stop the effect he had on her.

"So, where's he now?"

Salma had just given her a brief rundown of the events of the day leading up to the call that Grandma Olly was in the hospital. She left out the reason for Qasim's visit or the conversation they had. She had yet to process them herself. Her eyes darted to the timer on the microwave. It was almost one thirty in the morning. When they arrived back at the Manoir several minutes ago, after her grandmother was settled, she requested tea. Salma looked at the cup in her hand. It had had some time to cool a little, and she needed to head up the stairs.

"I'm staying here tonight, so he went to get something to change into because he wanted to stay with me." Salma turned off the light and exited the kitchen.

"That is so sweet."

"Don't make up any fairytales in your head."

"Well, from what I hear, he is a praying man, so half the battle is won."

"Good night, Zay," Salma said, disconnecting the call.

Salma nervously stepped into her grandmother's dimly lit room, comforted by the familiar scent of her favorite perfume and lavender. Her gaze rested on Grandma Olly, and she felt an intense mixture of love and apprehension. Her grandmother was leaning against the headboard of her bed, her Bible cradled in her lap and eyes closed in prayer. The bandages around her wrist caused a knot in Salma's chest that tightened.

"Grandma?" she called softly, concern clear in her voice.

Grandma Olly lifted her head, exhaustion visible in her eyes. "I thought you got lost."

Salma smiled and moved closer to the bed, setting the mug down on the bedside table before sitting on the edge of the bed. "Never that," she said firmly.

Grandma Olly smiled weakly. "Even if you did, I'm positive that young man would move mountains to find you."

Salma shifted uncomfortably, not wanting to talk about Qasim. She had been hoping to keep him away until morning, but apparently it was too late for that now. Gathering her courage, Salma looked her grandmother in the eye.

"Grandma, can we not," she said firmly.

Grandma Olly sighed, understanding the underlying meaning behind Salma's request. She put down her Bible and took Salma's hand in hers.

"Of course, my child," she said softly. "How about we talk about you instead? How are you holding up, really?"

"Me? I'm worried about you."

"And you see there is nothing to worry about." Her grandmother sighed. "I told them not to call you."

Salma chuckled. "You know they're more afraid of Musa than you, right?"

Grandma Olly shook her head and pointed to the teacup which Salma handed her. After their grandmother's hip surgery, Mustafa had left a standing order that one of them should be called immediately if their grandmother experienced any kind of discomfort. They all protected their grandmother fiercely, but Mustafa was in a category all by himself. One that annoyed their grandmother sometimes, but she also understood that watching over her was something he needed. Especially since he felt he didn't do that for their mother.

They sat in silence for a few minutes, the only sound being the soft ticking of the clock on the nightstand. Salma found comfort in the silence, and she knew her grandmother did too.

"*Parle-moi, mon enfant.*"

Salma sighed. "I don't have anything to say. I'm still processing, *Grand-mère*. Bottom line, he wants us back together."

"What do you want?"

That was the question she'd asked herself since Qasim stepped foot in Tweede Kans Cove. The fact that she couldn't give him an unequivocal no bothered her. However, it wasn't something she would discuss tonight.

"I promise, we'll talk tomorrow." Salma stood. "Please drink your tea and rest. I'm in my bedroom and since you invited Qasim, he'll be here too."

"Hush. Child. You know that man wasn't leaving you here alone. He loves you."

Salma frowned. "And how do you know that, oh wise one."

"He told me."

Salma folded her arms across her chest. "Huh, when?"

"You might not have talked to him in years. That doesn't mean I haven't."

He kept in touch?

"*Grand-mère*—"

"I must rest now. We'll talk in the morning."

Salma grinned. *Yeah, now she's tired.* It was now almost two, so Salma decided to leave the questions for the morning. After kissing her grandmother on the forehead, she walked to the door and turned off the light. Her grandmother was using the bedside light to read her Bible and drink her tea.

"Remember, you might not know what you want, but God knows what's best. Ask Him."

Salma nodded, said good night, and left the room.

~

*S*alma sat up and pulled the throw blanket around her shoulders. With her legs dangling off the side of her canopy bed, her eyes darted to the window at the sound of the rumbling thunder. Her heart raced as rain relentlessly pelted the windows. Breathing through her nose and out of her mouth, she tried to relieve her anxiety. Rain and thunder brought her back to the anxieties of childhood, and she had worked hard to develop a series of strategies to cope. But nothing provided relief like her villa—her own sanctuary away from it all.

Another option would be the man two doors down. Qasim was still her best anxiety reliever. But the only way he could do that was by holding her in his arms, and their lines had been blurred enough for one night. As much as she tried to guard her heart against his effect, the nostalgic memories of Qasim gathering her in his arms, rubbing her back and whispering the same words he used to whisper anytime she was afraid, putting her mind in a state of peace.

"Our Father is our refuge and strength, a present help in times of trouble. We will not be afraid."

A feeling she was ashamed to admit she hadn't felt since they parted ways. When they'd arrived at the hospital, without missing a beat, he was back to the man who anticipated and took care of her every need. Growing up the way she did, she had mastered the art of taking care of herself. However, there was something calming about having a man step into those shoes so she wouldn't have to. She saw the way her brother was with Zaina and the way Kojo was with Yasmine. She yearned for that. She had it, once. Then he had to go and ruin it with lies. One thing she learned from her mother – second chances were expensive. Salma didn't give them.

She released a heavy breath, letting her chaotic thoughts drift away while trying to forget the emotions that had resurfaced during dinner. She was an expert at keeping these feelings in check, and she refused to let them overwhelm her now. She knew that as much as she was anxious about the rain, she was better off practicing a breathing technique than waking up a sleeping lion. As she debated with herself, she heard a light tap on the door. Her heart skipped a beat; she closed her eyes.

Of course, he'd come to check on me.

Salma hesitated. She wished for a moment she could be like other women who had stories of their estranged husbands or exes being terrible humans. Qasim wasn't that. He was the sweetest, kindest, most loving man she knew, but he was also a deceitful liar. And that was a deal breaker.

After another tap, she got up from the bed, wrapping the blanket tighter around herself. As she walked towards the door, she could hear the rain intensifying outside. She opened the door and her eyes widened at the sight of a bare-chested Qasim. Her eyes immediately darted to the small tattoo of her name on the upper right side. His pajama bottoms hung loose on his hips while his silk durag was secured on his head.

Yeah, he knows exactly what he's doing.

Standing at the half open door, Salma quickly tried to camouflage the obvious effect he wanted his exposed skin to have. "'Sim, what are you doing here?"

"I see we're making progress." He leaned his shoulder against the door frame.

"What are you talking about?"

His lips pulled up in a grin. "This morning and at dinner, I was Qasim. Now, I'm 'Sim. I'll be back to honey soon enough."

Salma fought her smile and smirked instead. He had always teased her saying her term of endearment for him was for old people. After a while, she told him the reason she called him "honey" was because that was what her grandparents called each other. They were the first representation of healthy love for her. Salma recalled Qasim peppering kisses all over her when she disclosed that information, vowing to be her "honey" in this life and the next.

"You're remembering that day, aren't you?" He winked.

That was another thing she hated. His ability to read her like no one else could. Years of being friends first contributed to that, but still it irked her. Especially at times like this.

"In your dreams…"

"If you say so, but you'll call me that again. Sooner than you think."

"I think I want to go to bed now. It's late."

"I know how late it is. I also know what thunder does to you. So, are you going to let me in, or are we going to stand at the door all night?"

Her eyes roamed his frame again. "You know this is my grandmother's house. Where's your shirt?" She walked back into the room, and he followed.

"If you're concerned about grandma, I'll be dressed by the time she gets up." He sauntered over to the bed. "For you, these pj pants are the best I can do. You know I sleep in my birthday su—"

"I don't know anything."

"Yes, you do. The fact that you're angry with me doesn't change that." He sat on the bed and patted her side. "Now, woman will you get in, please, so I can hold you. You need to sleep."

Salma scoffed and draped the blanket over the padded bench at the end of the bed, revealing her cotton shorts pajama set. "Don't act like you're doing me any favors."

With his hands intertwined behind his head, Qasim stared at her. "Oh, I'm not. This is mutually beneficial."

She hesitated, digesting his words. "Don't get any ideas in your head. Nothing is happening."

"Woman, if you don't get in this bed… I'm a grown man who can control himself." He smirked. "Now, I'm not saying the big guy down there won't react to having his owner rub up against him. But absolutely nothing is happening until you and I are on the same page."

Before she could get the words out, the heavens seemed to

open in an angry symphony of thunder and lightning. A tree branch slammed against the window as if it was warning her to stay silent. She jolted with fear, her heart threatening to burst from her chest.

Qasim sat up, concerned etched in his eyes. "Star, come here…"

Salma climbed into the bed and Qasim drew her nearer. Spooning her, he kissed the back of her neck.

"You still pray right?" he asked.

"I should elbow you…what do you think I am?"

He chuckled. "Hey, I had to ask. Those texts you sent me after your grandmother's party had heathen written all over them."

"You should ask yourself why," she said.

Qasim grunted. "Father God, with a contrite heart, we thank You for today. We bless You for Grandma Olly's healing. Watch over us through the night and grant us peace. In Jesus' name."

"Amen," they said in unison.

Qasim softly kissed the top of her head. His lips lingered for a moment, sending chills up her spine as his breath warmed her skin. She smiled, wishing him good night before allowing herself to drift off into sleep.

"Do you feel that?" Qasim asked a few moments later.

"What?" she murmured groggily.

"Restored equilibrium," he whispered.

"Good night 'Sim."

She had no comeback to refute the accuracy of his statement. She did feel it, but their physical connection was never off-kilter. It was their hearts, minds, and souls that were out of harmony.

CHAPTER 8

The morning sun gently filtered through the curtains, illuminating the traditional Moroccan breakfast spread as they waited for Grandma Olly to make her appearance. Qasim wasn't really a breakfast person, but with Salma, he needed all the help he could get. Therefore, declining Grandma Olly's breakfast invitation would've been the wrong way to go. He replied to Qadir's text regarding their upcoming call in two hours. He didn't know how long he would stay in Tweede Kans Cove when he left Ibadan since he couldn't predict Salma's reaction to him. One thing he did know was that he wasn't leaving without her. Because of that, he set up an office area in his hotel suite, so that he could conduct business while there.

Last night, he had the best sleep of recent years. That was a feeling he was no longer willing to exist without. His eyes trailed Salma hungrily as she took a call from one of her managers. She'd never looked so sexy to him. The light brown sweater over white, loose-fitting pants that clung to her curves so nicely, had him remembering the silk pajama set she wore last night that showed much more skin. His body quivered with intense heat emanating from his core, in anticipation of their lovemaking once they got on the same page regarding their marriage.

It had taken all the willpower he had and a plea to the Holy Spirit for help for him not to ravish her last night. As she lay in his arms, oblivious to his struggle, he almost gave in to his desire and changed his mind about not taking things further yet. Her sweet skin was pressed against his bare chest as he fought to keep them both still.

Memories of a time in their relationship when they couldn't keep their hands off each other flooded through his mind. His brothers called them nasty, but if he couldn't get freaky with his wife, then they had problems. He loved that her sexual appetite matched his, but that also made the last five years so hard. When he wasn't drowning himself in work, he was in the gym or busy with other activities. His gaze remained glued to her as he envisioned the decadent ways he'd make love to her when the time came.

Salma hung up the phone, her eyes trained on the table where he waited. She crossed the room slowly and lowered herself into the chair.

He peered at her inquisitively. "Everything okay?"

She raised a brow in disbelief. "Err...yeah."

"What's that face for?"

Salma shifted in her seat and shrugged slightly. "I'm not used to this...to you coming to my rescue like this." She grabbed her orange juice glass and took a sip, avoiding his gaze.

"I've never stopped. However, it's hard to rescue someone who acts like you don't exist."

"Can we not?"

"We're going to have to."

Salma stood. "It won't be now. I have to get going." She walked toward the kitchen.

Qasim followed. "You're going to leave me here with your grandmother?"

She opened the cupboard for a Tupperware container and walked back to the table. "Yep. You're the one that wants back into the family. Also, according to what I'm told, you've remained in contact with her."

Qasim watched as she packed some food in her container. Voices coming from the stairwell stopped her. Moments later, the doctor who'd arrived earlier on Salma's insistence appeared, ushering in Grandma Olly. Qasim walked up to them and took the older woman's hand in his. She looked much better than when he saw her the night before.

"Doc, how is she?" Salma asked.

The doctor looked at Grandma Olly whom Qasim had helped take her seat at the head of the table.

"She's fine. All she has to do is rest her wrist and she'll be back to new in no time." After a few more instructions on medication dosage in the event of pain, the doctor left.

"I'm surprised you're still here," Grandma Olly said to Salma.

Qasim chuckled as he prepared Grandma Olly's plate based on the items she pointed out. He could feel Salma's warning eyes on him, but he ignored them. Her grandmother knew exactly what he knew; his wife ran away at the slightest inconvenience.

"Why wouldn't I be? I had to make sure you were okay," Salma said.

Qasim placed the plate in front of the older woman and poured her some mint tea.

"Thank you, my dear." She lifted her eyes to Salma. "I'm fine child, but I expected you to avoid what you don't want to tackle..."

"Sorry to disappoint both of you, but I can't even avoid him if I tried."

"Not anymore you can't," Qasim added.

Strolling toward her grandmother, she kissed her on the cheek, rolled her eyes at him and headed for the door. Qasim turned toward Grandma Olly and excused himself. He caught up with Salma as she was about to put her coat on. He took it from her and helped her into it.

Qasim's lips curled into a smirk. "My car is waiting outside. The driver will take you," he said.

Salma stood still, her shoulders rising and falling with each heavy breath. She refused to turn around and acknowledge him.

"Don't tell me you're upset." Qasim chuckled.

Salma spun on her heels to face him, her eyes flashing angrily. "That you and my grandmother ganged up on me? No, why should that upset me?"

Qasim's laughter filled the room as he pulled her close with the lapel of her coat. "There goes my brat," he said fondly, despite the tension in the air.

Salma swatted his shoulder and yawned. Last night had been eventful and even though their slumber was peaceful, they'd only had a few hours before they had to get up to start the day.

"You're the boss. Why not call in and play hooky with me?" Qasim kissed her forehead. "Show me the town. It's been years since I've been here, and you weren't scowling at me."

Salma lifted her brow. "Maybe we haven't gotten to that part yet."

Qasim smiled. "We're moving forward, not backward."

"As tempting as that sounds, I have a meeting in an hour, then an inspection." She leaned her head on his shoulder.

Qasim threaded his fingers through her silky tresses and massaged her nape. She had her hair down, so he didn't run the risk of her complaining he was messing it up. A moan escaped her lips before she grunted and stood to her full height.

"You're going to make me fall asleep."

"Good to know that my fingers still have that magical touch."

"They're dangerous too...let's not forget dangerous." Salma turned and walked out of the house.

Qasim watched as his driver approached her, took the briefcase from her hand, and opened the back door. Once the car started moving, Qasim headed back inside. He planned to have breakfast with her grandmother then head to the hotel. Aiming to be done with work by noon, Qasim had plans to take his wife outta town. They needed privacy before her brothers returned by the weekend.

Walking back to the dining area, Qasim rejoined Grandma Olly at the breakfast table. Her face was an unreadable mask as he sat down.

"Now that my granddaughter is gone, would you like to tell me what you're doing here?"

Qasim swallowed hard and forced a smile. One thing remained true about the matriarch of the DuBois-Arazi family: she held no punches. He'd been to Tweede Kans Cove a few times before, but he hadn't been able to bring himself to come back here in the last three years. When he got the invitation to her birthday party, his attendance had been strategic because of the reports he had gotten from Paul.

When he and Salma first broke up, he came after her, hoping against hope to get her back. But she had avoided him at every turn, filling her calendar with out-of-town trips right before he arrived. Then he wasn't sure what she told her grandmother, but he could feel the coldness radiating from her. A sharp contrast from the look in her eyes now.

"I want my wife back," Qasim replied. There was no use delaying the inevitable.

Grandma Olly raised an eyebrow at his statement. "And how do you plan on doing that?" she asked, sipping her tea.

Qasim took a deep breath. "I don't know yet. But I can't keep living without her. She's everything to me."

Grandma Olly sighed. "I don't know how much time I have left on this earth before my Father calls me home. One of the greatest joys of my life has been watching my grandchildren grow up and become who they are."

Qasim took in the distant look in her eyes as she stared out the window.

A few beats later, she turned to him. "You're no stranger to how they came to live here. I'm not sure how much my baby girl told you, but those kids endured a tragedy no child should have to endure." She took another sip of her tea. "Watching them find love has been a blessing. But the pain I saw in Salma's eyes when she returned home is something I never want to see again." Grandma Olly fixed her gaze on him. The warning behind her tone was clearly understood.

Qasim nodded ruefully. "I know and I regret that."

"I've always liked you. From the first time you visited with Omar, to the times you started pretending he was the only one that brought you to Tweedes…"

Qasim chuckled. He first met Salma when she was in college at NYU. However, it wasn't until a few years later, when she was completing The Certified Meeting Professional program in New York that their relationship grew. She had his head all messed up. Anytime his schedule allowed, he flew to New York, or he would fly her to London. By that time, Omar had returned to Tweede Kans Cove full time. Grandma Olly was right. There were times when he needed his "Salma fix" and she would be visiting home. On those occasions, Qasim would fly down.

"I love her."

"I know you do. But sometimes love is not enough. Out of all my grandchildren, Salma's scars are deepest. Underneath the bravado is a little girl who is still hurting. Hurting from the loss of her parents and the loss of a love she allowed herself to believe in."

Qasim nodded again. There were things he wanted to say, but the person who deserved to hear them first was his wife. He knew all about Salma's wounds. Unfortunately, to prevent her pain and preserve his sanity, he made a decision that caused those wounds to bleed on them both. Instead of voicing that, he promised Grandma Olly he would do things right this time around. A vow he planned to fulfill.

"*Iya mi*, you do know I know how to win over my wi... a woman." Qasim caught himself just in time and quickly amended his words. His mother was daughter-in-law hungry, so even hinting that she already had one wouldn't be in his best interest.

"This isn't just any woman; she's the one you let get away."

A few hours later, he climbed in his truck headed to his hotel and his mother's call came through. Qasim hadn't talked to her since he'd arrived and as tired as he was, he knew that not answering her wasn't the best move. All he wanted to do was to shut his eyes for a minute. He'd spent the morning convincing Grandma Olly he wasn't going to lose Salma again. He knew how much the older woman meant to Salma, so even during their estrangement, he called her often to check in. She was also the keeper of their secret. After the question-and-answer segment of their talk, she began advising him on what he needed to do to get Salma back.

Be honest.

He knew Salma said she wanted honesty, but he wasn't sure she could handle the truth. He would always be who he was...an Adesina. Being a part of the family business forced him to accept who he was and take the good, bad, and ugly that came with his name. He'd spent five years untangling his family from illegal dealings, but that didn't mean they were free from enemies. The only difference now was that he had the means to protect his wife. His past naiveté made him underestimate the Brotherhood before, but that wouldn't happen again.

Deciding not to debate his mother, he listened as she went on and on, giving him tips on how to win Salma back. Now that the women she brought around him at family functions hadn't been able to help him get over his broken heart, and his brother had no intention of marrying his fake fiancée, she was becoming antsy about being a grandmother. Getting Salma back suddenly became a mission his mother decided was her own. He knew she liked

Salma, but they had stopped speaking of her years ago, until recently. Qasim made another attempt to block his mother out when something she said struck a chord.

"Son, since she is truly the love of your life, fight. Fight every obstacle that comes between you and her living the life you both deserve."

Growing up, their parents instilled in them the importance of honoring the ties that bind them. At that moment, he realized that what his mother didn't know was that the obstacle in his way might be the very thing she held dear: their family. As the driver pulled up to his hotel, Qasim told his mother he'd call her soon before sending Salma a text.

Hey, checking in. How are you?

He got in the elevator and rode to the top floor while awaiting her reply. As soon as he entered his suite, it came.

My Star: I'm okay. You survived breakfast…lol.

You have jokes.

My Star: At your expense? Always.

Don't get mad when I return the favor.

She sent him an emoji with the tongue out and a laughing one. Smiling, Qasim dropped the phone on the counter and opened the refrigerator. The beauty of his best friend being his lover and wife was a fulfilling and rare experience. Picking up his phone and walking into the office area, he reminisced about the first time he saw her.

He was still playing professional soccer when he and Omar met at a party in New York about ten years ago. After the party, they stayed connected. Omar was the rich Arab and he was the famous soccer star and they both partied hard. Through them, their older brothers met and started having business dealings together. Qasim had heard of Omar's twin, but hadn't met her until a year after he met Omar.

Qasim and Omar had gotten their wires crossed, causing Qasim to show up at Omar's New York condo when he was actually back in Tweede Kans Cove. By this time, he'd seen pictures of Salma, but when she opened the door that day, his world stood still. Her beauty immediately snatched the breath from his lungs. Breath, he was not even ashamed to admit she hadn't given back.

Salma invited him in. His exaggerated reputation must have preceded him because she turned her nose up at him. He teased her until this day about how rude she'd been. For some reason, unlike everyone else, he desperately wanted to change her mind about him. He partied, yes, spent money like water, yes, was the stereotypical bad boy, all true. But he didn't sleep around or have a string of women like the media said.

God and Mother Nature were on his side, because while he was there, the heavens opened to a blizzard that snowed them in. That weekend was the game changer. By the time he returned to London, he had gained a friend. No matter what people said, or how cliché it sounded, the fact that Salma had her own money and didn't give any care as to who he was, turned him on and sent him on the chase. A chase she immediately vetoed—when she friend zoned him for a year.

My Star: Bring it on. I'm not scared of you.

Salma's text came in bringing him back to the present. He powered on his laptop. Qadir had been able to push the meeting. It was now set to start in ten minutes.

Be ready by lunchtime.

My Star: 'Sim, I have a lot of work to do.

You're the boss and I want your time. Be
ready to leave in two hours.

He smiled when she sent him an eye-rolling emoji. He was on a mission to get his wife on the same page regarding their marriage. Avoiding the DuBois-Arazi brothers for now was wrong, but necessary. Everybody couldn't be like Yasmine's husband who Salma told him went through the brothers first. He was an Adesina—they operated differently. Everything else could be handled later. Whether through conversation or by force, one thing was certain.

His wife was coming home with him.

Some hours later, Qasim stood at the periphery of the bustling resort lobby. He spotted Salma the minute he entered through the double doors. She was in the corner with about five employees huddled around her. Her hair was now pinned back, and her sleeves were drawn up slightly. As she spoke, her grace and authority were illuminated by the sun streaming through the large windows, casting a warm glow on the scene unfolding before him.

As the guests walked by, her serious expression morphed into a warm smile. Qasim took the time to study a side of her he rarely saw. Her passion for her work and the genuine care she showed for her team was admirable and gave him an idea. He'd ask her to consult on the rebranding of the farm's Farm to Table initiative. He hoped it would give her an added incentive to come back with him.

Salma was a boss. Beauty, brains, and sex appeal all in one, and she belonged to him. His jewel, so rare, to be protected and cherished. Having his fill of watching her and intent on satisfying the desire to touch her, Qasim lifted off the bar he'd been leaning on and made his way to her. Their first reservation was in four hours. He wanted to be settled way before then.

CHAPTER 9

She'd always thought that the thing about residents of a town being oblivious to its attractions until a tourist came in and raved about those same attractions was just something people said. Now, standing on the balcony of the penthouse suite of the Royal Mansour in Marrakech and taking in the skyline of the city, that sentiment proved to be true. Being a DuBois-Arazi and the demands of her job afforded her the ability to travel far and wide. She had stayed in different resorts and hotels, making her no stranger to luxury. However, nothing, at least not in recent memory, compared to this hotel Qasim, her husband, had booked for them.

My husband.

That term had become foreign to her. After she got over her initial impression of Qasim, although she was smitten with him, she refused to be wrapped up in his charm. He was a famed footballer who lived a continent away. Although he courted her, she insisted they remained friends. Even after she gave up fighting their attraction, referring to him as anything other than 'Sim or Qasim was still strange to her. The night he told her he loved her, he became "honey." Salma smiled. She hadn't referred to him as anything other than a jerk in so long that now referring to him by his rightful title would take some getting used to.

After he picked her up from work earlier, they swung by her villa so she could pack just the necessities as Qasim called them.

"Make it quick, Star. We'll be gone for three days only..."

"Since you won't tell me where we are going, I need to make sure I'm covered," she'd said, walking down the hall to her bedroom.

She'd ignored his grunt and second warning, which turned out to be a mistake. A few minutes later, as she was staring at her closet, her husband walked in and started packing for her. A smirk crossed her face as she observed him pack the exact products she needed from her bathroom. Her amusement quickly turned into annoyance at the thought that he seemed too familiar with women's products. Her stomach twisted in knots at the thought of him probably packing for another woman.

Folding her arms across her chest, she leaned against the door frame. "I see you know your way around a woman's bathroom."

He glanced over at her. "Fix your face. I know my way around *your* bathroom." Lifting her packed toiletry case, he walked into her bedroom and grabbed her duffle bag. "Let's go, baby. If you need anything else, we'll get it along the way."

"Forgot how bossy you can be."

It didn't take long before they reached Grandma Olly's home. Salma had a feeling her grandmother already knew where they were headed, probably explaining why the older woman didn't bombard her with questions. As Qasim spoke with the driver, Grandma Olly took Salma aside.

"If you still want to be married to him, don't forget that love keeps no records of wrong. Both of you must learn how to communicate better. Don't listen to respond—listen to understand. It's easy to throw those three little words around, but marriage is more than that. Compromise, commitment, and sacrifice are important." Grandma Olly squeezed her hand. "Don't keep your husband waiting." After another kiss and tight hug, her grandmother ushered her out of the house.

Blinking away the memory, she reached for her phone in her back pocket. Salma took a few pictures of the breathtaking skyline and walked back into the suite to find said husband. Glancing at her phone, she responded to the group chat she had with Yasmine and Zaina. The same one that Yasmine's overfriendly behind created even before the ink dried on Zaina and Mustafa's marriage certificate.

We just got here abt 30 mins ago. Can you girls chill for a minute? LOL

Yas: Not an excuse, the minute you arrived, you should've sent us pictures.

Zay: Agreed.

Is this how it is? Get married and start minding other people's business?

Yas: You should know.

Zay: Meaning?

Salma shook her head, walking toward her own room. Salma didn't know who *this* Yasmine was. There was a time when getting information from her sister was a high-level sporting event. Now she leaked like a faucet.

Yas: Nothing

Zay: I know you're keeping something from me... but that's fine.

Salma laughed, before texting back.

> Yas watch out. That's code for I'll whine and guilt trip you until you tell me the truth.

Yasmine sent a couple of laughing emojis while Zaina sent one rolling her eyes. Salma was on the verge of responding when she heard Qasim's raised voice. The bellman was about to give them an overview of the two-bedroom suite when Qasim's phone rang. Lines of agitation appeared on his forehead. He planted a kiss on her temple then he excused himself. That had been a while ago, but she had occupied herself by exploring the place they would be staying for the next couple of days.

> Zay, I need you to decide on the stuff I sent you for the baby shower.

Her brother the overprotector overheard Salma and Yasmine planning the shower and didn't like the idea of the celebration being a surprise. Mustafa claimed that in a documentary about pregnancy and motherhood he'd watched one night, they talked about surprises and unexpected jolts being bad for expectant mothers. How that happened or if that was really what the documentary said, Salma didn't know. But to her brother, it was gospel and made him apprehensive, so she went with it.

Her sister-in-law had about four months to go, so she needed to finalize things soon. While the three bubbles appeared indicating Zaina was responding, Salma went in search of her husband.

The door of his room was open, but she still tapped on it to alert Qasim to her presence. He turned to face her, his expression apologetic. On the flight over, she fell asleep while he worked on his laptop. He had promised her over and over that once they landed, he was all hers. She understood that sometimes there were things that couldn't be helped, so she wasn't upset. Yet she wondered what it was that got him so rattled. She understood the basic workings of his family's farm, but being CFO of the whole enterprise had to be a daunting job. His earbuds were in his ears while both hands were shoved into his pockets. He was dressed down today. Black drawstring pants and a simple grey t-shirt that hugged his muscles. Lifting his hands, he beckoned her to him.

"Anita, get with Mr. Canto. I need those figures by morning. You know how important the crop yield figures are to the quarter revenue projections. It must be included in the package for True Foods. The minute you were made aware of an issue, I should've been your first call."

Salma sat on the bed and watched as he listened to the person on the other end of the line. From Qasim's demeanor, nothing the person was saying was good enough.

"All I hear are excuses. If I have to do your job, I don't need you now, do I? My brother is expecting us to close this deal. He needs it for the R&D expansion that has already been communicated to our partners. If we don't have accurate data, we risk losing this contract, and it will have a ripple effect on our entire operation. All this, I thought you already knew!"

Salma could feel Qasim's energy as she approached. As if drawn by an invisible force, she found herself leaning into him as his arm snaked around her waist. His palm traveled across her back and settled with a burning heat right on the curve of her buttocks.

He felt like home. That realization caused her to shiver.

With her arms around his neck, their eyes met and danced with a shared hunger so great that it was almost palpable in the room.

"Look, I gotta go. Get the team working around the clock if you have to. I need those numbers by tomorrow."

Qasim gave one final command before ending the call. Salma's breath hitched as time stilled in their embrace. Qasim was the only one who could unravel her. With one hand still anchoring her to him, he used the other to remove his earbuds and tossed them on the bed. It had been a minute since her body had been tethered to his. The previous night in his arms, she was comfortable, but her mind also spent the time deathly afraid of her decision being clouded by their sexual chemistry.

"Everything okay?" Salma lowered her eyes while trying and failing to detangle herself from his embrace.

"Look at me," he commanded. His tone forced her obedience. "Are we that bad that you can't meet my eyes while in my arms?"

"Being in your arms isn't the problem," she said softly. "I'm afraid of what comes after."

Qasim chuckled and took her hand, guiding her to the bed. "'Sim…"

"Relax. Didn't I tell you that nothing's happening until we're on the same page?" He sat on the bed and pulled her to his lap. His arm circled her waist.

"Mighty confident, aren't you?"

"With you? Always. I know every inch of my wife's body and when the time comes, you'll be begging me to quench the fire."

She swatted his shoulder. "Nasty…"

Qasim went into a full-on laughing fit. She missed hearing the rumble that vibrated from his chest when he laughed. That should have been her clue after they got married that something was wrong. Suddenly he was stressed, and his laughter seemed more forced than from the pits of his belly like she had been used to. She'd been in such wedded bliss that she didn't listen to what her grandmother ground into her and Yasmine's head as kids.

"Listen to your gut. A woman's intuition never fails."

She didn't want to believe that the love of her life was anything but honest with her when she had asked him repeatedly if everything was okay. She had a strict rule of cutting off anyone at the first sign of their dishonesty. No one would have made her believe *her* Qasim was capable of not only lying to her, but also exposing her to danger.

Forgiving a man for his transgressions was what got her mother killed. She forgave her father repeatedly after he put his hands on her. There was no way she was repeating her mistakes.

Her grandmother's words about being open fluttered through her mind and she blinked her eyes to get rid of the memory.

"So, is everything okay?" she asked.

"It will be. I should've had some numbers to send to Q this afternoon. Instead, I'm being told the person responsible dropped the ball."

"If you have to work, I completely understand."

"Nice try. But no. My only goal for the next three days is getting you to tell me what I gotta do to fix us." Qasim buried his face in the crook of her neck. "Don't you miss me, baby?"

Salma closed her eyes and took a deep breath. The scent of his cologne and the coolness of his breath threatened to take her under. The number of years she'd been celibate had to be a record somewhere in the world. But she was about to break her celibacy streak if she didn't get away from Qasim now.

"I thought we..."

Qasim's lips grazed Salma's neck, silencing her question. His teeth nipped her lightly and she released a moan of pleasure. Her quest to remind him of their dinner reservations was quenched by his desire to taste her. He threaded his fingers through her hair as his mouth continued its descent, kissing and sucking down along the exposed part of her chest the V-neck t-shirt allowed. Captured by the euphoria of their embrace, she barely had the energy to speak.

"I thought...we...had dinner reservations?" she struggled to whisper.

He paused, then pulled her head down to his. His lips almost touched hers. "Our reservation is in two hours."

Before she could respond, he captured her lips in a deep, passionate tango. As she leaned into him, he broke their exchange. Salma grunted, her body hummed, and she frowned.

"Don't look at me like that. You take forever to get ready," he said with a grin.

She rolled her eyes. "This you knew before—"

"Sue me. Do you know how long I've been waiting to kiss you?" Qasim winked, pecked her lips, and patted her thigh.

Salma sucked her teeth before standing and strolling to the door.

"Star baby..." Qasim called out.

"I'll be ready. "Salma chuckled as she walked through the connecting door to her own part of the penthouse. A cold shower and the privacy of her own space would give her the time she needed to refocus her thoughts. As she stepped into her room, her thoughts went to her twin and her chest tightened. Once she and Qasim became friends, Omar was skeptical. He thought they were in a relationship, but they weren't...then.

"He's a great friend to me, but Sal, he'll be a terrible boyfriend to you," he always said.

According to him, a celebrity football player from a wealthy family who was among the highest paid in the league was a dangerous combination. On some level, he was right.

She started dating Qasim several months before he got injured. And although they continued to claim they were just friends because of the press, Omar knew and didn't approve. They broke up briefly, but she didn't tell Omar when they got back together. Once they got back together, Qasim took her to Paris one weekend and proposed. He was leaving Europe for Nigeria, but she was still in New York.

Salma dreaded the look in her brother's eyes when she came clean in a couple of days. Would he forgive her? Would he forgive Qasim? Starting the shower, she decided to focus on the present with Qasim. The outcome would determine how big or small the damage might be.

～

A little over an hour later, Salma studied her reflection in the mirror. She still wasn't sure what Qasim had planned for the night, only that he wanted her dressed in something "smart casual." Her eyes drifted over the black, one-shoulder jumpsuit she'd chosen to wear. She fluffed her hair, pressing her lips together to even out her lipstick before snapping a photo and sending it off to Yasmine. Her sister was about to drive her nuts asking for updates she didn't have to give.

Yasmine was more on edge than she was about Mustafa and Omar. If she had her way, she would be in Tweede Kans Cove this weekend to provide Salma a buffer. However, Salma told her this was a situation she had to face alone. Moreover, she'd be home for Zaina's baby shower in a few weeks.

Turning to pick up her light pink clutch, her phone buzzed in her hand. Looking down, her lips turned up in a smile. Yasmine had liked the photo and sent a response.

> Yas: You look sexy, Sal. Remember, hear him out.

Salma sent her a couple of heart emojis, then there was a knock on the door. Her heart skipped a beat when she saw Qasim on the other side of the door. Qasim smiled. She moved aside, allowing him to saunter into the room. He was dressed to impress in an all-black ensemble that showed off his broad shoulders. A dress shirt with the top button open was tucked into his well-tailored pants. To complete the look, he donned a sleek black sports coat.

He stretched out his hand. She took it and he twirled her. She could smell the subtle musk of his cologne mixed with raw male energy that seemed impossible to resist or escape. Their chemistry was so tangible, it was almost too much to bear.

"You look stunning, love." He placed a gentle kiss on her cheek.

"You don't look too bad yourself. Although I see you're still trying to copy my style." She winked mischievously and put her phone in her clutch bag before stepping out into the hallway with him.

Qasim chuckled at her comment, playfully putting an arm around her shoulder as they walked towards the private elevator. "If I must copy someone, I think my wife is the best choice."

"Come on, smooth talker. I'm starving," Salma replied, rolling her eyes affectionately as they entered the elevator together.

He reached out for her and leaned her against him, her back, flush with his chest. As the elevator took them to the lobby, he hummed the chorus of "Crush" by Yuna ft. Usher in her ear. The moment felt surreal for Salma as Qasim wrapped his arms around her. It reminded her of their time together before everything crumbled. A few minutes later, they were entering their car on the way to the restaurant.

A sense of déjà vu swept over Salma as the sun dipped over the horizon. She'd always known Qasim had more access than most because of who he was. She thought nothing else could surprise her. Yet dining on the rooftop of La Terrasse de la Brillante on such short notice astonished her.

The restaurant was situated on the roof of an expensive boutique hotel near the Bahia Palace in the middle of Marrakesh. The exorbitant prices were well worth it. Not only was the cuisine divine, but the polished yet discreet service and the beautiful ambiance with stunning views of the city below provided an experience wrapped in luxury. They could see the majestic Atlas Mountains in the distance and Koutoubia – Marrakesh's biggest mosque.

When they first arrived, Salma couldn't resist taking a few pictures of the breathtaking view. The lights of the city sparkled below them, and the aroma of roasted lamb and exotic spices wafted through the air. As they dug into their meals, Qasim told her stories of his recent deals and business pursuits. Although he no longer played soccer, there were still brands that wanted him as their spokesperson. Salma listened intently, marveling at his dedication to his goals. Apart from the delicacy with which he treated her, totally the anti-sport celebrity stereotype, the fact that being born with a platinum spoon didn't deter him from his dedication to whatever he set his mind on was so sexy to her.

Yet, an overwhelming sense of betrayal when she discovered the truth about him rocked her to the core. His deceit crushed her confidence and crippled her trust in her own judgment, leaving behind a painful residue of disappointment and heartache.

Salma looked up from her dessert when she felt Qasim's hand over hers. Their eyes locked in a passionate exchange, which spoke volumes without a word. They'd been having such a good time laughing and catching up. Now reality had set back in. Salma knew they needed to have a difficult conversation about their relationship – one that could change everything.

"So, what we doing, Star?"

"Can I finish my meskouta first?"

"That's your second helping. You'll be all right."

Salma placed her hand across her chest. "You dare dessert shame me?"

Qasim chuckled. "I'm not fooling with you, woman. You do remember the many nights I fed you dessert in bed, right?"

With her mouth open, Salma looked around. "Must you be so nasty?"

"First, you love me for it. Second, you are my wife. I'll be that way with you wherever I want and lastly, get your mind out the gutter. I was talking about lemon cake. What were you talking about?"

Salma smirked. "Hmmm..." A few beats passed between them. She used the comfortable silence to gather her thoughts. Tucking her hair behind her ear, she took a breath and met his eyes again.

"Why did you lie to me? I bore every part of me to you. Why did you lie?"

"I didn't lie to you—"

She raised her hand. "'Sim stop! No matter how you want to sugarcoat it, you didn't tell me the truth. If you did, I would've been prepared...ready."

"Would you? Remember when you always made comments calling me perfect?"

Salma remained silent. She knew what he was talking about, but she didn't necessarily need to give him an answer. He was perfect...well until he wasn't.

"Baby, you expected me to be the perfection you didn't see growing up. The picture of perfection your brothers make you believe they are–"

"Oh, so we're dumping on brothers now. Because I have—"

"Stop being difficult and listen to me..." He sighed.

Salma felt her body heat rise as she listened to Qasim's words. She could feel his energy soaring, becoming desperate and frustrated.

"Once the light shone on what came with me...despite all the love I showed you, all the reassurances I gave you before that incident I'll spend my life making up for...you ran. You ran Salma, my heart be damned, you ran. The painful part is you shut me out like I didn't exist. Like what we had didn't mean anything.

"Out of respect for you, and giving you time, I didn't come blazing. I had to hound your grandmother to see how you were. I'm not the kind of man who hides his woman from the world, nor the one who lets what belongs to him slip away, let alone my wife. But for you, I've calmed down my beast. But that's done. I want you to come home."

Salma lowered her head. "Do you know that until a year or so ago, I had to have one of the resort's drivers fuel my car?" she said, her voice, barely a whisper.

Whenever she encountered a whiff of gasoline, her heart would race, and a rush of anxiety would overwhelm her. The memories of the day she was taken resurfaced, bringing back the vivid images of confinement, vulnerability, and the struggle for survival.

She had just said goodbye to her friends after a great lunch. As she walked towards her car, two men suddenly appeared out of the shadows. She froze in fear when they requested she follow them, or they would kill her. For six hours, she was held captive while they spoke French and what she knew to be Yoruba and Hausa. They never laid a hand on her or mistreated her, but she shouldn't have been there in the first place. When she'd found out why, anger boiled within her.

Qasim's thumb swiped the tear cascading down her cheek. She wasn't even sure when he moved his seat closer to her.

"I'm sorry. I underestimated the Brotherhood. I was trying to clean up the mess my grandfather and father made." Qasim ran his hand over his head. "Blinded with rage that my brother hadn't disclosed the depths of our involvement, I completely shut him out. Since I was flying solo, I didn't think they had eyes or would dare come after you. That's on me! It's a regret I live with every day. I promise it'll never happen again, but I need you back home, baby."

Salma looked into his eyes. They communicated his sincerity, but she knew what second chances could do. Sure, her brother and sister had their second chance, however, a crime family or former crime family and an underground organization weren't in play.

"I'm not sure if I want to come home yet..."

Tension hung in the air as Qasim studied her. Without responding, he called for the waiter to order another lemon cake to go. A few moments later, the bill was settled, and the two of them strolled out hand in hand. As they reached the bottom of the stairs and walked into the cool night, Qasim kept her hand in his, but steered her away from his vehicle.

"Where are we going?" She looked over her shoulder and the guy who normally rode in the front seat, who she now knew as Jide, was behind them. "We're being followed. You might want to tell the big guy to chill out."

Qasim turned, said a few words in Yoruba and they continued their journey. Soon after, Qasim helped her into an ornate carriage with its wooden frame adorned with intricate carvings. A friendly coachman dressed in traditional attire and a warm smile greeted them. Her eyes lit up with excitement. She hadn't gone on a carriage ride in forever and she loved them as a little girl.

He's not going to make it easy for me to deny him.

As the carriage meandered through the historical town, they passed by the majestic Koutoubia Mosque. Its elegant minaret reaching toward the starlit sky. The air was infused with the scent of spices and fresh blooms, creating an intoxicating blend of aromas. Qasim put his arm around Salma, drawing her closer as they snuggled together under a blanket that seemed to come out of nowhere. With her head on his chest, he leaned down and nipped her neck with his teeth. He blew on it a moment later, sending shivers through her.

"I can still hear your voice, ringing in my ears like a chorus of promises. You vowed to be with me through the good times and bad, always being there to share my joys and bear my sorrows. You said you'd open your heart and talk with me honestly when anything was wrong. I believed every word you said then..."

"'Sim..."

"You are opinionated, fiery, compassionate, kind, full of life, smart and sexy. But one thing I never took you for is a liar."

Salma was jolted from her position. "And I'm not."

"I can't tell..."

"Meaning?"

"Those were your vows, none of which you fulfilled." His gaze was intense and pulsing with energy.

A familiar heat crept up her neck. "You vowed to protect me, or don't you remember that?"

His voice softened, but the power behind it grew stronger as his hand wrapped around her upper thighs and pulled her closer. "I do and I failed, but I'm trying to fix that. You on the other hand..." His gaze never left hers, he used the back of his hand to caress her face. "...your body hums in my presence. Your breath quickens and your pulse races when I'm nearby. The reason I know this is because my chest tightens, and my stomach does that flip thing I despise. I love you, Salma. So much so that I realize I can't stand you as well. I hate the control you have over me. I'm not ashamed to admit that because you're my wife. But you, pretending what's between us is dead can no longer fly with me. I refuse to be in limbo—between where we were and where we could be—it's driving me crazy. And there's no way I'm ready to give up on what hasn't even begun."

"The person I made that vow to turned out to be someone else. Don't you get that?"

"No, I don't. Because I'm the same person. You know me, even if you insist on believing you don't. Come back with me. Get to know me, and my family. Our feelings for each other demand your best effort. If after that..."

Qasim let his words trail, but the weight of his unspoken words hung between them. No matter how hard she tried to keep her heart at bay, emotions welled up inside her. Salma opened her mouth to speak, but no words came out. Qasim was still so attuned to her that he knew when she'd reached her limit. He gently placed her in his lap, wrapping his arms around her waist. She nestled her face in the crook of his neck and allowed his scent and the beat of his heart to soothe her. The rhythmic trotting of the horse reminded her that she was missing the view of the city she rarely saw, yet nothing could break her away from the security she felt in her husband's arms.

CHAPTER 10

The following evening, with her arm wrapped around his bicep, Salma leaned her head against Qasim's shoulder as they strolled through the Medina in Marrakech. She couldn't remember the last time she had given herself permission to be free. To just be. Over the past five years, she'd used every mechanism she knew to escape the unfulfillment rumbling within her. Earlier she and Qasim had a traditional Moroccan breakfast on the balcony of their suite. Surprisingly, he hadn't brought up anything about their conversation the night before.

Last night, in the comfort of his arms, within minutes she'd drifted off to sleep. When the carriage came to a stop, Qasim carried her to the car and placed her in the back seat. Several minutes later, she was showered, clad in silk pajama shorts set and in bed. She'd pleaded with Qasim to stay with her. However, he declined, reminding her that they were both in a vulnerable state, and he didn't want sex to cloud their decision-making.

"No matter how much willpower I have, baby, I can't sleep in this bed and not ravish you. Not tonight," he said, standing at the foot of the bed.

"'Sim..." she murmured.

"Please don't say my name like that..." Qasim walked to the

head of the bed and leaned over her. Running his index finger down the curve of her jawline, he traced the contours of her lips. She shivered, and he smiled down at her. "Star baby, you own me. But until you become my wife again...in the real sense of the word, you can't possess me."

Her brain was in a chaotic frenzy as she got lost in their intense gaze. He let his hand travel down the length of her bare thighs before parking behind her knees. The waves of pleasure caused her to let out a soft moan.

"You...you...you're not being fair..."

Qasim brushed his lips against hers, teasing her slightly before he fully captured her lips. He gripped her chin as his tongue glided inside her mouth, inviting hers for a dance. Their exchange started off sweet, then thorough, before progressing to aggressive. Salma was on the verge of sinking under raw desire when Qasim broke contact. Blinking, she frowned, her question unspoken.

He pulled the blanket up to her neck and kissed her forehead. "All's fair in love and war. I'm fighting to win." He sauntered toward the door and opened it.

"Ugh...I can't stand you." She threw a pillow at him which he dodged.

"I know and that's why I love you. Goodnight, my Star." He chuckled and shut the door behind him.

Salma sucked her teeth, remembering how she had tossed and turned, trying to find a position that would help her fall asleep after he had wound her up.

Qasim stopped walking. "What's wrong with you?" he asked.

"I just remembered I can't stand you."

He stared at her then laughed when he recalled what she was talking about. "You survived, didn't you? I told you to take a cold shower...I did." Shrugging, he pulled her along.

They'd spent the day exploring colorful markets, tasting exclusive gourmet meals, and visiting traditional craft studios. Hand in hand, they shared the history of the city. In the span of forty-eight hours, Qasim brought out the little girl in her. Something only he could do.

All day they were like kids, enjoying life to the fullest, all their worries forgotten. After enjoying an intimate picnic lunch at Menara Gardens, they returned to the hotel, and retired for a nap. It didn't seem as though she'd been out for long before he was waking her to get ready for the surprise he had for her.

Salma couldn't contain herself when he took her on the most amazing hot air balloon ride, ever. The ride had ended about an hour ago and she wanted to end the night with drinks on the rooftop, but he insisted he had somewhere to take her before they retired for the night. The next morning, they would be headed back to Tweede Kans Cove...and reality. Something they hadn't discussed at all since last night.

"Where are we going?" she asked. "I should be the one taking you around, but I'm not even sure I know where we are."

"This is my date...trust me. You ever been to Bahia Palace?" Qasim asked.

"Huh?" Salma looked around, taking in their surroundings. Her brows furrowed. "You mean the touristy place tourists go to? No, I haven't."

Qasim smiled. "Hater. No one told you to stay in Tweede Kan Cove, working day in and day out." He glanced over at her briefly before returning his focus to the street. "I hope Mustafa is compensating you appropriately."

Salma laughed. "You do know it's a family business."

"And so? Ilẹ Oloro is family-owned, but I don't CFO for free. Neither should you be traveling into enemy territory for free all in the name of providing stellar excursion experiences for Grand Amour guests."

Qasim maintained a hold of her hand while Salma doubled over in laughter. She knew without a doubt that he was referring to Hamza and the winery. Salma wasn't oblivious about her looks and the way men were drawn to her. She also loved that Qasim wasn't bothered by any of it. She could confidently say that in their years together, he'd never gone all "King Kong" on her. He maintained she was his and that was that.

Qasim continued to talk smack about her brothers for intentionally putting her over guest services and experiences because of her beauty. Beating his chest, he promised to fight the "misogyny of the Grand Amour institution" now that he was back. All she needed to do was say the word. Salma couldn't contain her laughter. She really missed the times when he would keep her in stitches.

She wiped the corner of her eye and turned to him. "For someone who claims I shut him out, you seem to know an awful lot about my movements."

Qasim shrugged. "I don't know what you're talking about..."

"'Sim, if you've had someone spying on me, I'll kick you and whoever's behind when I find out."

"You're too pretty to be fighting, baby." He kissed her cheek.

A few moments later, they entered the palace. A man who she presumed to be a tour guide approached Qasim. Planning was her thing, but she admired the fact that Qasim could make plans for them without her being involved. She wondered when he planned all of this, but wasn't surprised he knew how. Since he arrived in Tweede Kans Cove, she'd been struggling with the man who pulled at her heartstrings and the man whose family had a deadly past. Since their talk, she had been searching for the answer to one question.

Can I take the risk of following my heart despite the potential danger?

"Follow me, this way..." the tour guide began walking through the courtyard.

Turning to Qasim, she whispered, "You wanted to see an empty building?" They were ushered through the historic site built in the 1800s.

"You know it's not just an empty building. It's a piece of history."

He wasn't lying. The beautiful palace was a mix of Islamic

and Moroccan architecture, with an intricately designed court-yard and a beautiful garden. The mosaic and incredible arabesque windows and doors were said to be some of the most intricate in the world. For a place that was built to serve as a harem decades ago, it was well preserved. The architecture was amazing, but none of the original furniture remained.

Salma was about to ask why he decided to bring her here when Qasim came to a stop in front of one of the doors. The tour guide had walked away, and Qasim wrapped his arms around her. She settled into his chest.

"What do you see?" he asked, his voice slightly above a mumble.

Salma set her gaze on the bluish-green mosaic before them. This kind of design or something like it was all around the palace, but this one stood out. She looked at the piece before her to see if there was anything she was missing. After a few moments, she shrugged, giving up.

"Try harder," he coaxed.

"I mean, it's a mosaic. I don't see anything particularly special about it. It's beautiful but—"

"Remember at dinner the other day, you talked about things going back to the way they were, and—"

"You said you wanted us to make a mosaic..."

He chuckled. "I knew you were still the sharpest pencil in the box..."

Salma nudged him with her elbow. "The pencil that will poke your eye out if you don't get to the point."

Qasim squeezed her waist. "What did I tell you about directing your violent tendencies towards me?"

Salma chuckled. "Stop saying that. Someone passing by might hear you and really believe I'm violent."

"You are..." he brushed his lips against her neck. "...but I love it. Anyone that has a problem can come see me."

A moan escaped her. "Stop 'Sim. This isn't America, London, or Nigeria. We're in Maghreb country and in public; kissing in a historic building may have consequences. Besides stop getting me riled up..."

He grunted. "You right. See how quickly you distract me." A few beats passed between them before he continued. "All the pieces of this mosaic were necessary to complete and make it beautiful. For us, every moment that has gotten us here – laughter, intimacy, tears, fights, love – has shaped us and done just the same. You're my center, baby. Don't let me do this life alone."

Her throat clogged from raw emotion. The significance and weight of his plea thudded in her chest. After a few moments, she let out a sigh. "I guess I've focused too much on the individual pieces of our journey, discarding the whole picture."

"I'm not saying you didn't have a reason to. Not trying to sound like a broken record, but that will never happen again. All I'm saying and asking for is for you to put us out of our misery. I've been off balance for five years, but I couldn't bring you into an environment I wasn't sure of. Now I am."

Salma nodded. Understanding what he was asking her. There were so many things to consider, but none of them trumped her returning to her happy place.

Him.

~

"Father, I've become one of those Your children I never thought I'd be – always asking for help any time I talk to You. Since that health scare, I feel like I'm in an 'asking for help' era. But I know You said the heavy laden can come to You and ask for wisdom, so here I am. Neither Grandma nor Yas can give me the answer I need. Please help me make the right decision, in Jesus's name. Amen," Salma muttered.

Clutching her robe tighter, she looked out into the early-June night sky. After getting up a few moments ago to use the restroom, she stepped onto the balcony of their suite. After they'd returned to the hotel, she and Qasim decided on a movie. One moment they were laughing at Will Smith in *Hitch*, the next, she found herself tucked under him.

Despite the comfort of the contour of his well-toned arms, rest eluded her. Her mind went over every possible scenario of the fallout to come once she and Qasim returned to Tweede Kans Cove. She'd learned from Zaina that Mustafa had met up with her in Botswana and they were on their way to Tweedes. Not to be on anyone's bad side as far as communication was concerned, Salma had kept in touch with her older brothers since she'd been away. However, she left out the details about being with Qasim. Salma knew her grandmother wouldn't tell any of her secrets.

Five years ago, the woman had looked her in the eye and said, "You were an adult when you said, 'I do' behind your family's back, so you're going to have to be an adult when it comes time to tell everyone the truth."

Salma looked down at the phone in her hand. She reread the Bible verse on the screen. ***I will instruct you and teach you in the way you should go; I will counsel you with my loving eye on you.*** Psalm 32:8. After reading it a few more times, she exited the app to return to the home screen.

Two thirty-five a.m. I need to get back to sleep.

"What are you doing out here?" His tired timbre tickled her senses.

Salma took in his washboard six-pack made visible by the open shirt of his black pajamas. She bit down on her bottom lip, then wiggled her brows. Qasim chuckled, sitting on the chair, and pulling her down on his lap.

"You better set that lip free, unless you're ready to back it up."

"You're not going to let me live down the fact that I fell asleep."

"Nope. You were rubbing on me all the way back to the hotel. Then get knocked out after two scenes of the movie."

"You're the one that fixed me a warm bath and a glass of wine. You should really be blaming yourself."

Qasim cradled her closer and she leaned on his chest. "Talk to me. Why are you out here at almost three in the morning?"

"Come morning, we go back to the real world. My family, yours, our careers, the distance. I mean, I wish all we had to consider was just the two of us."

"First, it *is* just the two of us. We have obligations and love for our families, but it is just you and me. But I get what you're saying. Baby, I know you love our bubble, but I'm not doing that secrecy thing again. Second, years ago, you weren't fully in your role at the resort, and I was just a few months into mine. However, we've done distance before and made it work. Although I'm not trying to live apart from you again, for now, we'll do what needs to be done. Lastly, I know you're worried about your brothers, but leave that to me. I got us, Star."

Salma smiled.

Years ago, she was happy but afraid. Qasim on the other hand was always sure about them.

A tear slid down her cheek. "This might destroy you and Omar."

Qasim thumbed it away. "As long as it doesn't touch you, I'm fine with that. O will be all right after we talk. Your brother isn't as irrational as you think."

Salma repositioned her body, so she was straddling him. Qasim leaned back, his eyes hooded as she locked them in her gaze. She placed her hands on his shoulders. "For years, I was so angry with you. Growing up, the house was always chaotic, so I craved calm. You gave me the calm I yearned for, then snatched it away without warning. But...I love you...believe me I tried to stop. I know everyone says this that it has become cliché, but my soul really loves you, Qasim Adesina."

Salma watched his Adam's apple roll up and down as he struggled to control his emotions. His hands went underneath her nightshirt, and he caressed her back.

"The day you let your guard down about how your childhood trauma affected you, that was the day I swore to always be your calm. But baby, calm in a relationship can also be a false veil for the avoidance of any kind of discomfort. If we don't experience discomfort, we can't grow. I failed in my part to measure the discomfort we experienced. Instead, I avoided it by keeping secrets.

"We relied so heavily on our 'calm' that we didn't trust God to help us through our shifts. God's got me and I most definitely got you. Trust me to guide us through the rough patches, to hold your hand when things get tough. I promise to be your rock, your support, your everything...after the Big Guy that is." Qasim pointed upward.

Salma's lips lifted in a small smile. His words sank into her gut, sending warmth and love through her veins. When she and her siblings moved in with their grandmother, they started attending church. However, it was Qasim that really introduced her to a relationship with Jesus. One she neglected when they severed ties, until recently.

Qasim's eyes remained steady, giving his words validity, and erasing her doubt.

"God is my refuge and strength, a present help in times of trouble..."

"Therefore, I will not be afraid," he finished the verse from Psalm 46:1. "You remembered..."

One night, years ago, after a devastating loss for his team, they were on the phone while she tried to comfort him. That conversation led to her telling him about one of the horrible nightmares of her childhood. He shared the verse with her, and it had become one of their favorites through all their trials...except the one that mattered the most and eventually tore them apart.

"Everything," she whispered.

Her fingers traveled to his nape while his hands gripped her waist. The tension in the atmosphere was palpable and electric. Leaning in, she pressed her lips softly against his. As they kissed, she knew this was the beginning of a new chapter in their lives. All uncertain thoughts faded to oblivion when their gentle touch quickly gave way to a hunger that could no longer be restrained.

Qasim reached up and took her hair out of the loose bun it was in. He deepened the kiss and their mouths molded together in a fervent dance of passion. Their tongues entwined in a sensual tango, exploring each other with a mix of curiosity and familiarity. Their hands sought one another with urgency, exploring the curves and contours of their bodies. His fingers ran through her hair, caressed her cheeks, and traced the outlines of her shoulder. The heat between them intensified, their bodies drawing closer until there was almost no space left between them.

Suddenly, Qasim stood, scooping her up in his arms, and carrying her back into the penthouse. Once they entered the room, he gently laid her on the bed.

"I adore you..." he whispered in her ear.

Brushing his lips against her forehead, cheeks, and neck he continued peppering her with light kisses while showering her with affirming promises.

"I'll spend my life cherishing, loving, respecting and protecting you and our unborn children," he said.

Moans that she didn't recognize as hers escaped her lips as heat rose within her. Her brain was too fuzzy to verbally respond to his declarations. Words that were like balm on her soul.

"I want to hear the words. Tell me." He grunted.

"*Dans cette vie ou dans la suivante, mon âme te trouvera toujours*," she whispered.

They submerged themselves in the heat of passion, reconnecting in an intense melodic dance only their souls knew. Salma closed her eyes and felt the warmth of his hands roaming her skin. His lips brushed her ear, demanding she repeat the French words she spoke when she agreed to be his wife. Granting his request, she repeatedly vowed, "In this life or the next, my soul will always find you."

"*Y*ou promised to behave."

The next afternoon, Salma glanced at Qasim as she tucked away her Kindle. He regarded her briefly before smirking and returning to his phone. When their plane landed, they both switched back into business mode. Although it was Saturday, their assistants were on call. After checking in, Salma picked up her Kindle to occupy herself while Qasim responded to emails that needed his attention.

She was about to speak when he paused, grabbed her chin, and drew her close. Qasim kissed her deeply, then squeezed her thigh. Through his silence, he communicated that he heard her, and she shouldn't worry. The light feeling she'd had since she and her husband reconnected in the wee hours of the morning was lifted the minute she entered Tweede Kans Cove. Qasim's driver turned the corner leading up to the gate of the DuBois Manoir. They should be approaching her grandmother's in about ten minutes. Putting away his phone, Qasim turned to her.

He narrowed his eyes at her. "How many ways do I have to show you that your comfort will always be my first priority?" His tone was terse.

"I'm sorry, honey. It's—"

"Nah, hold up, say it again."

Salma smiled. After last night, he deserved the right to be called honey. He relished it and had been making her repeat it any time she said it.

"Be serious," she whined.

"I'm waiting..."

"Honey," she chuckled and shook her head. "You're ridiculous."

He took her hand in his. "Good, you're laughing. Look, relax, I'll let your brothers have their say. O knows how I get down, so if he swings, I'm knocking him out. Musa will just mean mug me, but won't say anything too bad. He might take it up with Q."

"Oh my gosh..."

"I'm kidding..."

Salma gave him a warning look before leaning her head on his shoulder. A few minutes later, the gates opened. The thought of giving her marriage a second chance no longer plagued her. Despite her confidence, the weight of the guilt from her brother's reaction loomed large.

CHAPTER 11

The car came to a stop in front of Salma's grandmother's house. The windows of the truck were tinted so he knew he had a little more time to reassure his wife. After last night, he expected her to be more relaxed. He extended grace because he knew why she was so wound up. Under any other circumstances, he would be irritated because he felt like she was doubting his ability to handle the situation they were about to step into. His wife didn't shy away from conflict, but she welcomed only the kind of conflict she was sure she'd come out of as the winner. Apologizing for her wrongs was something she struggled with.

Keeping their nuptials a secret was what she was struggling with the most. He was going to have to endure the same thing when he got home. But Salma was the baby of the DuBois-Arazi bunch, and his feisty woman was an undercover softie whose family approval meant everything to her. As he told her last night, for her he'd take anything, but she knew even he had his limits. Good or bad, she was his, and whatever was going to happen was about him and not her. He needed her to understand that.

"Star baby, I need you to breathe. I can handle myself, but if I notice you're being affected negatively, then I lose my mind. We don't want me to lose my mind, so I need you to breathe and let me handle it." He squeezed her thigh.

She nodded. "I just don't want—"

"I know, but we're here now, so we gotta deal with it."

She folded her arms across her chest. "I don't need their permission to be with you. You know I love you. I just wish I handled things differently." She sighed. "I should've been like Yas – up front. Musa and O knew Kojo—"

Despite what Salma thought, her brothers knowing Yasmine's husband wouldn't have meant a thing if Yasmine was not on board. Same for them. That's why it was critical he got his wife back before facing the brothers. That part he'd keep to himself. Instead, he worked on calming her nerves.

"Hey, stop that. They know me too, but that ain't the problem." Pulling her closer, he brushed his lips against hers. "You ready?"

She nodded.

Qasim opened his door and walked around to open hers and helped her out. Pinning her against the car door, he stared into her eyes. "I let you have your way most of the time, but this isn't one of those times. Don't get involved, Star, let me handle it." Grabbing her hand, Qasim led Salma around the car and up the stairs to the front door. "That wasn't a suggestion, baby."

"I got it. Can we go in now?" she quipped.

Qasim chuckled. "I'mma punish the sass outta you later tonight, but let's go."

Salma opened the door and the first person they saw was a very pregnant Zaina. A vision of his own wife, swollen with their child appeared before his eyes, causing him to smile.

Zaina waddled over to them with a wide smile on her face. He met the auburn-haired woman during Grandma Olly's birthday party. She seemed nice but reserved. Watching her pull Salma into an embrace told him she was fully acclimated to the family now.

"And who do we have here?" Zaina asked.

"Zay, if you don't move out of the way...

Zaina laughed. "Excuse my rude sis—"

"Hello Zaina, nice to see you again." Qasim stretched out his hand. "I see congratulations are in order. How are you?"

Zaina took his hand and playfully stuck her tongue out at Salma. "I'm doing okay. You look well. I trust she behaved herself."

Qasim grinned and shifted to glance at Salma who scoffed in response. "Where is Musa?"

"He's not here yet." Zaina gestured toward the family room.

They headed that way, but abruptly stopped when they heard clapping coming from the stairwell. Every head turned in that direction and met Omar's scowl.

"So, it's true. You came to my city, paraded my sister all around Marrakech and didn't think to say anything…"

Zaina held her stomach protectively, a wave of nervousness dancing in her eyes. Qasim squeezed Salma's hand. He expected some kind of flack but didn't expect his friend to come out swinging.

"I didn't know I had to ask permission." Out of his peripheral, he saw Zaina give Salma a weary smile before continuing down the long foyer.

"When you have my sister, you do." Omar was now at the bottom of the steps.

Omar was about an inch shorter than Qasim, so his position put them at eye level. Qasim took a step back.

Salma began, "O, what are—"

Qasim glanced at Salma causing her to purse her lips together. "As you can see, your sister is fine. We had unfinished business that didn't concern you."

Omar snickered then turned to Salma. The disdain in his eyes caused her breath to hitch, but Qasim was happy she didn't take the bait.

"I thought this was over. I warned you not to pursue her in the first place," Omar said.

"You and I know that I don't listen to instructions from anyone regarding my heart."

"Your heart? Were you thinking of your heart when we were in the club with Leticia?"

Salma tried to pull her hand from his, but he held it tight. Qasim thumbed his nose and sneered. "That's what we're doing? I know you're mad, but you don't have to go that low."

Omar turned his wrath to Salma. "And you, I knew something was up with all this sneaking around you've been doing. Didn't he hurt you enough already?"

"It's not what you think, Omar. If you'll wait a minute, I'll tell you everything," Salma pleaded.

The hurt in her voice tightened Qasim's chest. He knew how close they were. Being a part of their circle for years demonstrated that the brother and sister were indeed forged from the same mold. And yet, now Omar seemed to have forgotten how much he meant to her. Qasim could understand why Salma wanted to try to reach her brother—but if Omar thought for a second he would disrespect her, no amount of understanding would let Qasim allow that.

Qasim stepped forward. "Now, hold on O," he said sternly. "Nobody set out to deceive you. We can talk about this like adults, but you're not going to talk to my lady that way."

Omar glared at him. "Your lady?" He turned to Salma, eyebrows raised. "His lady?"

She lifted her chin and met his gaze. "Yes."

The steadiness in her voice caused Qasim's chest to swell with pride.

"Well, *his lady*, don't come to me crying the next time—"

"I ain't trying to make her cry. I live for the smile on her face."

"I can't believe you, Omar," Salma said, her voice low.

Qasim heard the tremble in her voice, despite her bravado. She was close to tears, and he'd had enough.

"So, we're friends, but I'm not good enough for your sister?"

"You had her—"

"We both made—" Salma tried again.

"Star...," Qasim whispered, pulling her behind him.

Omar laughed mockingly. "Oh, you speak for her now?"

Qasim shook his head. "She speaks for herself, but she also doesn't fight any battles on her own."

"Battles? I'm not going to fight you over my own sister." Omar pointed at them. "Whatever you think you have with her is over."

Several weeks into their relationship, Qasim and Salma had a huge argument. Things were said, and they decided to take a break. One that didn't last long, but they decided to keep their reconciliation to themselves. But Omar was full of "I told you not to go after my sister." The big brother thing was cute, but Qasim was done arguing with him. Omar was hurt and before he said anything he couldn't come back from, he needed to leave.

"You know you have no say in what happens between us..."

Hearing Salma whimper, Qasim pulled her to the side. He cupped her face and used the pad of his thumb to wipe away the tear in the corner of her eye. Clenching his teeth, he stared into her eyes.

"Stop it. You're gonna pull me outta character." His eyes darted toward Omar who was glaring at them. "Never shed a tear for any man... not even me."

"Let's just go."

"Nah, this is your family, stay for family dinner. I'm not trying to break up family tradition. O's problem is with me." He kissed her forehead. "Say hi to your grandma for me. I'm gonna head out."

Qasim tried to step away from her, but she clutched the hem of his shirt. The plea in her eyes almost broke him. Part of him wanted to whisk her away and put an end to this, but he knew there were so many other factors that had to be considered. Respect from their families would only come with them facing the battle head-on.

"Let him go, Sal," Omar taunted. "Don't beg him to stay."

Qasim turned to Omar. "Make no mistake, I'm not going anywhere. I'm temporarily removing myself from a volatile situation before things get worse." He caressed the side of her face. "Call me when you're done, and I'll be back to get you."

Omar furrowed his brows. "He's been your man for what...two days and suddenly he's protecting you from us?"

"I'll protect her from *me* if I have to," Qasim said.

"Omar, stop. When you calm down, I won't be so quick to accept your apology."

"So, what are you saying Sal? You'll pick him over—"

Qasim smirked. "And here I was telling Star you're not that irrational..."

"I'm always irrational when it comes to my twin, and you know that."

"But I got her, man—"

"What makes this time any different? Because she's been your *lady* for two days?"

Qasim scoffed and glanced at Salma. The warning in her eye told him that she knew exactly what was about to happen. He had tried, but Omar knew just the right buttons to push. Questioning his integrity was one of them. He had almost got roped in another player's mess years back and Omar knew about it. He had nothing but his word. Even with what separated him from his wife the first time, he hadn't lied—just omitted the truth.

"No, because she's been my *wife* for five years." This wasn't how he envisioned this scene playing out, but here they were.

"Your what?" Omar roared. The storm of anger pooled in his fiery gaze.

As his eyes darted between him and Salma, Qasim also noticed betrayal and disappointment. In the blink of an eye, Omar came charging toward him and threw a punch, but missed. Salma screamed at her brother and stepped in front of Qasim. He yanked her to the side and turned to make sure she wasn't hurt. The temporary distraction caused Omar's second punch to land on its target.

His jaw.

Zaina rushed into the foyer with Grandma Olly a few steps behind. The older woman called out to Omar, but he had tunnel vision. Zaina scurried to Salma who was now yelling at him and her brother. Qasim wiped the corner of his mouth. Looking at his thumb, he saw that Omar drew blood.

"That was your one and only time," Qasim seethed.

Omar's chest heaved; his jaw clenched while his fists trembled with repressed anger. Without another word, he walked forward. Qasim clenched his fists; he was done playing nice. Salma and Zaina raised their voices in protest when the front door opened. The eldest DuBois-Arazi entered. His dark eyes roamed the scene before settling on his wife.

"I don't care what's going on here, but if my wife is hurt, somebody's going to pay," Mustafa growled.

Qasim looked over at Mustafa, but ignored the comment. Instead, he walked over to Salma. "Come walk me out." His expression gave no room for protest. He needed to leave to prevent things getting worse, fast. He grabbed her hand and walked around Mustafa. As they approached the door, Mustafa called out to Salma.

"She'll be back," Qasim said, without a backward glance.

When they got to the car, Qasim opened the door for her. Once she was in, he went around and got in the car. He shut his eyes and leaned his head back. He took a couple of breaths before opening his eyes and facing Salma. The apprehension in her eyes didn't go unnoticed, but he had to let her understand a basic rule...again.

She lifted her hand to touch the corner of his lip, but he caught it before she could make contact. "Didn't I tell you to never, ever get between me and another man."

"Honey, it was only O. I was trying—"

"I don't care if it's our grown son. Don't do it."

"I was—"

"Salma! We're not debating this. Never put yourself between

me and another man, especially in conflict. Do you understand me?"

Her pout appeared but at this moment, he didn't care. His woman was strong-willed, but there would never come a time when it would be okay for her to do what she did back there. Apart from the fact that her actions caused Omar's punch to land, she could have been seriously injured.

"Salma?"

"Yes, I understand. I'm sorry...for everything." She folded her arms across her chest, leaned her head back and sighed. "Now everyone hates me."

He pulled her closer. "Nobody hates you. No matter what O said, you'll always be the sister he loves. Now, our friendship might not survive, but that's not for you to worry about." He kissed her lips. She tried to deepen the kiss, but he winced in pain.

"I'm so sorry."

"Stop apologizing. I'll put some ice on it. Go back in there, call me when you're done. And cut O some slack."

Salma rolled her eyes, making him chuckle.

"You know you would've done worse if he showed up married and didn't tell you."

Salma grunted, but she knew it was true. He'd heard about her run-in with Mustafa's wife. The DuBois-Arazis were protective of one another, and Qasim understood it because his family was the same. However, Salma was also an Adesina. That trumped everyone and everything.

~

My Star: O is still a jerk, Musa acts like I'm invisible. Grandma said her piece, and Zay's getting on my nerves hovering around me like I'm some charity case.

*Q*asim read Salma's text again. He'd been back in his hotel room, showered, and laid on the bed running through the events of the last hour. After his shower, he ordered lunch from the restaurant downstairs. He and Salma had skipped lunch in Marrakech because they wanted to be back in time for Saturday dinner. An event that turned into a disaster. He'd run through every potential scenario in his mind. What happened was nothing like he'd imagined.

> You want me to come get you?

> My Star: I want to say yes so bad, but my grandma seems so shattered.

> It's your call baby. Say the word and the driver is en route.

> My Star: I'll stay until my grandma goes to her room.

> Ok, when the driver gets there, stop by your place, and grab a bag.

> My Star: Honey, my keys are in that green tote. Why can't we stay in my villa?

Qasim's eyes darted to the doorway; he saw the green tote she was referring to. Since they had come straight from the airport, their bags were still in the car. He had his driver bring them up when he got back. After last night, there was no way he was sleeping apart from her again. Unless it absolutely couldn't be avoided. The reason he chose this hotel was that he wanted privacy for them.

> My Star: Don't worry, with the way my brothers are acting no one will be stopping by.

Qasim smiled. She still had the ability to read his thoughts. After texting her back that he'd be waiting, Qasim tossed his phone on the bed and stood. It would be easier for her to get ready for work at her place instead of bringing her stuff here. He flung his suitcase on the bed just as his phone buzzed. He picked up the device and chuckled.

> Nze: 'Sim, just got home. Let me get some
> time in with my princess and her clingy mama.
> I'll hit you back.

Qasim sent a couple of laughing emojis before responding.

> I'mma tell Jas you say she's clingy. Besides
> you like it.

> Nze: Like? Cuz, I love it. Hit you in a few.

> Bet

Qasim tossed the phone back on the bed and made his way to the closet. Arinze or Nze Kalu was his Aunty Bola's first child and only son. He was an award-winning actor who lived in Atlanta with his wife and baby girl. Growing up, although Arinze lived in the east and Qasim lived in the west of Nigeria, the cousins spent a lot of time together. His aunt and dad were determined that their kids would be as tight as they were.

Unlike the two-year age gap Qasim had with his younger siblings, he was four years younger than Qadir. Qasim and Arinze were the same age, so gravitated toward each other and had a tight bond. Arinze knew everything that went on with him and Salma. He had also been instrumental in getting Qasim and Qadir on speaking terms again after Salma left him.

Several minutes later, Qasim was in the back seat of the truck heading to Salma's villa. Qadir called to check in and Qasim gave him a quick update. He made sure to omit everything about his encounter with Omar. Tensions were already high. Qadir and

Mustafa's business dealings or friendship didn't have to be affected by any of this.

When they were younger, there were so many people Qadir had messed up or cut off permanently for messing with him or their younger siblings. His brother's cut-off game was strong, and Qasim didn't want to be responsible for that.

After Qasim assured him that everything was okay, Qadir gave him some updates on outstanding projects. There was a meeting Monday morning that he needed Qasim to be a part of. Until they decided on the next steps, Qasim would be working out of Salma's home office. He couldn't stay in Tweedes indefinitely and he needed his wife by his side. So, they'd be making that decision sooner rather than later.

Qasim was ready for his future to start and that wasn't possible without his heart. He smiled remembering a very pregnant Zaina and the way Mustafa was ready to clear the room if she had been hurt in any way. Nothing mattered but her and his unborn. Before their separation, he and Salma had the same goals and desires when it came to starting a family.

He glanced at his phone again. Salma hadn't texted back. He was losing his mind trying to be patient, but he needed to know how she was doing. It was taking everything in him not to barge into her grandmother's house and demand Salma come with him. He was about to set the phone back down when Arinze's call came through.

Qasim answered on the second ring. After the preliminary greeting, Qasim began to tell Arinze what happened between him and Omar. The cousins had been in close contact since Qasim touched down in Tweede Kans Cove. Since Qadir and Arinze were the only people who knew he and Salma were married, they were the only two he could talk to. With the way he was feeling when he left the Manoir earlier, his brother wasn't an option, so he had hit Arinze up.

"At least one hurdle solved. You got your wife back," Arinze said.

"You know O isn't a problem for me, I just want my wife happy. She can't be that if she's beefing with her people."

"I'm glad I don't have that problem. What's about to be a problem for me is Ella."

Qasim frowned. "Who is Ella?"

"My wife's horse."

Qasim laughed so hard that his stomach started to ache. He didn't even have a frame of reference for what his cousin was going through. He had seen Jasmine cry on the spot if that horse was in any kind of pain. He admired Arinze though, because although none of them were raised to treat animals like humans, Arinze learned for his wife's sake, and that was admirable.

"I see you didn't take Cheta's advice to put something in the horse's food so she can sleep."

"Man, I've been married less than three years. Don't even joke like that." Arinze chuckled. "He said that crap not knowing Jas was around the corner. Now Ella might die a natural death and my wife will swear I did something to her."

Qasim laughed again. Arinze was frustrated because although the horse had a special value for Jasmine, she was old and in pain. But Jasmine refused to let the horse go, so they kept pumping money into medical care to sustain her.

"Anyway, enough about me. I can't believe her brother brought up Leticia though...in front of his sister at that," Arinze said.

"I mean he came out swinging and he knows for a fact nothing happened between that girl and me. He was there." Qasim shook his head and listened to Arinze threaten to kick Omar's behind whenever they crossed paths.

Leticia was a woman he had dated casually off and on. They were never in a relationship per se, or put a title on what they were. However, they did appear to the public as a couple. Qasim was still playing for Viva City FC when a story broke out about him and her leaving a club together. It was an industry party, and even though they hadn't arrived at the party together, they did leave the building together but went their separate ways.

He and Salma were new, and they'd just had another argument about her wanting to keep their relationship a secret. He misinterpreted her want for secrecy to mean she didn't want to be seen with him, and didn't trust him after everything he had done to show her that she was his heart. Keeping what they had private he could understand, but secret, he couldn't. So a lot of hurtful things were said, among which was him telling her he could find other women who'd love to be on his arm.

It was just his luck that Omar was in London then. They hung out and Leticia strutted her way into their section. The reason Omar knew nothing had happened was that both of them were on a plane heading to Lagos when the news broke. He and Salma later reconciled, but it was still a touchy subject for her.

"Your relationship with her brother will work itself out. The main thing is you've gotten your wife back. Soon, you'll be completely free of the Brotherhood. The future is bright."

"Cuz, I see my wife and I see my future."

"I feel you. But I promise, you're a better man than me. Separated from my wife for five years..."

"Those were the hardest years of my life. But I had to die to my need for her. I messed up big time when I failed to protect her the first time.

"But you didn't know.

"That's true, but I was also arrogant. I had just moved back to Naija. I forgot that I was in a different environment. I acted on my own, started cleaning up shop without studying my opponent or praying for God's guidance. You see that 'lean not to your own understanding' verse..." Qasim let out a weary laugh, "...that thing is real. Because the more I acted on my own, the more secrets I kept, and the more I underestimated my opponent.

"I was also so mad at Q that I didn't ask him for help. With Chief recovering from surgery in London and my mom with him, I was wilding out, heavy. That cost me my wife. Now I don't move without consulting the Big Guy and I know my oppo-nents...and best believe, they know me."

Arinze grunted. "They sure do. Big Cuz might look scarier, but your name rings bells. Does Sally know that part of you?"

Qasim chuckled at the name he called Salma. "Don't let my brothers help you get your behind kicked with that nickname y'all insist on calling her."

"Shoot, I heard Q call her that..." Arinze chuckled.

"But nah, she doesn't know my alter ego. That's not who I ever want her to see me as."

"Cool, well looks like everything is on the up and up. Hit me up when you head back to Naija or if her brothers jump funny again. Then, I'm on the next plane out."

Qasim laughed before telling him about the golf tournament slated for early October. Arinze promised to see if he could make it, if not he'd see him in Montego Bay for his wedding ceremony.

After he got off the phone, he felt lighter. Thinking about Nigeria, Qasim did a mental inventory of things he needed to make Salma comfortable in their home. In Marrakech, when they talked about his everyday life and the business, she referenced where he lived as "your house." Although the house was his in the literal sense, he couldn't wait to see the look on her face when she realized it was "their home." Excitement coursed through his veins. He had *almost* everything he ever wanted.

Leaning his head back on the leather headrest, Qasim said a quick prayer of thanksgiving. Before opening his eyes, his mind went to Omar, and he muttered, "Lord, I need You to help me navigate this right." Immediately he opened his eyes, a text from Salma came through.

"Daniel, you remember the way to that mansion, right?"

"Yes, sir."

"Make a U-turn. Let's go get my wife."

CHAPTER 12

"Zay, come on let's go."

"Sis, hold on. She's gonna box this one for me." Zaina pointed to the orange blossom infused vanilla cake.

Salma rolled her eyes. They'd been at the Tweede Patisserie for the past hour, choosing a cake for the baby shower. The celebration was not for another two weeks, but Zaina hadn't liked any of the previous places they had gone to. The Patisserie was a specialty bakery that specialized in high quality baked goods such as croissants, tarts, cakes, cookies, and other delicate desserts.

They were often booked solid, which was the reason they weren't an option in the first place. However, Zaina got a call from them the previous day that they had an opening for a consultation. Salma wasn't in the mood to talk about any kind of celebration, much less plan one. But her personal troubles aside, this was for her unborn niece. The fact that she was the designated planner and more fluent in Arabic was another reason she didn't let Zaina come by herself.

So here she was, on a Wednesday afternoon with Zaina who couldn't seem to make up her mind on what flavor she wanted. As the attendant boxed up Zaina's order, the delicate chime of the shop's doorbell announced the arrival of another customer. A gush of fresh ocean breeze rushed in and mixed with the sweet aroma of the flavors that lingered in the shop. The weatherman hinted at some rain later in the day. All Salma wanted to do was get out of here, take Zaina home and head to her villa to wait on her husband.

"I'm ready. I got you the red velvet cake. I hope it gets your attitude together because you're becoming unbearable," Zaina said, walking toward the door.

Salma opened her mouth to respond to her, but decided it wasn't worth it. Zaina was right. Instead, she grunted as they stepped onto the sidewalk. Once they got in the car, Salma instructed the driver to head to Zaina's villa. Qasim had to go to Marrakech for a meeting, so he left Jide with her and took Daniel.

"I'm going to talk to Musa again because the three of you are getting on me and Grandma Olly's nerves," Zaina fussed. "Not to talk of Yas. The only reason she isn't here troubleshooting is that the kids are ill."

Salma waved her off. "Please don't. Musa is fine wi—"

Zaina chuckled. "Is that what you think? That man is walking around like his first-born child ran away and enlisted in the army."

Salma laughed. "No, he's not."

"He is Sal. He's hurt and disappointed. Unlike Omar, he doesn't care who you date. But you getting married and keeping it a secret all these years...you hurt my husband's feelings and you need to fix it."

This was the reason she avoided everyone. It was late July and about ten days since the blowout at her grandmother's house. Dinner that day had been so awkward with the thick cloud of electric tension that hung over the table. Once she got back to her villa, Qasim ran a bath for her and had some food heated up when she got out. He was right to guess she hadn't had much of an appetite at her grandmother's.

That night, she cried in his arms while he made her promises of everything being okay eventually. He said a prayer over them before they fell into a restful sleep. The next day, she and Qasim tried to talk to Omar, but he'd sneakily left for Accra, and Mustafa conveniently had meetings that couldn't wait. Taking Qasim's advice, Salma gave them the space they needed. She and Qasim concentrated on their jobs by day and dating, rekindling, and deepening their bond by night. The news traveled fast around Tweede Kans Cove, because while they were out and about, they got curious stares from strangers.

"But I've tried. Even my husband—"

Zaina shook her head. "No, you need to worry about your relationship with your brothers, first. Them seeing you with Qasim before things are right with you guys will have them fighting all over again." A few beats passed between them. "I love my Mar-Mar, but even I know that the restraint Qasim showed was a one-time thing only. Did you see his eyes? Anyway, my brother can take care of himself."

Salma gave her a pointed look. Zaina's father was Tanzanian while her mother was Nigerian. That fifty percent of Zaina's DNA had her referring to Qasim as "her brother" any chance she got. She didn't allow two sentences go by without saying "my brother this, my brother that."

"You know it's so funny hearing you say your husband."

Salma shrugged. Sometimes it was funny to her too. She had spent so much time suppressing that part of her life that its resurgence seemed strange.

"I can't believe you gave me all that flack about marrying Musa in London when you got married in secret too."

Salma narrowed her eyes and waved her off. "Please don't go there. Besides, it's not the same thing…"

Salma had been on the phone for several weeks planning Zaina and Mustafa's wedding. At the time, Zaina was in London finishing up something for work. Zaina participated in all the Zoom calls with her mother and Salma as they planned the event. Suddenly, Zaina said she was stressed and in typical Mustafa fashion, he shut everything down. Next thing Salma knew, Mustafa flew to London, and he and Zaina got married privately, then flew to their second home in Zanzibar for their honeymoon. All that planning, the time spent, everything down the drain. She became annoyed all over again when she thought about it.

"Hmmm, whatever. You got to plan the surprise one we had, so stop whining."

Some months ago, Mustafa called Salma and asked her to plan a surprise wedding ceremony in Casablanca. According to her brother, his mother-in-law couldn't keep a secret, so Salma ended up planning it with Zaina's best friend, Ibiso Danjuma.

Salma missed those times; everything was so simple. Well, they were simple because she repressed parts of her life that she hadn't wanted to deal with. She glanced over at Zaina who was now on the phone with Mustafa. It was so strange for them to be together, and for Mustafa to not speak to her when he called.

Wiping the tear that formed in the corner of her eye, Salma looked out of the window and took in the charming sights of Tweede Kans Cove. Colorful storefronts lined the cobblestone streets, while locals navigated their daily routines, some in traditional djellabas and others in modern attire. The aroma of street vendors' tagines and the scents of spices seeped through the slightly wound down front window, intertwining with the fresh pastries Zaina had. Textiles and flowers adorned windowsills, adding a touch of vibrancy to the picturesque scene.

"I know you volunteer at Beautiful Eyes today. What time do you have to be there?" Zaina asked.

Her brows furrowed. "In about two hours. Why?"

"Your brother is home," Zaina said. "This ends today."

Salma's heart thudded in her chest. She missed her brother, but at the same time was at a loss for what to say. She had no regrets about marrying Qasim. She had many regrets about the way she went about it and the way she handled the marriage itself. Her grandmother said for her to be able to restore relationships, she had to first be restored to her Savior. However, it seemed that ever since she returned to the Father, things hadn't gone as smoothly as she had thought. She wasn't naïve to think her life would be smooth sailing, but Salma wasn't used to this type of tension.

Pulling out her phone from her purse, she saw that Qasim had sent her an image of the saffron farm he was visiting. She liked the image, then sent him a text.

> Hey honey! I miss you.

> My Honey: My Star, I miss you too. Well, I really miss those...

Salma smiled when his next message appeared with a winky face, a spread hand, and a peach. Heat rose within her remembering their passion-filled tango in the morning before she left for work.

> Stop...lol

> My Honey: I adore my wife's body and what it does to me. Sue me.

> And I adore yours too but that's not the point.

> My Honey: What's wrong? Are you okay?

The way he could read her always amazed her. That's why the night she knew she would be leaving him in their New York home, she had to put in extra work to make sure she didn't tip him off.

> I'm going to see Musa.

> My Honey: Good. Remember, to speak your mind, baby. But his feelings are his own, all you can do is explain your side. The worst has already happened.

> I love you, honey.

> My Honey: I know. But not more than me. I'll
> tell you all about my meeting tonight.

She absentmindedly traced her thumb along the edge of her phone case, her fingers flipping it over and back in a restless rhythm. Sighing, she leaned back and closed her eyes. The family would soon get together to celebrate Zaina and there was no way she wanted their current turmoil hanging over their heads.

The car soon came to a stop in the driveway of Mustafa and Zaina's villa. Salma had visited numerous times since the couple had been married, however this was the first time she felt she wouldn't be welcomed.

Once they got inside, she and Zaina were met by Mustafa who was coming around the corner. Her brother was dressed down in jeans and a black, long-sleeved jersey shirt. Something he wouldn't have been caught dead in before he got married. Her brother had changed drastically, and she was happy for him. In her opinion, Mustafa was still grumpy and a man of few words, but he was lighter. The love he shared with his wife was good for him. He was still obsessed with her as he had always been. Evidenced by the way he was currently kissing her as though he hadn't seen her in forever.

Salma couldn't be mad because it was the same way Qasim had been all over her since they reconciled. However, she wanted to get this over with, so she was going to have to break this up. She cleared her throat.

Zaina pulled back. Using the pad of her thumb, she wiped the corners of her husband's lips. "Behave," she warned Mustafa before turning to wink at Salma and heading for the kitchen.

It was only when Zaina was no longer in sight that Mustafa looked at Salma. The disappointment in his eye caused her to lower her head.

"Pick your head up, *aikhti alsaghira*."

He turned and walked toward his home office. Any other time

the "little sister" name would have garnered a response, but he was at least talking to her, so he could have it.

Salma followed. The feel of his house had really changed. Instead of the various shades of grey and black he had before, the house now showed the presence of a woman with an elegant touch that had infused the space with a palette of soft pastels and warm earthy tones. The once stark furniture was now adorned with cushions and throws. Fresh flowers graced the tables, their fragrant presence filling the air. Salma couldn't help but smile. Zaina had transformed the house into a welcoming and harmonious haven.

When he entered the office, Mustafa settled his husky frame on the sofa and crossed his legs at the knees. Salma watched him before her gaze swept across the room and caught sight of the aged bowling trophy on his bookshelf. She recalled that same trophy from two years ago when she had visited this office. He won it with his then girlfriend, now wife. It was a memento from their time together and he'd held onto it for seven years. She recalled pushing for him to get rid of it because of the painful memories she thought it dredged up. Then, Mustafa had unequivocally told her to mind the business that paid her. How the tables had turned.

"I know you didn't come over here to admire an office you've been in several times." His voice was terse.

Salma paced the length of the office and sighed. "I'm sorry, okay? What did I do that was so wrong? How long are you going to treat me like an outcast?"

His gaze burned through her, and she wrapped her arms around her body. She wished he would say something and stop looking at her as though she was a stranger. She shifted from one foot to the other before he spoke.

"Sit down."

Salma stared at him, then did as she was told.

"You've always been spoiled, and I take full responsibility because I made you that way. But one thing I also taught you was to own your decisions, good or bad." He spread his arms across the length of the sofa. "If you do not know what you did wrong, then what are you sorry for?"

Salma contemplated his question. According to Zaina, he wasn't angry about who she married, but that she had gotten married without saying anything. She sighed and gathered her thoughts.

"Once we left the orphanage and went to live with grandma, I saw the way you and Yasmine, but especially you watched over me and O. You took on the responsibility of our father even though grandpa was there. So, I tried to do everything I could not to make your lives any harder. Yeah, our grandparents played a role in that, but it was mainly for you and Yas. I went to school all the way up to a master's degree. I checked all the boxes expected, then came and worked for the family. I did everything by the book. But in doing that, I didn't let myself live. I curtailed the little girl in me that longed for adventure. Qasim came along and allowed me to be that."

One of the best parts about their secret relationship was the way Qasim would drop everything and they would travel to places she mentioned wanting to see. It would be for a weekend or a day trip, but he made it happen. Sometimes she would just mention something she wished she had done as a kid, and he would recreate it. Salma quickly flicked away the tears that rolled down her cheek.

"I was old enough to remember that Baba and Mama did have times when they were happy. But something happened to make it go so wrong between them. So, I refused to fully embrace what Qasim made me feel, so we remained friends for a while. But when I finally did embrace it, you and Yas were so sad because of your own failed relationships. I didn't feel right sharing my joy. I know it's silly..." she shrugged, "... but I didn't. It was a random trip to France. 'Sim proposed, and we got married there and then. I didn't do it trying to hurt anyone. I planned to come clean and tell everyone once I moved back to

Tweedes after completing that certification. However, the marriage crumbled before then…"

The silence that ensued felt like a dagger slicing her heart open. The more time passed, and his stern gaze remained on her, the more she wanted the ground to open and swallow her.

"I'm not stupid, *aikhti alsaghira*. And I thought you knew, I'm protective and resourceful. When I saw your shifty reaction after I told you to invite Qasim and Qadir for our grandmother's birthday, and your unease when they got here, I did some digging."

"Wha…what?"

"Have you Googled yourself before?"

"What? No. Why would I? Oh my gosh, is anything on there?" Salma stood. "Let me get my phone."

"Sit. There's nothing there for anyone who isn't looking, but I had a professional look into it. You and 'Sim were not as discreet as you thought. There was one article, but it was in French." Mustafa stood and walked behind his desk. He opened a drawer and pulled out a folder. He tossed it on the desk.

Salma scurried over and picked up the folder. She couldn't read French, but there was a picture of her and Qasim in front of the Eiffel Tower. They were wrapped in each other's arms, but the rings on her fingers were quite visible. Those rings were in a safe in her villa. The four carats, round cut she had on now, Qasim gave to her when they were in Marrakech. To his displeasure, she'd removed her rings when they arrived at her grandmother's house that night. Now, she wore them with pride.

"I…I don't know what to say." Her eyes met his.

"You didn't say anything all these years, so I didn't believe it. The sister I knew would've said something. You disappoint me."

"I didn't mean to," she murmured.

Mustafa rounded his desk and stood in front of her. "I should give him the hard time you gave my wife."

Her eye widened and her pulse quickened. "No, please…it wasn't him. It was me."

"Why?" he asked, staring down at her.

She raised her brow. "Why what?"

"Why did the marriage crumble?"

Since her brothers were friends with Qasim and Qadir, she assumed they knew about the family's past illegal dealings. However, she was never going to let what happened between her and her husband leave her lips to anyone. Some men taking her, even if it was years ago and only for a few hours, would never go down well with her older brother. She was trying to dissolve the tension, not heighten it.

She also didn't want to lie so instead she said, "I wasn't ready to commit."

Mustafa studied her. He probably knew she was hiding something. But that was the truth to some extent. She wasn't ready to be as committed as her mother was and keep giving second chances to a man. Qasim was nothing like her father, but what happened between them was their business. If her brother didn't say anything, neither would she.

"*aikhti alsaghira*, I have always only cared that the man you end up with loves you the way you deserve to be loved...wholly. It wasn't your job to carry my burden or Yas', just as I have learned it wasn't my job to carry our parents' burden. I'll talk to your husband..." he smirked, "...if anything touches you, I'll touch him. I don't care what army he has behind him."

Stunned, Salma could only nod. Mustafa pulled her against his chest, and she felt the tension melt away in the embrace. She inhaled deeply, then released her breath.

One down, one to go.

~

*T*wo days later, the chilly gust of the airconditioned hallway brushed against Salma's face as she left her office. It was Friday, and this meant the resort was swamped with guests checking in and checking out. She was swamped with preparations for VIP reservations and the ballroom for this week-end's wedding. All that coupled with the meetings she had to attend made the day exhausting.

Although she had a manager in charge of day-to-day operations, Salma still had to deal with housekeeping issues at their Botswana location, a messed-up VIP reservation, and even worse—a guest who was threatening legal action because his wife mistakenly drank coconut water instead of normal water from the mini bar. Both bottles were labeled clearly and apparently the missus couldn't read. Salma huffed in irritation when she remembered that was the first thing she had to deal with as soon as she stepped through the doors. Despite the massage her husband gave her that morning and the coffee he put together before she left the villa, nothing could've relaxed her enough for that.

The day had left her feeling drained, though not to the extent that she would skip the play her husband had planned for later. Salma stepped off the elevator, her tailored blazer draped over her arm, and her heels clacking purposefully against the marble floor. As she entered the grand lobby, her gaze drifted up to take in the gleaming chandelier that hung from the ceiling before continuing to where a distressed guest stood waving her arms wildly at the front desk. Salma pursed her lips and reigned in her agitation.

"Good evening, I'm Salma, how can I assist you?"

The reassuring smile on her face was a sharp contrast to the anger rising within her when she couldn't spot any supervisor or manager nearby.

The older woman sized her up. The expression she wore was one Salma had seen many times on guests who didn't know who she was. Salma had long ago stopped giving her full name unless the occasion absolutely called for it. When she did that, she ended up having to pacify aggrieved guests more than necessary.

A few moments later, probably after feeling satisfied that Salma was someone of importance, the older woman began telling her how she was in Tweede Kans Cove for her granddaughter's wedding and her villa wasn't with the block of villas that had been reserved for the wedding party. Speaking with the attendant, Salma proffered a solution that pleased the woman who expressed her gratitude. With a final nod, Salma strode to the entrance.

Just as she approached the automatic doors leading to the front of the resort, her phone rang. She'd silenced it the first time it rang, so she answered just as the black truck Qasim insisted she rode in pulled up. She grunted. Her moving around in the back of a black truck with tinted windows in the small town was enough to give the locals something to talk about. For years, she'd walked around or driven herself, but suddenly she rode around like she was on a covert mission. All the points she'd made to Qasim as to why it was unnecessary floated through one ear and out of the other as he peppered her face with kisses.

"Hey Yas," she said, her voice slurring.

"Don't you sound exhausted."

"I am," she admitted. "But what's up? How are my kiddos?"

She loved her nephew and nieces, but recently, the more she thought about them, the more regret threatened to pull her under. Everything was going great, and Qasim never revisited the question of why she still left even after he explained everything to her that night. He assumed it was because of what she went through and that she was scared. It was, but the deeper reason lay beneath. One she dared not voice or their newly built house could come crumbling down. Over the past several days, the closer they got, the more she knew she had to come clean, but she didn't know how.

"Sal?"

"Yes, sorry... what's up?"

"Are you okay?"

"Yes, I'm good. How are the kids now? I mean for Kojo to be giving a refund for a government official's son's wedding, they had to be bad."

"No, it was a cold. But you can't tell KJ anything when it comes to his kids, so I let him do what he thought he needed to."

Salma laughed. Kojo grew up in Beautiful Eyes orphanage. So

the way he was with his kids could seem extreme, but Salma understood it. Her sister and brother-in-law had been at it since they were sixteen and eighteen years old respectively. Even after an almost twenty-year separation, it was as though they hadn't skipped a beat. Everyone in the family knew not to get involved in whatever squabble they were having when they did have them.

After the sisters caught up on the latest—it wasn't much since they had talked two days ago—Yasmine asked that she make a detour to their grandmother's house to pick up her orange sweater.

"Yas, come on. Can't it wait till you come home?"

"You know your grandmother is always clearing things out for charity. If she gives away my favorite sweater, I will be vexed."

Salma shook her head. The sweater couldn't be that sentimental if she just noticed it was missing after three months. Although Omar was still hiding out in Accra, the tension in their family was calmer. Even though she felt Yasmine was bluffing, she didn't want to cause another issue. After conceding, she told Jide to head to the Manoir as she texted Qasim that she had to make a detour.

Half an hour later, Salma rang the bell. When the door opened, she felt her heart stop at the sight of her twin. His eyes roamed over her, but he remained silent. Turning his back on her, he removed his phone from his back pocket. With measured steps, Salma followed him down the hallway. He entered the kitchen and Salma heard her sister's voice come through the speakers of his cell phone.

"Sister, is this why you made me come back here?" he growled.

Salma leaned against the frame of the archway listening to him and Yasmine. The bite she heard in his tone was one he'd never in his right mind use on their older sister. So, it was obvious that he had lost his mind somewhere.

"Don't speak to her like that. Yas, you shouldn't have bothered. I don't care if he doesn't want to talk to me."

"Salma, wait! Omar, you've had the space and time to be upset. I understand, but that's your sister. Now, hash out whatever this is." Yasmine cleared her throat. "If this tension still exists between the two of you when I come to town with the kids, you will not get to see them."

Salma's eyes darted to the phone. She heard her brother gasp before he thumbed his nose and chuckled. There was nothing humorous in the sound.

"You would really keep my niece and nephews from me?" he asked.

Salma knew her twin and the reason for his confession of never wanting to have children of his own.

"Try me. Sal, own up to your misstep and you guys get it together." Without waiting for a response, their older sister hung up the phone.

Omar turned back to the stove and began mixing something. He was either prepping for family dinner the next day or making something for their grandmother to eat once she returned from her Friday evening mass. Her stomach rumbled, breaking the tension in the room. She hadn't had anything since mid-morning. When Qasim called during lunchtime, she'd promised him she was going to eat, but something came up.

She walked over to the massive island and pulled out a stool. Before she could gather her thoughts to speak, Omar placed a bowl of kefta and some bread in front of her. The aroma of the stewed meatballs wafted up her nostrils filling her senses with the scent of savory spices. Despite her hunger, she narrowed his eyes at him, then looked down at the bowl before slowly picking up the fork.

"What? I'm infuriated, but not enough to kill you. Your so-called husband on the other hand..." Omar let his words trail off.

Salma shook her head but decided to fill her stomach a little before addressing him. A few minutes passed between them as Omar continued prepping and putting bowls filled with different chopped vegetables in the freezer.

"Are you going to talk to me or keep acting like I'm not here?"

Omar chuckled. "I'm not Mustafa. Either get on with explaining or exit stage left. As for Yas, I'll get Kojo to handle her." He folded his arms across his chest and leaned against the countertop.

"I'm not sorry about marrying Qasim. I'm sincerely sorry about keeping it from you."

"You didn't just keep your marriage from me. You kept the fact that you got back with him after that media fiasco, then got married to him. Let's keep it straight."

"Okay Omar, I did and I'm sorry, but don't you want to know why?"

He shrugged. "Spill."

"I understand you being older than me...older is a stretch since it's by only three minutes—"

"Salma!"

"Okay. You hold on too tight, O. You've been the keeper and protector of my heart since we were little, and I love you for it..."

When they were kids and the commotion between their parents would start, she would climb into her brother's bed, and he'd sing to her to help block out the noise. Over the years, she'd dated but something about Qasim triggered Omar. Salma suspected it was because he sensed her deep love for him and knew he had the potential to shatter her heart.

"When Qasim came along, I denied him for my own fears, but yours as well. Then I took the chance, and you hated it. It caused a rift between us. When that thing happened with his ex, we broke up...you allowed me to cry on your shoulder, but you also spent the time telling me you told me so."

Qasim refused to directly admit it to her, but when they separated, Omar blocked every attempt he made to reach out to her.

"Because I did! Now thinking back to when you returned to Tweedes...I was right. It was him you were sulking over...he broke your heart, twice."

Salma lowered her eyes. When she left Qasim and came back

to Tweedes, Omar was by her side through her heartbreak. He suspected it was a man but didn't push. Instead, he did things they did when they were kids to make her laugh and feel better.

"I agree, he bruised my heart, but if it can be bruised, that means it still works. I don't want to grow up alone, O. If I don't love again, that means I let my trauma win."

"So, what? You're healed of our childhood pain?" He walked over and sat next to her.

"I read something when I was praying some weeks ago. It's from Psalm 147:3. He heals the brokenhearted and binds their wounds. I can't erase our trauma and some things will still trigger me." She took a breath, then exhaled. "This means Jesus will help us out if we let Him. So, I'll be brave and trust Him. I won't allow the enemy to play with my mind anymore and deprive me of this joy. I refuse to."

The revelation the Holy Spirit just gave her sunk in and she nodded. Salma watched her brother's eyes gloss over. He joked a lot but the scars he had from their father's constant verbal bashing hadn't healed. It played a role in most decisions he made. Salma stood and drew Omar in for a hug. She stomped her feet when he refused to wrap his arms around her. He chuckled but finally hugged her back. Intentionally squeezing her so tight that she squealed until he loosened his grip. As she leaned her head on his chest, Salma prayed that soon her brother would consider casting his burdens on Jesus so he could find rest.

Real rest.

CHAPTER 13

Friday evening one week later, Qasim hummed a tune as he climbed the steps of Gentlemen's Groom Haven. The pleasant fragrances of sandalwood and citrus filled his nostrils as he strode through the gleaming glass doors. As soon as he opened them, a gentle chime rang out, announcing his arrival to the salon employees at the front desk. He advanced to the reception desk and presented his VIP pass for authentication. The soft carpet muffled his footsteps as he traveled towards the private lounge. Jazz tones and calming water trickling from a fountain created a tranquil atmosphere.

The lounge was an all-inclusive, high-end oasis tailored specifically for men's grooming and relaxation needs. The services ranged from customized haircuts to traditional straight-razor shaves to energizing massages and soothing sauna treatments. Patrons could also savor the pleasure of premium cigars, professional men's stylists, and a selection of upscale drinks. Qasim and Qadir didn't come to Tweede Kans Cove very often, but they had purchased memberships to the lounge at the insistence of the DuBois-Arazi brothers.

As he made his way through the galley, a smile crossed his lips. Even though no one knew they were in a relationship, Salma disapproved of him lounging here with her brothers mainly because women weren't allowed in. That was the main reason he hadn't told her where he was now. She'd been talking about the almond and cinnamon pastilla from La Belle Étoile since they dined there some days ago. He intended to use it as a bribe when she started asking questions. She might not go for it, but it was worth a try.

After a month of cold silence, Omar texted and asked him to meet here. He had reconciled with his sister recently, so Qasim figured it was now his turn. Whatever the motivation was, he was ready for this overdue conversation. He had to return to Nigeria in a few days and he wanted his wife's complete peace of mind. The only thing he wanted her to bother about was missing him. Initially, he'd planned on going back home with her, but after much persuasion, he saw just how daunting the task might be at present. Nevertheless, his journey home needed to happen in a few days.

Qasim stepped into the VIP lounge area, decorated with deep red walls and plush velvet armchairs. His eyes quickly found Omar, who was reclining in an oversized leather chair, a tumbler of amber liquid held comfortably in one hand. Ice cubes tinkled softly against the glass as he raised it to his lips. Qasim slipped into the chair opposite him. A few beats went by, and Omar hadn't lifted his eyes to acknowledge him. He'd always known Omar to be petty, but Qasim had endured just about enough. He lifted his hand to signal the waiter. After ordering a drink, he returned his focus to Omar. His friend was three years younger than him and now it showed.

Qasim grunted. "Yo, I know you didn't invite me here for me to watch you nurse that drink."

Omar leaned forward in his chair and locked eyes with Qasim, who raised a brow, leaned back into his seat and crossed his legs at the knee.

"I'm still trying to understand how you can sit in my face all these years knowing you were foul. My sister!"

Qasim frowned when Omar's hand curled into a tight ball. He gritted his teeth and scooted forward. He'd answer any question that needed to be answered or give whatever explanation he thought Omar deserved. But what would never happen again was Omar feeling he could put his hand on him.

"Let's get one thing straight, first. We can talk like grown men..." Qasim's eyes went to Omar's fist. "...Or you can swing, and I promise to lay you out. Don't act like you don't know how I get down," he snarled.

"You figure?" he challenged.

"Oh, I know..." Qasim held his gaze, then spoke again. "I was hoping we could salvage our decade plus long friendship. It's important to your sister. Me too if I'm being honest, but it's not something I'll lose sleep over either. If we don't come to an understanding after this, at least I can tell your sister I tried."

"Here I thought you were at least remorseful. Same old Nigerian arrogance. What you did was wrong and you're not—"

"Your sister was afraid of the way you showed your behind when we got together the first time. She didn't need the drama again, so she asked not to tell you. You know me...at least I thought you did. I love that woman with my being and shouting it from the rooftops was my plan. But her happiness means more than my ego. That was wrong, but it was what she wanted." Qasim took a breath to let his words sink in. "But hear me, there'll never come a day when I apologize to any man for giving my wife what she desires...not even her twin."

"That's my sister. I don't want her heart broken. The first time you did it took her back to a past we try to forget."

"And the first time didn't really happen. You know that. Salma got wind of the story and ran with it, and because you weren't onboard in the first place, you enabled her. I should be the one mad at you."

Omar chuckled and took a sip of his drink.

Qasim sighed. "Look, I can't claim to understand what you

guys went through in the past, but all I want...and need is to love my wife, man. And make babies..."

Omar frowned. "I don't want to know that."

Qasim laughed. "Get used to it, because I intend to slob her down whether you're in the room or not."

Omar grunted. A silent understanding passed between them. Qasim was okay with leaving things the way they were.

"Handle her with care." Omar sighed.

"I got her. You trust me with everything else. So, trust me with my most prized gift."

"Hmm, you won't be saying that when she's driving you crazy."

Qasim chuckled. "I've seen all your sister's crazy. In fact, I'm sure you decided to meet here so I can get another dose. You know she hates this place and will give me hell if she finds out I'm here."

Omar smiled and Qasim knew he was right. The man was petty.

"I do not know what you're talking about."

"Of course, you don't. But you forget, I also know how to tame that crazy." Qasim winked at him. "I got the magic touch."

"Ugh...I don't want to hear that!"

Qasim laughed from the depths of his stomach. Omar's face twisted in agony. He was really pained at the notion of a man and his sister. From what he was told, Omar didn't have a problem with Yasmine's man. So why was he so upset? It must be because he was overly aware of the media attention Qasim got when he was in the league. The press used his celebrity status to sell magazines. Stretching the truth and making up their own. Omar believed him when he denied the stories, but Qasim figured when his sister had the potential of being affected by those stories, he took a different stand.

"She refuses to tell me what went wrong with the marriage. But I hope it doesn't have anything to do with your family and their dealings."

Omar and Mustafa knew of his family's businesses. The legal

and illegal ones. They didn't talk about it often, but it lingered in the air between them. The Adesinas were a magnet for the media. Mainly because a veil of mystery surrounded them and what people didn't understand, they attacked and speculated about. Over the past month, their publicist had done some damage control with the recent bad press, but they couldn't control everything the media wrote about.

"I'm not gonna sit up here and make my family out as one of those happy-go-lucky, kumbaya families. But just as you would go to war for yours, I'll do the same for mine. And my wife is my number one priority. Always…"

Qasim's words trailed off as he and Omar lifted their eyes to Mustafa who entered the area. Qasim groaned because he wasn't ready to duel with another brother. Earlier in the week, he ran into the older DuBois-Arazi when he stopped by the resort to take Salma to lunch. They had a brief discussion that was malice free. The guy reminded him of his own older brother, so he didn't expect much of anything else. A waiter came over and asked if Mustafa wanted anything to eat or drink. After placing his order, he asked them to prepare a to-go order of fekkas for his wife.

Qasim laughed as Omar teased his older brother about being a softie for his wife, he admitted it was a good look, but he never expected to see the day. Qasim couldn't curb the vision of Salma swollen with their child. He looked forward to it. Omar made a few more jabs about how his unborn niece would have Mustafa wrapped around her finger. Mustafa grunted a few times. After another bout of light laughter between the men, Omar turned to Qasim.

"Talking to you now, I can without a doubt tell that you love my sister. I've never seen her so happy, or fight for something so hard as she's fought for her right to be with you…"

Qasim refrained from responding because he could feel a "but" coming on. He needed to get out of here soon, so it was best to let Omar get whatever he needed to off his chest.

"I also know you well enough to assume that now that you

have her back, you won't live apart from her. But...if at any time, you can't protect her from whatever your family has going on, please promise to bring her back to us. Or call and I'll come get her."

Qasim shook his head. "I hear you, but I can't make that promise. What I can say is, if that ever happens, I'll walk away from my family. But my wife...she stays with me." He held the gaze of both men. He needed them to know how serious he was about his position. Even when Salma wasn't with him, he had someone watching over her. She wasn't going to like it, but Jide was going to stay with her here in Tweedes until she eventually relocated to Nigeria. Paul, who put in his resignation with the resort when Qasim arrived, was currently on vacation.

"Fair...but like I told Salma, if anything touches her, I'll touch you," Mustafa said.

Qasim met his eyes. "Fair."

With the way he had things set up back home, nothing was touching his family and that included his wife. So, he wasn't worried about Mustafa's threat. What he would be worried about if he didn't get out of here was his wife. Her text just came through asking where her pastilla was.

~

"**H**ave you heard from Musa?" Salma called out.

She came scurrying from around the corner and walked into Qasim. He steadied her and tucked her hair behind her ear. With one hand on her waist, he used his other hand to toy with the pear-shaped diamond pendant on her neck-lace. His eyes traveled down her frame that was perfectly clad in an orange and white, off-the-shoulder jumpsuit. He bit down on his bottom lip. Flashes of their time earlier that morning danced around in his memory.

Salma shook her head, lifted her hand, and released his lip from the clamp of his teeth. "Stop that. If not for your 'just a little bit more' I would've been out of bed in time to stop Musa on this silly journey he embarked on."

Squeezing her waist, he groaned then leaned to kiss her forehead. She wasn't telling the whole story, but she was stressed out, so he was going to let her make it.

"Star...I need you to breathe."

"I can't when everything seems to be falling apart," she whined.

"You're being dramatic. Nothing is falling apart. Everything will be fine." Qasim pecked her lips. "I know how important it is for everything to go smoothly, but don't make me pull the husband card and bench you."

Salma sighed in resignation. "Honey, I'm fine. One headache and now you swear I'm stressed."

"No, one migraine that lasted two days and ended with a diagnosis that said you need to eat better and rest more."

In all his reporting, Paul omitted to tell him how much Salma worked. For the past several weeks, Qasim had watched her remain constantly on the go. It was as though there was something that always needed her attention at the resort. His wife had a hard time delegating and her staff had come to rely on her always stepping in. He hated it because he felt they took advantage of her need to ensure perfection. He couldn't even count the number of times he'd had to demand she leave work. He understood it because sometimes he could be the same way. However, he didn't have to like it and neither did it have to continue.

"I'm serious, baby."

"Okay, I hear you. It's just that Zaina is about to lose her mind and it's driving me crazy."

It was late Saturday afternoon and the day they'd been waiting for had finally arrived – Zaina and Mustafa's baby shower. Unfortunately, daddy-to-be was missing in action. Zaina's mom had arrived Marrakech on schedule last night, but there were setbacks with the DuBois-Arazi jet taking off from there this morning.

Instead of just sending his driver to pick up his mother-in-law,

Mustafa decided to tag along. Salma had jumped out of bed this morning when Zaina called frantic that she hadn't heard from Mustafa since they left. This was his first time seeing Salma since then. She had linked up with Yasmine who arrived with her family two days ago and they had been with Zaina ever since. Omar talked to Mustafa earlier, even Zaina did, so they knew they were okay and on their way back, but the fact that they hadn't arrived had Zaina in a frenzy.

"She has a right to be. You, on the other hand, are supposed to keep her calm."

"That's what Yasmine is doing now. You know that's not my strong suit."

Qasim chuckled. Salma kissed his lips before telling him she had to go and check on the photographer and make sure the picture backdrop was to Zaina's specifications. He watched her go for a minute. His chest hurt at the thought of having to leave her in a few days. He didn't want to uproot her life, but he'd be lying if he didn't acknowledge the gut-wrenching pain he knew was coming.

His mother was disappointed he wasn't coming back with Salma, but he knew she'd be more upset when he told her of their marital status. If what Salma went through with her family was any indication of how his own family would react to their secret nuptials, he would much rather have all that handled before his wife arrived in Ibadan. The scenarios might not actually be the same, but that hint of betrayal would still be present. One good thing was that his family knew Omar, so the notion that Salma would want him for his money wouldn't even be in play. His wife had enough of her own.

Qasim's thoughts were interrupted when one of the vendors tapped him on the shoulder inquiring about Mustafa.

"He's not here at the moment," Qasim responded.

The man looked at the clipboard in his hand again. "What about a Salma DuBois-Arazi?"

Qasim frowned, then took notice of the tag on the man's

shirt. Kassim Motors. His eyes scanned the area. The space was set up with a combination of rustic and elegant décor. Wooden round tables draped with soft pastel tablecloths were in the center of the room. The only reason he knew they were pastel was because his wife nearly took someone's head off earlier because they messed one up. Qasim saw Salma and Yasmine talking to a photographer in the corner and pointed that way. The man thanked him and moved in that direction. Qasim observed the interaction between the man and Salma. He bopped his head to the soft acoustic music playing in the background when he felt a presence behind him. He turned and saw a grinning Kojo beside him.

Qasim settled his hands in his pockets. "You gonna tell me what you're grinning at or keep being weird?"

Qasim was introduced to Kojo at Grandma Olly's party. After the party that night, Qasim, Qadir, Kojo, and the DuBois-Arazi brothers got to hang out. Qasim and Kojo were low-key fans of each other and hit it off immediately.

"I'm just making sure you don't tackle the man on his way out," Kojo said.

Qasim chuckled. Salma knew who she belonged to so there was no need for him to flex his muscles. However, seeing as the Hamza guy didn't get the message that she wasn't available, Qasim was extra cautious. Under the guise of their business dealings, Hamza found different reasons to send his wife texts, pop up in her office and send her lunch. Qasim was angry about most of it, but Salma pleaded with him not to confront the man while she attempted to soothe his anger in other ways.

One day, her sexual antics didn't succeed at taming his beast when he saw the jewelry Hamza sent her. That day, he and Salma had their first heated argument since reconciliation. She knew what his reaction would be to the gift, so she hid it on the top shelf in her closet. Although there was a sticky note on it that said "Return," Qasim couldn't get it out of his head that she was somehow encouraging the guy. The next day, Qasim went to the winery and took the gift back to Hamza himself with a clear message.

Stay away.

"Man, get outta here. Like you won't be the same way," Qasim said.

"Oh, in a minute. Yas is my whole world and the mother of my kids...man, I dare anyone to try me like that."

Qasim smiled. "I hear you but shoot, she better be. Eighteen years, that could never be me. I don't know how you had your heart galivanting this earth without you for that long."

"Being knuckleheaded, fighting my heart, doing everything but the work I had to do to be right for her...for me. For us." He took a breath. "Two broken people coming together is a recipe for disaster."

Qasim nodded. He couldn't say he wasn't without his share of baggage. Being one of the Adesina boys came with its own share of issues. There was constant pressure to perform. In school, socially and sports. It often felt like the better he and his brothers excelled, the more their father loved them. The opposite was also true if they underperformed. Not dealing with his issues was one of the reasons he was no longer in the league. Seeking perfection, he made a wrong turn on the field and instead of passing the ball, he forged ahead. That game was his last.

"If I've learned nothing in the time I've been away from my wife, I believe without a doubt that God makes everything perfect in His time." He shrugged. "Sometimes we're not ready for what we think we're ready for."

Kojo smirked. "Same thing I told Yas, but she wasn't trying to hear it. That woman gave me hell when I returned."

Qasim watched Kojo look over at Yasmine who was now walking with Salma to the front with the man leading the way. He understood where Kojo was coming from. Their trauma wasn't something they were responsible for, however doing the work to heal was. He smiled with the knowledge that both he and Salma had the courage to take the necessary steps.

There was commotion at the front of the door and he and Kojo began walking towards it when Mustafa and Zaina's mom walked in.

"Thank Jesus, now my wife can calm down," Qasim said.

"Yeah, 'cause she was becoming too aggy. I was about to put her in a chokehold." Kojo laughed.

Qasim raised his brow. "Watch it now. I'd hate for Yas to have to nurse you back to health."

"Man, get outta here. That's always gonna be my annoying little sister. Meanwhile, I'mma send you the bill for all the Zeidu Fashion sets I've had to get her..."

"Oh, I see, you're the *cheap* big brother." Qasim smiled, nodding. "I gotchu, run me the number."

Both men laughed as they listened to Salma yell instructions for pictures. Zaina was wrapped in Mustafa's arms, crying. He was trying to get her to calm down, so Qasim knew the pictures would take another minute. Because that man didn't move unless his wife was good.

A few hours later, the shower was winding down. Salma had outdone herself, but Qasim had no doubt she would. Everything was planned and executed to perfection. Games, dancing, and videos of Zaina and Mustafa as babies had played on the large projector, drawing laughter from the guests. It was an intimate affair with about thirty to fifty close friends and associates of the parents-to-be.

The food was light, a perfect blend of Moroccan, Nigerian and Tanzanian cuisine. Soon after, Mustafa presented his wife with a snow white 2023 Bugatti SUV. The guy from earlier was asked to deliver it to Salma in Mustafa's absence. One thing about the burly Arab, he didn't talk much, but he always showed out for those he loved. Qasim was impressed.

Omar was all over the place ensuring things were going smoothly. It was amazing to see how Yasmine's kids followed him around the place. He and Omar were on better footing, but there was still an air of awkwardness between them. Qasim now understood that it was no longer about him being with Salma, but more about being excluded from the process. Qasim was hopeful that things would smooth themselves out soon. As long as he and Salma were back on solid footing, Qasim wasn't too concerned.

Qasim watched the camaraderie between the DuBois-Arazi siblings and suddenly missed home. No one except Qadir knew he was on his way home, so he looked forward to surprising his mother. Seeing his wife preoccupied, Qasim made his way to the restroom. As he was about to turn the corner, he felt Salma's eyes on him. He winked at her and pointed to where he was going. After her subtle nod, he continued his journey.

A few minutes later, Qasim returned, and his blood boiled at the sight before him. *This man didn't seem to understand the concept of staying away.*

As he took determined strides to the bar at the back of the venue where Hamza stood with Omar, questions swirled in his head. What was Omar doing with Hamza Alami? Why was he here? Salma told him that Omar was aware of the encounter he had with the unrelenting man. Was Omar so mad at him for marrying his sister that he would work against him? With each step he took, Qasim felt his adrenaline fueling his rage. His stride was suddenly cut off.

"Aye! Not here."

"Kojo, move," Qasim seethed.

"Nah, I can't do that. I'm trying to save your behind. You see all this work your wife put into this event. If you cause a scene, and mess it up, she'll be tight."

Kojo's words settled in his mind as blood rushed to his ears. He couldn't let this go unchecked. But Kojo was right.

Qasim kept his eyes ahead. "I just want to talk to him."

"I can't stop you, but—"

"I'm good. I promise."

Kojo stepped aside and Qasim continued on his path. Kojo fell in step beside him. Omar and Hamza had their backs to them.

"Look, I suggest you leave quietly. This is a private event," Omar said.

"I'm sure your sister won't mind. She told me about this baby shower when I took her to lunch."

"That was months ago, and I know she didn't invite you..."

"How do you know that? I just—"

Omar hissed. "Because her husband might look calm, but he's crazy."

Qasim's heart rate returned to normal, hearing that Omar was on his side after all. However, it was time to bring this to an end.

"I mean, I tried to tell him when I popped up on him, but I don't think he got the message."

Both men spun around, though Qasim kept his gaze locked onto Hamza. He outstretched a hand for a fist bump, which Omar responded to. Qasim could tell that Hamza was furious, and it was clear he was really smitten with his wife. He blamed himself because in all the years he was separated from Salma, Hamza was the one person he allowed to get too close.

"You do not scare me. I looked you up! I know all about your criminal family," Hamza whispered harshly. The protruding veins in his neck were bluish, showing his anger. "Typical Nigerians...if you're forcing my Salma to..."

My?

That word blinded Qasim and everything Kojo said earlier went out the window as he took a few steps forward. He was intercepted again by Kojo and Omar.

"'Sim, he's not worth it. Let's go," Omar said.

"Even if it wasn't me, it would never have been you. She might have tried to make it be you, but it never would've worked. That woman's soul is intertwined with mine." Qasim let his words sink in. "This is my last warning. Since you know so much about my family, you should know that we have no problem rewarding bad behavior."

Qasim turned, then pulled out his phone. He texted his private investigator.

> I want a file on a Hamza Alami of Harmony
> Winery. I want everything, up to what side of
> the bed he sleeps on at night.

Qasim was ready to leave the man alone, but it seemed as though Hamza wanted to play. Qasim was about to show him what a grown-up playground looked like. A few moments later, a response came through.

> PI Rah: On it.

Qasim pocketed his phone when Salma walked up to him. He pulled her close and wrapped his arm around her waist. Her arms snaked around his neck, and she stared into his eyes. He knew what she wanted – to know what happened – but this wasn't the time to discuss it. Instead, he kissed the crook of her neck and whispered in her ear.

"You still owe me for this morning. I'm ready to collect."

Her laughter was music to his ears. Mustafa clinked his glass, signaling he was ready to end the evening with a toast. Qasim pulled her with him to get their glasses. He was ready to get out of here so his private party could begin.

CHAPTER 14

"*H*oney, stop whining. I'll see you in less than twelve hours." Walking into her kitchen, Salma kicked off her shoes and placed her keys on the counter. She glanced at her phone's screen into the eyes of her strikingly attractive husband. It'd been six weeks since Qasim left Tweede Kans Cove and she missed him terribly. But she had to do what was required before her trip to Nigeria the next day.

On his final night in Tweedes, they agreed that she would get most of her operations in order so that she could stay in Nigeria for a few months. While there, she'd become accustomed to her new family and atmosphere before making the final move at the top of the year. Like Yasmine and Kojo, they agreed to keep her villa in Tweede Kans Cove as their second home. However, because there was no Grand Amour in Nigeria, she'd mostly work remotely, but return to Tweede Kans Cove once every month to work from the main office.

"I don't whine. This is me grumbling," Qasim said.

Salma giggled, leaning her phone against the flower vase. "We saw each other two weeks ago. You'll live."

"Two weeks is fourteen days. Do you know how many minutes that is?"

Not willing to deal with their separation any longer, two weeks ago, Qasim booked them a romantic weekend in Cape Town, South Africa. As she opened the refrigerator to remove the left-over couscous chicken bowl from the previous night, she couldn't help but think back to that weekend. He had wined and dined her, then they went to see some historical sites before retiring to the hotel room where they enjoyed each other until it was time for her to catch her flight back home.

The moments she thought would never be hers again were back. The man and life she fell in love with and made vows to. While he was in Tweedes, they had spent so much time dealing with the past and her family that they really couldn't enjoy each other. In Cape Town they were free of any inhibitions. Qasim had shown her pleasure beyond her wildest dreams, leaving her breathless and begging for more.

"I see that smile on your face, so I know you feel it too," he said.

Salma put her plate in the microwave and leaned against the counter. "Yes, I do, but it's your fault I had to be here an extra day."

"You're the one that decided to go into business with a petty man."

She sucked her teeth. Everything had been planned out for the trial trip to the winery, but when the day came, the chief wine-maker had an excuse that caused it to be canceled. Salma was disappointed, but didn't think too much about it until it happened again. Although they'd signed a contract and finalized the schedule, Hamza was nowhere to be found when Salma demanded a meeting. It wasn't until she was giving an update at the staff meeting that Omar let it slip that Hamza must be afraid of Qasim. Neither he nor Qasim were forthcoming with the reason why. However, none of that was important when it came to honoring their contract.

"He's being a sore loser—"

"Loser? Star baby, he was never in the running." Qasim stood from the chair in his office.

She rolled her eyes before they darted to the timer on the refrigerator. He draped his jacket across his arm. It was a little after eight at night and he'd been working nonstop for the past two weeks so he could be totally available to her when she arrived. She'd initially disagreed with his reasoning since Ibadan would eventually become her home, so she wanted them to carry on as normal. Qasim nixed the idea, saying there would be plenty of time for normal. He wanted to be available as much as possible since this was her first trip.

"Cocky, are we?"

"No, just stating facts. But baby, I gotta go."

Jide entered the frame and picked up Qasim's briefcase. Although she was against it, Jide had been with her in Tweede Kans Cove up until two days ago. Although Qasim didn't like it, she had insisted he didn't need to remain as she was right behind him the next day, or so she thought.

"Hi, Jide," she said, settling down on the barstool to eat her dinner.

"Good evening, Mrs. A."

"I didn't forget your pastillas. They're already packed."

"Appreciate it, Mrs. A. I'll be at the airport to get you tomorrow."

Qasim scoffed. "Didn't I tell you that my wife is not your friend?"

"'Sim leave him alone. Jide is my buddy. Isn't that, right?"

"She's calling me 'Sim because of you. I'm about to exchange you for one of Q's men," Qasim threatened.

Jide laughed and said goodbye before he departed the office. Salma had a huddle with her team early the next day, then she and one of her managers planned to go to the winery. After threatening legal action, Hamza conceded to a meeting with her. Afterwards, she'd be traveling to Marrakech before taking a flight to

Lagos. Qasim would meet Salma there and they'd drive to Ibadan the following day.

After Qasim reiterated that he didn't want her to go see Hamza by herself, he left his office, trailing Jide to his car. He had a late meeting with Qadir and a representative from the state ministry of tourism. The farm had recently soft-launched its agritourism arm. They'd decided to open their farms to visitors who were interested in experiencing farm life, participating in workshops on organic farming practices, or simply enjoying rural landscapes.

Many nights, they had been on the phone and Qasim had run the ideas his marketing team had come up with regarding guided tours, workshops, farm stays, and on-site stores selling their products directly to visitors by her. Salma and Qasim continued to talk until he arrived at his destination. After professing their love for each other, they said their goodbyes.

After tidying up the kitchen, Salma paused in the middle of the hallway and took a deep breath before continuing to her bedroom. For so long, she had been in this room alone and was totally comfortable. Now, Qasim's smell was everywhere. His favorite cologne lingered in the air.

She tried to swallow the lump growing in her throat as she steeled herself against the sudden swell of longing that threatened to overwhelm her. When they talked, she worked hard to maintain her composure and not show just how much she longed for him. She knew he had a lot on his plate and didn't want to take away from that. If he caught wind of her sorrow, he would drop everything and come to her.

After tossing her shoes in the closet, Salma put her hair in a bun as she slowly walked over to the dresser. She opened the drawer, and gently pulled out one of Qasim's undershirts. She placed it on the bed before heading over to the bathroom. She turned on the Bluetooth speaker connected to her playlist and started the shower.

As she stepped into the shower, "Yet" by The King Will Come

began to play. The uncertainty of what her trip might hold weighed heavily on her. Qasim wasn't the only one who withheld a secret. Hers might be worse. All these years, she'd convinced herself that she'd been justified in leaving Qasim. While that might have been true, the loss that occurred as a result wasn't only hers to mourn.

Forgive us our sins as we forgive those who sin against us.

The words of the Lord's Prayer kept playing on repeat in her mind as she stood beneath the hot, cascading shower water. For the past several weeks, she'd been obsessively focused on those twelve words. Salma leaned on the shower wall. Tears ran down her cheeks. Regret and fear seeped into her heart at the prospect of her happily ever after being taken from her again.

Letting go of what happened to her in New York was easier than forgiving Qasim for it. The choice to heal rather than hold was for her peace of mind. But even after all these years, she had never forgiven him. Over the years she tried to, but her anger remained. Anger that caused her to hold onto secrets she should've shared. In hindsight, Qasim had a right to know. He had a right to share in the pain that probably would have brought about their reconciliation faster.

After a few moments, Salma turned off the shower and stepped out onto the plush mat. She dried herself off and brushed her teeth. After applying lotion to her body, she slipped into the undershirt she had since traded her expensive lingerie for. Salma slid into her side of the bed. Hugging the pillow that Qasim used during his stay, she closed her eyes, asking God to give Qasim the strength to show her the mercy she was hesitant to grant him.

~

Saturday morning, a week later, Salma stretched, rolled onto her side, and picked up the handwritten note that was on Qasim's pillow.

My Star,
Had to leave for the Country Club with Q and Sif.
Call me if you need me. Be back soon.
I love you.
Your Honey.

She lifted her hand to rub her eyes when she felt the cool metal of a bracelet she knew she didn't have on when they went to bed the previous night. She admired the delicate star charm that dangled from it. Smiling, she reached for her phone under the pillow. Noting the time at a little after nine a.m., she sent Qasim a text.

The charity golf tournament event was later this evening. It was also the day that she would get to meet the patriarch of the Adesina family.

Saying a prayer of thanksgiving, she scooted up in the bed, leaning against the headboard. When Qasim returned home weeks ago, he told his family about her and their nuptials. Understandably, they handled it way better than her family did. Before she arrived in Ibadan, she'd had a brief phone conversation with his brothers, mother, and cousin. The only person she hadn't talked to or seen was Chief Adesina. He was to arrive in Nigeria from London late last evening.

According to Qasim, Chief as he was fondly called, was quite upset that a "daughter" of his lived outside his direct protection. Truth be told, his stance and wanting to appease him was partly the reason she let Jide stay with her in Tweede Kans Cove for so long.

Salma didn't know what to make of the man. When she met him years ago, he seemed so dissatisfied that she was who his son chose. Now as his son's wife, he was angry that she wasn't living in Nigeria. When she told her sister, Yasmine believed time and certain circumstances changed people. Granted, he might not have changed much if he refused to talk to her over the phone, but Salma could only hope that he wasn't hostile to her when she finally saw him later. Any friction between them would break Qasim's heart. Although he kept promising to walk away from his family if anything that compromised her safety would arise, she didn't want that for him. Because she couldn't imagine it for herself.

She had sat down to dinner with the whole family the night after she arrived. After the initial awkwardness, Qasif and Qamar teased her about being the runaway wife. Qasim's mother and his cousin, Shola, kept harping on an official wedding. Mrs. Adesina was warm and welcoming. She was so excited that an outsider looking in would think Qasim was her only son. It was almost as though Salma was her only chance at having a daughter-in-law. The couple pacified her by promising to have a wedding reception early next year. Qadir was just as intense as she remembered. Since Mustafa had been that way for years, Salma knew it was only a matter of time before the love of a good woman melted whatever had him so tight. His fiancée would also be in Ibadan today. She shuttled between Lagos, Ibadan, and the US. Qasim refused to tell her who she was, claiming he wanted her to be surprised. He did, however, share that their engagement was strictly business.

Running her fingers through her hair, she mindlessly scrolled through social media for a few moments. As she was about to log off, she received a notification from Instagram. Clicking on the notification, she was led to Qasim's page. A wide grin spread across her face as she gazed at the picture of her head on his chest on the ride back from Lagos. The caption read: *My heart is home.* Underneath, she responded *forever and always*, then logged out of the app.

Getting out of bed, she walked over to the walk-in closet to retrieve what she would be wearing after her shower. Afterwards, she headed to the bathroom to wash her face and brush her teeth. Putting on a set of workout clothes, Salma tidied up the room and made her way to the home gym.

When she arrived, she understood what Qasim had meant in

Tweede Kans Cove when he said he was living in their home. All the things they had talked about having in a home were in this one. The three-story, six-bedroom with all en suite bathrooms mansion had a comprehensive smart home system. The lower floor was where the gym, indoor pool, sauna, and wine cellar were located. The living space took up the second and third floors. The bedrooms were spread out between both floors with the master on the third. There was an elevator, two home offices, a gourmet kitchen, and a home theater.

What really warmed her heart was the beautiful children's playroom. When Qasim showed it to her, he wrapped his arms around her while she leaned her back into his chest. He whispered the vision he had of their kids playing. Later he took her around the perfectly manicured, landscaped yard. There was a pool, an outdoor kitchen, and a half soccer field. What really made her cry was when he took her to the mini observatory he had built in the backyard. It was equipped with different sizes of telescopes that would provide the perfect view of the Milky Way.

Stopping in the kitchen, Salma got a bottle of water before continuing to the ground floor. Once she adjusted the dials and stepped on the treadmill, her phone rang. Seeing it was Yasmine, she put her ear pods in, then answered the phone.

"So, when are you coming to Accra?"

Salma laughed. "Hey to you, too. And can you allow me to settle in my own home first?"

"I like the sound of that and I'm so glad you are closer to me now."

"I miss grandma though."

"Yeah, me too. But this is what she wants for us. To be happy and content. Meanwhile... I saw you on the socials. Gosh, I'm so happy for you, Sal."

Salma laughed. "What were you doing there? I thought you swore off it after the last time."

Yasmine sucked her teeth and Salma laughed. Her sister had a love-hate relationship with social media because of her husband.

No matter what Kojo posted, there were thirsty women under his post trying to shoot their shot. When he posted himself and his kids only, it was worse. There were women who asked if they could be the stepmother to his kids. When they first got married, Yasmine used to respond to some of the ones she considered highly disrespectful. That would cause problems between her and her husband. He believed her stooping down to their level would give them something more to talk about. He was right, but Salma understood her sister's pain. She had to endure it silently when Qasim was still in the league.

"Anyway, how are my babies and KJ?"

"Everyone's good. I don't get to cook for them every day, so on Saturdays I like to make a big breakfast. For once Kwame and Anisa decided on the same thing...waffles."

Salma chuckled then a sense of dread fell over her causing her to be silent.

"Sal, *lam tukhbirih biedu*?" Yasmine asked.

A few beats passed and Salma was still silent. How could she tell him? She wasn't as brave as she thought she was.

"You must tell him. You're only prolonging the inevitable."

"He's going to be livid."

"Of course, he will. You're in the wrong, but you're his wife. So, you do what needs to be done. Just like he did for you...grovel."

It was easier said than done. How did she come back from hiding something so personal for them?

"After we got married, Kojo advised I see a therapist. Since it helped him, I did." A beat passed between them. "I always remember something my therapist told me any time I started to self-sabotage. She said that behavior comes from when I let my traumatized eight-year-old self dictate the actions of my present self. Even though technically everything is fine, when I am triggered by the slightest discomfort, my present self relinquishes control to my younger self and I self-sabotage.

"I understand you more than most, Sal. Running from 'Sim

was your six-year-old self, leading the charge. He'll be mad but stay there and fight. Trust his love for you. That man came to Tweedes alone. Knowing Musa and O would be out for his head. But he came for his Star. Don't let the enemy or that six-year-old brat rob you of your happiness."

Salma let her older sister's wise words sink in. She pulled the strength she needed from them to do what she had to do.

Switching gears, Yasmine asked about her experience since she arrived in Nigeria. Before now, she hadn't visited the country. As promised, her husband, Jide and Daniel were at the airport when her flight landed a week ago. From the airport, they went to Qasim's Lagos Island home. Instead of an overnight stay in Lagos, Qasim made it a few days. While they were there, he took her to the famous Nike Art Gallery, to watch a play at the National Theatre, and they had dinner at a restaurant she shared a name with, Salma. She hadn't had time to explore much, but the part of Lagos she did see was something to behold. Kinda reminded her of New York.

After getting her sister caught up about dinner with the Adesinas, they talked about their brothers who were holding things down in Tweede Kans Cove. The family was on high alert as they waited for Zaina to go into labor. Soon after, they ended the call with a promise to call each other again soon.

~

Several hours later, Salma had showered, had a late breakfast and was lounging on the plush white, oversized sofa. Qasim still hadn't returned, but he was constantly calling and texting to make sure she was okay. There was enough to do to keep herself occupied. She couldn't remember when she had kicked back in so long.

He had set up one of the home offices nicely for her, but she had promised him that for the first month, she wouldn't work. A promise she intended to keep. A mix of soft Afrobeats and R&B

tunes played from the satellite radio as she annotated the latest murder mystery book that currently held her captive.

Dipping her hand in the bowl of peanuts and chin-chin mix, she opened her mouth to toss them in when the security system announced someone approaching the front door. Before she could pull up the footage on her phone as Qasim had shown her, the doorbell rang. She walked over to the door as she tried to pull up the app. The compound was guarded so she knew it wasn't anyone who could do her harm. As she stared into the menacing face of Chief Qavi Adesina...she wasn't so sure.

Her chest heaved and her lungs struggled to supply it with oxygen. Taking a deep breath, she smoothened down Qasim's Viva City t-shirt she wore over blue jeans. She opened the door and was met with the older but slightly shorter version of her husband. His head was clean shaven while the mustache that connected to his well-manicured beard was completely snow white. He had on a dark blue kaftan, loafers and dark shades covering his eyes. The two men who stood behind him in black suits also had their eyes covered. She felt small and naked under their gaze.

"My dear...my dear."

"Oh my gosh. Good afternoon, Sir. Please come in." Salma stepped to the side and the three men walked in. She shut the door behind them and began leading them down the foyer. After a few short strides, Qasim's father halted his steps and raised his hand. The other two men immediately turned and headed out of the house.

When the door closed the second time, Qasim's father took off his sunshades and gestured for her to lead the way. He looked around, observing the space she occupied and sat in the chair opposite it. Salma picked up the remote and lowered the music, then faced him. She folded the blanket that had been tossed over her feet and started to tidy up when she heard the older man clear his throat.

"Please sit down," he said.

"Can I get you anything, Sir?"

"The only thing I want is your comfort. Please sit."

Salma sat. Adjusting her spine, she reached for the throw pillow and placed it on her lap.

"The Yorubas have a saying *Ẹni to bá ta ará ilé rẹ ni ọpọ̀, kò lè rí irú ẹni bẹẹ ra ni ọ̀wọ́n*. It means one who sells his family for a measly amount, won't ever buy them for good value."

Salma sat motionless, her throat tight with emotion. She glanced around the living room, desperately seeking an escape from the older man's penetrating gaze.

"From our first meeting, although brief, I knew that you loved my son," he said, his tone dripping with ice. "I wanted to see the woman that made my son go against the systems I had put in place. I didn't disagree with him. But I feared he was acting irrationally and not being strategic. Although I saw the love you had for him in your eyes, I also saw some skittishness. I knew that if things got rough, you wouldn't stay by his side. And I was right. You didn't. I'm not sure when you became my daughter-in-law, but I know that you weren't my choice."

Salma clenched her teeth as his words filtered through her mind. She balled her fists, causing him to raise an eyebrow in her direction. Refusing to give him the satisfaction of hearing her voice crack, she remained silent.

"However, I do not have a say in the matter, but I'm glad to see you have some bite." His gaze darted to her fists. "My son went to war with me and his older brother for you. The question I have is, can you honestly say you'll do the same for him?"

"Sir, with all due respect, I love Qasim—"

"Love is not enough, especially if it's not treated like a commitment. The men that laid a finger on you were handled immediately, but my son was broken by your departure. This Adesina name comes with its privileges, its burdens and sometimes horrors." A beat passed between them then the older man stood.

Salma did the same.

"My wife has been with me for fifty plus years and together we've built a dynasty. We've taught our sons the importance of family and building a life with the right woman. A strong woman who can stand in for them when they can't do it for themselves. I'll be honored to have you as my daughter, but only if you can handle being an Adesina."

"I can do that, Sir," Salma said.

She refrained from trying to prove a point to the elder Adesina. It was her husband she needed to show that to, not his father. In due time, her father-in-law would see what he wanted without her having to say anything. Salma followed as Chief Adesina walked through the foyer to the front door. Unexpectedly, he drew her in and wrapped one arm around her shoulder. "I hope to see you on the course later."

He simply nodded and left the living room with Salma once again trailing behind. Before he opened the door, he told her to reach out if she needed anything. Salma nodded and without another word, he opened the door. They froze as they stared into the dark eyes of her husband.

CHAPTER 15

Friday evening, Qasim stepped into the backyard of his home, when his phone buzzed from the pocket of his basketball shorts. Pausing, he read the text from his attorney. The wind was cool and gentle, and the sky was a dark blue spread.

Ivan: It's done.

Qasim smiled.

He was still on the flight home to Nigeria after departing Tweede Kans Cove when he received an email from his private investigator with information regarding Hamza Alami's situation. Recalling the memory of the man's conceived entitlement to his wife still had the ability to send rage coursing through his veins. If it had not been for Kojo and Omar, once Hamza called Salma "his" – despite numerous attempts to tell him he was barking up the wrong tree – Qasim would have tossed him across the room.

It turned out that not everything was as it seemed with the winery's finances. Apart from his role as CFO of Adesina Enterprises, Qasim had his own personal business under Sim & Co International. Under that umbrella, he engaged in strategic investment and restructuring. Upon finding out that Harmony Winery had defaulted on their bank loan and was desperately looking for an investor, Qasim asked his attorneys and personal accountant to broker a deal to buy into the winery.

Of course, Hamza had no idea that Qasim was the investor who was willing to bail the winery out of its financial trouble. Qasim did consider letting the man off the hook, charging his exuberance to him getting up there in age and not thinking properly. However, when Hamza started making things difficult for Salma after he left Tweedes, all bets were off. After negotiating an iron-clad deal in which Qasim would be a silent but majority owner of the winery, he bailed the winery out.

So, what's the final percentage?

Ivan: 65/35 in your favor, Sir

And he doesn't know it's me.

Ivan: No, Sir. I made sure of it.

Drop the paperwork by my office.

Ivan: Are you going to make your presence known?

No, Wale can continue to remain the face of Sim & Co. I'll only appear when the time is right. Thanks!

Qasim pocketed his phone and walked over to the outdoor kitchen area where his brother and his cousin, Arinze, were seated across from the pool. For dinner, Qasim had some goat meat kebabs on the grill which he intended to serve with fried rice.

"What are you smiling for?" Qadir asked.

"I told you I was gonna do it," Qasim responded.

Qadir's forehead creased for a second before he understood

what Qasim was referring to. He laughed then shook his head. "Dude must have been down bad to accept such a deal."

Qasim shrugged. Seeing Arinze's confusion, he filled him in on who Hamza Alami was, what he did and ended with how he responded.

Arinze's mouth remained open, staring at Qasim in disbelief. "What?!"

"He wanted to play. I showed him how it's done." Qasim waved him off.

"Aren't you supposed to leave vengeance for the Lord?" Arinze asked.

Qasim adjusted his t-shirt that read God's Own. "Guess who's made in His image." He winked then walked over to the grill. His motivation might not have been completely right, but he helped Alami while making sure the man learned a lesson about Salma Adesina.

His wife.

Salma had been in Nigeria for a little over a month, and things were going so well that he began to feel a strange churning in his stomach. The anxious feeling had him thinking something was amiss. Before their separation, things had been going so well between them that when she left, even after he explained things to her, he was totally blindsided.

After checking on the small cooler of rice, he looked up at his brother, with whom he had shared his concerns. "I don't know Q, I have this feeling in my gut—"

"That something will go wrong, and I don't understand why. Things are falling into place just the way you wanted them. So, what's the problem?"

"I'm with Big Cuz. What's the issue?" Arinze asked. He missed the golf event, but arrived in Nigeria the previous day and would be headed to Enugu in the morning.

Shola had waltzed in earlier and said she was kidnapping his wife for a night on the town. Shola was headed back to school in Luxe Noir in a few days and according to her, she wanted to party with her cousin-in-law since he had been keeping Salma all to himself.

Now that was where he called her out on the lie she was spinning. Between her and his mother, he was fighting for some alone time with his wife. After a month off, Salma had just started back working, so now he had to add that to the mix. Surprisingly, she even had a standing midweek lunch date with Chief.

Since the day he walked in on his father leaving his house, he'd tried and failed to find out what the two of them were talking about. His father claimed he was welcoming his new daughter while his wife maintained he came to see as she was getting settled. He didn't believe either of them, but since he didn't see any distress on Salma's face or change in her demeanor, he had to let it go.

The golf tournament was a success with the Adesinas winning. Later that evening, he was the envy of the charity dinner when he walked in with Salma on his arm. The vision of her in a body-hugging, black dress with the back cut out was hard to clear from his mind. All night he found himself uncharacteristically denying men who walked up to her wanting a dance. He didn't regard himself as the jealous or possessive type, but having Salma in Ibadan was making him question that stance.

After the event, he kept her to himself for several days. They went to plays, movies, museums, made a quick trip to Accra and most importantly, they christened every part of their home with passionate lovemaking.

Since both of them were back to work, they had established some kind of rhythm. Normally they'd rise, pray together, then hit the gym downstairs. Afterwards, they would have breakfast together at the kitchen island before separating to get ready for the day.

"I don't know. Maybe it's because of the impromptu change in the Brotherhood's leadership…"

"That shouldn't bother you. We have only four more weeks left in our contract with them. Soon Adesina Enterprises will be fully legal. They go their way, and we go ours." Qadir lifted his drink to his lips.

"I promised her that we'll be completely done with..." Qasim shrugged. "This new change has me—"

"'Sim, you gotta trust your wife the same way you want her to trust you," Arinze said. "If you're always worried that she's gonna run anytime things get rough, you're going to have a life full of worry."

"The last time nearly broke me..."

"And both of you found your way back to each other. So why is it so hard for you to let that go?" Qadir asked.

Qasim marinated on that question. Why was it so hard for him not to be affected by their past?

"Check this out and it's all I'm gonna say about it," Arinze said. "I ain't trying to tell my cousin's business like that, but when his wife died, he took it personal. Like she did something to him, and he allowed it dictate how he moved. He almost lost my niece and his new wife because he couldn't see that his former wife's death wasn't about him. It affected him, but it wasn't about him. What woman would want to leave her newborn and check out?"

"Even you knew that Sally had issues—"

Qasim laughed. "Q, you must be a sucka for punishment." He shook his head. "The other day my wife went off when you called her that crap. I guess it wasn't enough?"

Qadir waved him off. "All I gotta do is get her another modeling gig with my fiancée."

Arinze laughed before biting from his kebab. Qasim couldn't contain Salma when she found out that Qadir was engaged to the CEO of Zeidu Fashions. Qasim didn't pretend to know what his brother and his fiancée had going on, but the charity event was a family thing and she usually showed up for those. For this year's event, she wasn't so sure she'd be able to. When he returned from Tweede Kans Cove with the new knowledge of Salma's obsession with the fashion brand, Qasim wasn't about to leave anything to chance. He called his future sister-in-law and pleaded with her to ensure she attended the event.

"How you keep getting favors from someone you rarely have time for?"

"Focus on your issues and leave mine alone," Qadir quipped. "Anyway, to Nze's point, five years ago, her leaving wasn't about you per se. It was about her...I mean what she'd been through in the past."

"You know it's funny how we judge others by their mistakes, but when it comes to ours, we judge ourselves by our intentions." Arinze's phone rang and he stood to take the call. But not before yelling out. "Give Sal the same benefit of the doubt you'd give yourself."

Qasim walked back over to the grill and turned the meat. He thought about what Arinze said. He wanted his wife to forgive him, and she had, but had he forgiven her? Maybe that was why he couldn't trust that things wouldn't go wrong again.

"Free me from the unforgiveness that has me in bondage, O Lord," he murmured in prayer. He wanted to give his marriage an honest shot. Salma had her baggage, but he had his. Couples therapy might be good for them.

A while later, with the backyard restored to normal, Qasim, his cousin and brother walked back into the house. They made a detour to the kitchen to put away leftovers and wash their hands.

"I gotta be in Lagos early, so I'm out," Qadir said.

"I'mma head out too. Y'all's auntie is about to run me crazy. Anytime I land Naija, she's on my case, asking where I am. Like I don't live thousands of miles away from her," Arinze said.

"Fool, ain't that your mother?" Qadir grinned.

Arinze shrugged. "She was your auntie way before she became my mother."

Qasim's laughter was cut short when his phone rang and he saw it was Shola. His heartbeat accelerated. It was late, but he didn't expect them back this early. He had Jide and Daniel with them, so they should've been good.

"What's up, baby girl?"

"Brother, *E̱ kaale*. I—"

"Where's my wife?" he asked, cutting the rest of her statement off.

"We're outside. Can you come and get her?" Shola pleaded.

Qasim tossed his phone on the sofa and rushed toward the front door with Qadir and Arinze hot on his trail. Shola was near the tinted SUV with one hand on her hip. Qasim brushed past her, opened the door and his regard fell on Salma. Her hair was now down all over her face. She lifted her head and smiled, wide. She hiccupped, obviously tipsy as she hummed one of the songs from *Grease*, one of her favorite movies.

"What happened?" Without waiting for an answer, Qasim picked Salma up bridal style.

As he made his way up the stairs to the front door, he heard Qadir scolding Shola about letting whatever was wrong with Salma get to the point where she was delirious before leaving wherever they were. When Shola cried foul about not being allowed to have any fun, this was the reason why. Whenever she was around her friends, she often forgot who her family was. They could make mistakes she couldn't afford to. If the press had any footage of his wife and her in an inebriated state, they would have a field day.

He looked down at Salma who had now passed out in his arms. She wasn't getting away with this scot-free. Tonight, he would take care of her. In the morning, she had to explain to him how she got this way when she didn't even drink.

～

"I feel so bad that you had to cancel your trip for me," Salma whined.

Qasim looked over his shoulder. He took two bags of popcorn and put them in the microwave. "You should feel bad. Maybe next time you'll think twice before sampling what you've never had before."

"It's been two days, 'Sim, stop fussing. I said I was sorry."

Qasim didn't respond. Instead, he crossed his arms over his chest as he waited for the corn to finish popping. That night he had been scared out of his mind when she kept throwing up. He got in the shower with her, washed her hair and her body as he used his to keep her from slumping. After he dried her hair the best he could, he got her dressed and put her in bed. He placed water and painkillers on her bedside table, then put a small trash bag near the bed in case she needed it. Once she was settled, he went back downstairs and Facetimed his cousin.

With tears in her eyes, Shola apologized before telling him that she was drinking palm wine which Salma wanted to try. She didn't think it was that potent because it was in a can. Palm wine was a cloudy liquid tapped from the palm tree. It was mostly consumed in villages, but some beverage companies in the city bottled or canned it like beer or soda. The problem was that every factory handled the fermentation process slightly differently. Since that's what gave it its alcoholic content, one could never be sure how potent it would be.

Qasim was livid when he knew that was what Salma consumed. The only thing that saved Shola and his wife from his wrath was the fact that Shola had been instrumental in ensuring Salma's stay in Ibadan was comfortable. He didn't want to get in the middle of their growing friendship. However, Salma still felt his displeasure with the whole ordeal. Here it was two days later, and she was still feeling sick.

Salma wrapped her hands around his waist and leaned into him. He'd been working from home to ensure he was able to cater to her needs. He was supposed to leave for Abuja earlier, but he pushed it back. Qasim wasn't really upset about staying with her as he was with her putting herself in danger.

"I'm sorry. Now can we enjoy movie night without you pouting?"

Qasim turned in her arms and cupped her face. "Don't ever put yourself in danger like that again."

"Got it." She elevated herself on her toes and kissed his lips.

Smacking her behind lightly, Qasim poured the popcorn into a bowl and set it on the tray that had other snacks. Salma picked up the drinks and followed him to the back of the house. Since Salma wasn't in the mood to go anywhere, Qasim set up a little tent with a mosquito net in the back and a movie projector. He estimated that by the time their movie was over, the sky would be clear enough for her to look through the observatory telescope.

A few hours later, as Qasim pulled Salma up the small flight of stairs, their footsteps echoed gently on the polished floors. The air inside held a faint scent of metal and anticipation, ready to reveal the wonders of the cosmos. Qasim watched the soft moonlight play upon her face as her eyes sparkled. The movie was great; they laughed, recited some lines they knew from memory and fed each other popcorn.

He had been fine with them sharing a bowl until she got the urge to put red pepper flakes over hers. That was the nastiest thing he had ever seen, but she claimed it helped with the queasiness of her stomach from the lingering effects of the alcohol. He had made sure she drank enough water, but somehow, she wasn't any better. He wasn't sure when the night skies would be as clear as they were right now, so instead of insisting she go to bed, on her insistence, he was taking her to the observatory he had built. The look on her face was what he lived for.

Stargazing was their thing.

Truthfully it was hers. During one of their earlier talks, she cried as she told the story of how when her parents would get into it, she would climb into Omar's bed, and he would sing to her. She would fall asleep, but never for long. Not wanting to wake up her brother, she'd look out of the window and get lost in the stars as they twinkled in the dark expanse. It gave her comfort pretending to be one of them...so far away.

Qasim stood behind Salma as she peered through the telescope's lens. For a few moments, she was mesmerized by the stars. She spun around and into his embrace. He brushed away her tears with his finger, tucked a strand of hair behind her ear, and held her gaze.

He caressed her cheek. "You know why I call you Star, right?"

She nodded, so he continued, "You don't look too confident. So, let me remind you so you understand just how much you mean to me. How deeply in love with you I am. Just like the stars above, your light guided me through my dark days. When I could no longer play and thought my life had ended, you told me I could be effective and do anything I put my mind to. Like how starlight illuminates the night, you illuminate my life."

Tears streamed down her face. "I love you, honey."

"Not more than I love you." He bent to kiss her, but stopped when she heaved. A look of concern washed over his face, and he stepped back. "That's it. Tomorrow morning, we go to the doctor." He scooped her up in his arms and carried her out of the building, through the yard and straight to their bedroom.

The next day, Qasim squeezed Salma's hand as she sat on the examining table in the doctor's office. Dr. Dare had been the family doctor for several years. She was a petite, Black American woman who relocated to Nigeria with her husband.

Qasim's plan was to devote his complete attention to his wife, but today was one of those days that had started off very wrong. Panic swept over him when he was woken up by an angry Qadir. The financials Qasim sent last week to commission the first phase of the agritourism project for the public were in complete disarray.

Before Qasim signed off on the money, he had traced the source to a completely legitimate transaction that was done weeks ago. Now it seemed the funds were mixed with those of the Brotherhood's dirty money. Now the potential of this project being tied to illegal activities could jeopardize everything they'd been working on regarding expansion.

His eyes darted towards Salma who was dressed in a blue

paper gown. Her teeth pinned her bottom lip. She had been acting strange since they got up this morning. Luckily for him, Dr. Dare was able to fit them in. She'd completed her intake forms, been weighed, had blood drawn, and provided a urine sample. He knew about the cancer scare she had months ago, so he chalked her nerves up to that experience. Kissing the back of her hand, her eyes met his and he winked.

"Honey, I have—"

Her words were drowned out by the incessant buzzing of his phone. The email he had been waiting for had arrived. His assistant had laid out a detailed timeline of where and when the coupling started and how they would proceed with separating the funds. He scanned through the meticulous plan to transfer the Brotherhood's funds discreetly, masking their origins and avoiding any trace of connection to the agritourism project.

The top five members of his staff all signed iron-clad NDA agreements, so he wasn't worried about unsavory information being leaked. However, what bothered him was the web of deceit and danger that could be exposed if one person strayed. He prayed that all parties stuck to their word and the contract to completely cut ties in two weeks. This dual life was creating a tension that was bound to snap, causing an explosive rupture that would bring everything to the ground. He sighed and temporary relief caused him to lift his lips in a smile.

"Progress?" Salma asked.

He kissed her forehead. "A little."

She didn't know the details of the issue and he wasn't willing to share. She was about to say something when the door opened. In walked Dr. Dare with her white coat on and a clipboard in her hand. She smiled at them. After greeting them, she congratulated them on their nuptials and then shared a short story of her time in Morocco with her husband. She looked down at the chart before lifting her eyes again. Whatever she was about to say was interrupted by another buzz from his phone. This time it was Qadir. He needed to take it.

"Continue Dr. D, I'll be right back, but I need to take this." Qasim turned to Salma who nodded, then he opened the door to step out.

Qasim leaned against the door while Qadir informed him that he had found a community bank in Abuja that could help. If everything went well, they would secure funds that would temporarily relieve the pressure of having to separate the funds. Qasim would have to be there in person. That was good news. With this newfound backing, the project would launch on schedule, impressing partners, investors, and now there was the added benefit of local community support. Telling Qadir he'd take care of it, he turned and opened the door.

"According to this..." the doctor looked down at her clipboard, "... you're gonna be a mom again."

Again?

His heart thudded against his chest and his lungs struggled for breath he couldn't give as he waited for Salma's answer. His feet moved further into the room until he was standing right beside his wife, his fists clenched tightly in an effort to maintain control of the rage that threatened to consume him. She looked up at him with trepidation in her eyes. Her lips trembled and tears streamed down her cheeks as she wrung her fingers together.

"Wha...really?" she whispered.

Rage knocked the wind out of him, and a strangled gasp escaped his lips as he stumbled back. The doctor, furniture, and fixtures around them seemed to blur and dissolve into the background as his ears began to ring and his heart pounded against his chest. He knew without a doubt she wasn't hiding a child somewhere, so there were only two answers to this conundrum, and she better pray she gave him the right one. He bent low until they were eye to eye. He placed his hands on his knees and spoke in a dangerously low voice. One he didn't even recognize.

"Salma Adesina, I want you to think very carefully before you answer my next question."

Her fearful gaze didn't waver as she nodded, but remained

silent. Her fear was palpable, but it wasn't enough for him; he needed her terrified.

"Was it mine?"

Her eyes showed her offense, but he didn't care. "Answer me!" he roared.

"Yes," she cried through sobs.

"Good." He rose to his full height and looked down at her. "Now, what the hell happened to my kid?"

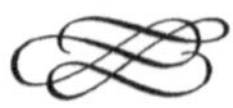

CHAPTER 16

Eleven weeks pregnant? Thank God for Nurse...ugh I forgot her name.

Salma tried to hold back the flood of tears that threatened to spill over her lashes as Qasim's question hung in the air like a weight. Just when she thought the tension would suffocate them all, the door opened, and a nurse walked in. The doctor used the opportunity to step forward and subtly nudge Qasim to the side. Salma knew that the only reason he allowed it was she had been their family doctor for almost two decades and he respected her. The gesture felt like an anchor, grounding her amidst the turmoil. Salma was thankful for the silent plea the older woman recognized.

Her husband kept it together while Dr. Dare gave her a prescription to help with the nausea, and information for an obstetrician. It never even crossed her mind that she might be pregnant. She'd been on birth control for a few years to regulate her cycles. Admittedly, engulfed in the bliss of the past few months, she'd missed a pill or a few here and there. But pregnant? This was her fault for not paying attention to her body. On the intake forms, there was a question about if she had been pregnant before. She'd answered truthfully but thought nothing of it. If for a second, she had thought pregnancy was a possibility, or that the doctor would choose that way to break it to her, she would have told her husband before they arrived at that office. It was a good thing she hadn't been drinking but for that sample.

Despite his anger with her, Qasim asked the doctor about the alcohol. She responded there was no need to worry.

Once they left the office, Qasim walked ahead of her. Salma's heart broke with each stride. It was as though he was trying to get away from her. He didn't even respond when she called out to him.

Except when she yelled out... "Please wait! I didn't kill her." Although she referred to her angel baby as a girl, the baby wasn't old enough for its sex to be determined.

That statement had Qasim coming to a grinding stop. He turned to her, but the rage in his eyes showed her no mercy, searing her soul. He didn't say anything, but opened the door of the car for her to enter. For the few minutes his eyes were on her, along with rage, she saw a profound sense of hurt and disbelief, as if his trust had been shattered into a million pieces. A feeling she desperately wanted to erase.

Once they got into the car, Salma attempted to do just that, but Qasim raised his hand ultimately silencing her. Logically, she knew it wasn't the right time. Not with his men in the front. However, currently sitting in the middle of their bed for the past half an hour, waiting for him to come out of their walk-in closet, nothing he was doing seemed logical.

He was packing.

Salma rose from the bed, her heart racing as she took silent steps towards the closet. She walked in, preparing herself for what she might find inside. To her surprise, he was sitting in the corner of the closet on a padded bench, his head cradled in his hands. She moved closer and knelt at his feet. His body tensed as he felt her presence, but he didn't look up or move from his position. Salma stayed there with him for some moments, trying to figure out where to start her long overdue explanation.

"Are you ready to tell me why you have been holed up in my house? And most importantly why that young man has been calling my phone?" Grandma Olly asked.

In the ten days Salma had been back to Tweede Kans Cove, she had successfully gotten her grandmother to keep her whereabouts a secret – a task made easier since all her siblings were out of town on various business engagements. The only person who might have blown her cover, Anisa, her niece, was spending some time with her grandparents on her late father's side. Thinking of her niece, Salma rubbed her stomach as the fall of her grandmother's steps told her the older woman was approaching the bed.

Salma drew herself up and leaned against the headboard. What she thought was the best solution to avoid harming her baby was the same thing that caused her to lose it. When she woke up three days ago with terrible cramps followed by excessive bleeding, she knew. A trip to her gynecologist confirmed it. At six weeks, she had miscarried her baby. Their baby, conceived by their love. Now, she had nothing to live for. Despite all her efforts, Salma had turned out to be just like the one woman she loved and hated at the same time...her mother.

Grandma Olly pulled the covers back and got in the bed with her. Salma leaned her head on her grandmother's shoulder. Sadness filled the air; a pool of tears that was hot and burning cascaded down her face.

"I married him, grandma. I made a mistake and married him. He's a criminal...the family is. I don't know. All I know is he wasn't who he claimed to be. I didn't want to be like her. Although he tried to explain what happened, I knew I couldn't stay there. She wasn't strong enough to leave. I was, but my child still paid the price," Salma cried.

Her grandmother allowed her to cry. A few moments later, she asked. "My child, I heard what you said, but none of it makes sense. Start from the beginning. Did you say you're married?"

Over the next several minutes, Salma gave her grandmother an overview of her relationship with Qasim up to her marriage and her leaving him.

Her grandmother gasped. "You young people take nothing as sacred anymore. How does he marry you without telling your family? Does Omar know?"

"It wasn't his fault. Because of how Omar was behaving, I told him I wanted to keep it silent. But we were going to say something when I moved back finally."

She had been in a certification program that she had another few months to complete. She wanted to wait until it was over.

"Something he shouldn't have agreed to. Do you know who you are?"

"I know..." Salma cried.

"If you're someone's wife, why are you here crying?"

The day she found out she was pregnant, Salma went to lunch and then to the mall with one of the women in her class. Qasim was in Nigeria and scheduled to be back later that night. She missed her new husband; he had been gone for a week. She had the perfect pregnancy announcement planned with a custom baby onesie she went to pick up: Daddy's Favorite. As she stepped out of the mall, she parted ways with her friend and walked to her car. There she was accosted by two men.

"They took me grandma. Held me in a room for hours. They told me that they wanted to make sure my boyfriend knew he could be touched," Salma cried. That night would forever be etched in her memory.

"Sit up. Now!" Grandma Olly stood from the bed. "You mean some men took you because of him? I need to call Musa."

Salma jumped up. In a kneeling position on the bed, she pleaded with her grandmother. No matter what had happened, she loved Qasim with her whole being. She couldn't be with him, but no amount of anger would allow her to bring him any harm. Salma sighed when her grandmother halted her steps. When she returned to the bed, Salma continued narrating the story.

When Qasim arrived, she wasn't at home. He dialed her phone repeatedly. Finally, the men allowed her to answer, but snatched the phone away from her. Within the hour, she was released to Qasim who took her home. She had never cried so much in her life. That night Qasim sat in the tub with her and held her in his arms as she trembled. Not ready to talk about it, she pretended to be asleep. When she felt the bed dip and he covered her to leave the room, she began looking up flights to Morocco.

"He kept explaining all through the next day, telling me about how it had something to do with the changes he was making to the family business." Salma shook her head. "I wanted to believe he would protect me as he claimed. But in the next couple of days, his father arrived."

When she opened the door and saw the older version of her husband with men who looked like they could kill with just the snap of his finger, she was terrified. The man sized her up and down. He expressed his sorrow for what she went through, and promised her that he would handle everything accordingly, but he had the look of disapproval that she was who his son picked for a girlfriend. Their marriage was still a secret.

"His family didn't know you were his wife?"

Salma shook her head.

"Both of you are unbelievable. I'll keep your secret, but when he calls me next, I will give him a piece of my mind."

"After his father's visit, I knew I couldn't stay there. I left to remove my child from a bad situation. Like my mother should have done for us." Salma wrapped her arms around herself. "It must be God's punishment, because three days ago I miscarried."

"My grandmother sat with me, prayed with me, then fussed at me," Salma said. She couldn't stop the tears when she raised her head and she saw tears in Qasim's eyes.

"And you didn't think I should know I lost my child? Bad enough, you thought I couldn't protect you, but..."

He allowed his words to trail off, then he stood and started zipping up his packed hand luggage. Salma walked over to him, her heart racing. She reached out to him and her heart broke when he recoiled from her reach.

"I'm sorry. Our baby died and I was so angry with you—"

"How were you angry with me? You decided to hop your stubborn behind on a plane and disappear," he roared. Rolling his shoulders, he shook his head. "I'm not even doing this. I have a flight to catch." He walked out of the closet with his luggage.

It was now late afternoon. She knew he was scheduled to go to Abuja...but now?

"'Sim...Honey..." she choked out, hurrying after him.

He paused at the top of the stairs, still facing away from her. "I know you're used to having your way, and I give you all your heart's desires." His voice was harsh and laced with a hint of sorrow. "What you can't have, and I won't do, is let you control the time you think I need to process and get over what you just told me. You've dealt with the loss of our child for five years; I've not had up to five hours."

Qasim turned around in one fluid motion and sauntered towards her. Before she could speak, he kissed her stomach softly before turning around and walking away. With every step he took, her heart splintered into a million pieces.

Soon after, Salma was lying on the bed in her bedroom, the sheets twisted around her body as she stared at the ceiling. She felt her phone vibrate in her hand and pulled it from under the pillow where she had been clutching it since Qasim left. A text message came through.

> My Honey: I've asked the chef and the housekeeper to come over. Jide is at your beck and call. If you need anything call me or Q. Eat something and relax.

Salma quickly dialed his number, but it went straight to voicemail. She knew he was mad, but he still cared. In the time she had been in Ibadan, she made the house her own, and knew her way around. Qasim was considerate of the kind of person she was – someone who disliked an entourage of house staff always being present in their home. They did their jobs and left at the end of the day. But none of that mattered right now; all she wanted was for him to be back here with her. With a sad sigh, Salma rolled onto her side and let her tears fall into her pillow until she eventually drifted off to sleep.

~

The soft warm light from the morning sun filtered through the partially opened blinds, casting gentle patterns on the tiled bathroom floor. This was one of Salma's many favorite rooms in the house. The white and grey marble walls and floors were adorned with golden accents. A large, soaking tub sat almost in the center of the room while the oversized shower was tucked in the corner. Soft towels were arranged on a heated rack, while a crystal chandelier hung from the ceiling to complete the luxurious feeling. The potted greenery in the room always gave her a sense of peace. A far cry from what her life was like right now.

Qasim had been gone for two days and even in their worst moments, she had never seen him this cold. She got quick phone calls to make sure she ate and had taken her medication. She also got his customary morning and goodnight text. What she hadn't gotten was his presence or his warmth. A trip that was supposed to be "one day" was now an "I'm not sure when."

The day before, she had wallowed in bed and didn't take calls from anyone. Salma turned on the faucet, thanking God that her parents-in-law were in London. Salma knew her husband wouldn't tell them about the baby without her present, but the mere fact that Qasim was out of town would have had his mother breathing down her neck. This morning though, she no longer had the luxury of staying in bed. Technically she could, but just like when she left her husband the first time, she needed to keep herself busy so she wouldn't lose her mind. She picked up her toothbrush and rubbed her stomach.

"Besides, your big head daddy won't be too happy if he calls, and you haven't eaten," she muttered.

Before getting up from the bed, Salma had taken her nausea medication, so once she finished washing up, she intended to have breakfast then head to her office. She clicked on the Calvary Is The Way YouTube channel. Zaina kept talking about a pastor she listened to online called Pastor Mensah. The day Salma went to check him out, she realized he was the same pastor that officiated Yasmine and Kojo's wedding and pastored the church they now attended in Accra. Salma attended church with her grandmother, but she was always open to hearing the word where she could get it. Propping up her iPad, she tapped on the sermon snippet she wanted to listen to, "Commit and Recommit."

As she brushed her teeth, her grandmother's words from several months ago came back to the forefront of her mind.

"Love is action, that also entails a commitment to the future."

As she washed her face, the preacher's voice began emanating from the device. His voice carried the deep sense of authority and wisdom she had come to expect.

"The value the Bible places on commitment is very important. It does not view it as something to be taken lightly, but to be revered and taken with caution. Our commitment to God cannot be by words alone, we must mean it in our hearts. In the Bible, we get to witness the deep-rooted commitment between God and His most trusted prophets and servants. From Abraham to Moses to Peter and most importantly, the Son of Man, Jesus, none of their assignments were easy, but they stayed on the course." Pastor Mensah paused, causing Salma to turn to the screen briefly before continuing her morning routine.

"That must also be the foundation of our purposeful commitment to one another. Peter was one of Jesus's three when He walked the earth. But even he couldn't remain committed to Jesus when things got rough. He believed he couldn't fall, and that arrogance led to him denying Jesus three times. We cannot remain committed to God or one another only when we get a certain pleasure or happiness from them and then quit as soon as the pleasure dies. This is why in everything, we must cling to Him for help to remain steadfast. We are called to be faithful to our commitments to God and to each other.

"Nothing I'm talking about has to do with commitment to a toxic or abusive environment. What I am talking about is, there's a season for everything under the sun and so sometimes things are good and sometimes they're not. Tides turn, your ability to pick yourself up, continually seek the face of God and recommit time and time again is what Paul is talking about when he speaks of perseverance and character. My brothers and sisters, do not be weary in doing good. Like Peter didn't allow his mistake to rob him of his ultimate purpose, don't allow yours to do that either. When you stay committed, something beautiful and lasting is born. That something can only be understood when it has stood the test of time."

As Salma continued to listen, her consciousness was transported out of her bathroom, and intense emotions grew within her as the words sunk into her spirit. She shut her eyes and allowed it to completely engulf her.

"Thank you for the chance to seek redemption. Help me to continue to grow in Your love so I can be the best version of me for me and those around me," she muttered a prayer, allowing the sermon to keep playing while she got ready for her shower and start of the day.

Later that evening, Salma sat in her kitchen while Yasmine cooked spaghetti. After her shower, she wrote Qasim what she would consider an epistle of a text since he didn't answer his phone. Technically, he did, but it was with a text asking if he could call her back since he was in a meeting. She couldn't wait as she had a burning sensation in her chest weighing her down.

After responding that she was fine, she got down to her apology. Granted, she was angry, but nothing could excuse her for not telling him. She admitted to only thinking of her feelings and the baby's wellbeing and not considering his when she left or when she miscarried. She poured her heart out and went about her day, eating breakfast and attending to Grand Amour affairs.

After about three hours, she was still met with silence from her husband. Salma couldn't take it anymore and called Yasmine to vent. Salma hadn't expected her sister to charter a jet to make the seventy-minute journey to her. However, she should've known that's exactly what she would do. She'd been with her the whole day, but she had to get back home later tonight. She and Kojo had an early morning meeting with one of the sponsors of his charity.

"Yas, I told you I've eaten. I—"

"That salad wasn't food. If you can keep it down, you have to eat." She spread some garlic butter on some slices of bread and put them in the preheated oven. "This won't be your first or last fight with 'Sim. You were wrong, so go into your woman bag of tricks and do what needs to be done. But that baby mustn't suffer because your husband has you in time out."

Salma rolled her eyes. As she was about to speak, her phone rang. She sighed when the screen showed Qadir's name. Yasmine chuckled. A few minutes ago, Salma told her sister that she knew Qadir would be calling her soon because she sent the chef away for the day. Salma loved her brothers, but the break from their overbearing nature was a welcome reprieve, especially from Omar. However, Qasim's brothers were happy to fill that role. Qadir more than others.

"Yes, sir," she said, once she answered with the phone on speaker.

"I was about to turn the car around to come see about you if you didn't answer."

His low monotone voice, she was sure, matched his stoic expression. He lived ten minutes away and she put nothing past him.

"How can I help you, Q? Have you spoken to my sister-in-law today?" Salma smiled because talking about his fiancée was a sure-fire way to shut him down.

"I see you're trying to get under my skin, but you got the wrong Adesina, baby girl."

Salma grunted, soliciting a chuckle from him.

"You sent the chef away. Do you want me to bring you anything?"

"Your brother…"

"I can't do that, baby girl. And I don't want to know what's going on between the two of you. You guys need to fix it because he sounds as pitiful as you," Qadir said.

Salma's eyes misted as she looked up at Yasmine who shrugged. She sniffed.

"He's working though and will be home soon. Now, do you want anything to eat?"

"No, Yas is here…she's cooking." Salma placed the phone closer to Yasmine.

"Good evening, Q," Yasmine greeted.

"Hey Yas, the Ghanaian chap let you outta his sight?"

Yasmine cackled. "Really, Q? How many times will I tell you his name is Kojo?"

"I'm still trying to determine if he's good enough for you…"

Salma laughed. Once he and Mustafa started doing more business together and he visited Tweedes more, Qadir swore he was their surrogate big brother.

Yasmine shook her head. "After three years?"

"I don't know what to tell you. He's the Ghanian chap until I'm convinced."

Yasmine waved him off because just like Salma knew, he was going to do whatever he wanted.

For the next few minutes while Yasmine plated their dinner, the trio chatted and caught up. Soon after, Qadir hung up, but not before telling Yasmine she needed to get to the hangar on time and Salma to call him if she needed anything. Salma moved around the kitchen, helping her sister clean up.

Every now and then, Yasmine would pause to remind Salma of all the sweet memories she'd shared with Qasim. When she pointed at the hand mold on the mantle of the living room, Salma smiled at the memento. The spur of the moment plaster cast of their intertwined hands in grey and black was something she and Qasim had made on an evening out bowling. Salma rubbed her abdomen affectionately as tears welled up in her eyes.

"You're right. This baby is making me emotional."

"Nope, don't blame our baby. But go take a shower while I head home," Yasmine said, warmly as she hung a kitchen towel on the oven handle. "We don't want the big Q to have a conniption."

Salma wrapped Yasmine in a hug of gratitude. "Thank you so much for always coming to my rescue."

"I love you too, *aikhti alsaghira*, now go."

"Not you too..." Salma stifled a yawn as she walked her sister to the car. She watched until Yasmine was safely inside, then locked up and trudged upstairs. Her hand moved to her pocket for her cellphone, only to remember that her husband still hadn't called all day. A heavy mix of sadness and resignation draped around her as she decided to give him the space he needed and focus on her evening ahead – a hot shower, a good book, and hopefully, some much needed rest.

CHAPTER 17

The wheels of the SUV crunched over the gravel as it made its way down Qasim's driveway, just passing through the entrance gates. Oncoming headlights caused him to lift his eyes.

"Dan, who's that?" Qasim asked his driver.

It had been a tiring two days and he was running on only a few hours of sleep. He knew Salma probably wanted to kick his behind, but nothing went according to plan. The bank had other stipulations and he ended up staying longer than intended. Handling the unforeseen demands by day and being on conference calls with his management team by night to begin work on separating the original funds from the Brotherhood's gave him little time for anything else.

Exhaustion was too small of a word to describe his state of being. The little free time he did have was spent thinking about the changes that had happened and those to come with him and Salma. The what-ifs almost had him spiraling, and he didn't want that. In the middle of the night, he woke up in a cold sweat, so sought the Holy Spirit. He was reminded of how thankful he should be to the Restorer. He had his wife back and a baby on the way.

"I'm not sure, Sir," his driver answered.

"Flash at them to stop," Qasim instructed, then put the phone back to his ear. "Q, I gotta go."

He wasn't worried about the danger whoever it was posed, but was more concerned about why they were leaving his house with only his wife at home at almost eight in the evening. Despite her job, his wife was sometimes asocial, so the likelihood of her inviting someone over was small.

The security setup for him, his brothers, and his parents' home was top tier. Two guards were stationed at the gates wearing plain clothes, but trained in close-quarters combat and tactical responses. Access codes were updated every three months, and fingerprint authentication was needed to enter.

"Okay, call me in the morning. And fix whatever is going on with you and Salma. I'm used to her smart mouth and not this sad face she got going on."

"How are you telling me how to handle my wife, when—"

"Fix it." Qadir hung up the phone.

Qasim chuckled. He hadn't told anyone of their news. He wanted to do that with Salma. But since he was out of town, he needed Qadir to check on her. The first night, Qadir told him how Salma gave him a hard time. Qasim knew that if he got on the phone, she would be crying and want to talk, and he couldn't do that with her at that time.

When both cars came to a rolling stop next to each other, Qasim stepped out of the car. When he saw Yasmine emerge, he smiled, but it was quickly replaced by a frown.

If Salma is in that car, I'm not gonna be responsible for my actions.

With brisk steps, he closed the space between them. Yasmine closed her door and leaned against it.

"Calm down. I couldn't pry her away even if I wanted to." Yasmine pointed at him. "And I'm gonna tell her you doubted her."

The beat of his heart returned to normal, he smiled and raised his hand in surrender. Yasmine stretched out her arms and they shared a brief embrace. He knew Yasmine's role in her sister's life, so if she was here, his wife must have really been in distress. That realization made his chest constrict.

"Is she okay?"

Yasmine shrugged. "For someone who thinks her life and marriage are over, I'll say she's hanging in there."

They both laughed.

"I'd love to stay and chat, but I got to get to the hangar." Yasmine began to walk away. "Take it easy on her. We all know she can be a brat, but she's yours and she loves you."

Qasim waved her off. "She's my guiding Star. We're locked in, forever." He stepped forward. "You, on the other hand...call up KJ. He's just gonna have to be mad, but I can't let you leave this late."

Yasmine shook her head. "It's a one-hour flight. Besides, the pilot is waiting."

"I don't care, Sis. You can't leave this late...not by yourself." Qasim walked around to her rental and told the driver to turn the car around. "I already gotta deal with your sister. Please don't fight me. Your brothers, Kojo, and even Q will have my head if I allow you leave my house this late."

After a brief stare-down, Yasmine let out a deep sigh, but got back in the car. Now that he had her compliance, it was time to get him and his wife back on the same page.

Once Yasmine settled into one of the guest bedrooms, Qasim made his way to the master bedroom. He took a deep breath, then turned the knob to enter. His socked feet against the carpeted floor muffled the sound of his footsteps as he approached their king-sized bed. Warmth filled his heart at the sight of his wife on his side of the bed, dressed in one of his t-shirts. Her hair was sprawled across the pillow and her Kindle lay next to her. She must have fallen asleep while reading.

The Psalms meditation playlist she loved to sleep to seeped through the speakers above. Psalms being narrated while they slept was something she picked up during their time apart and took him some time to get used to. He normally slept in silence, but the narrator was so low that the sound wasn't too much of a disturbance.

He needed to touch her, but he also wanted to wash the day off. Salma stirred but didn't wake so he used that opportunity to head to the bathroom. Quickly discarding his clothes, he stepped into the shower, savoring the rush of hot water that cascaded from the multiple jets. The water pounded his skin, kneading away every little knot and tension from his body.

Closing his eyes, he said a prayer. He wanted to be the best father, husband, son, brother, and businessman he could be. He knew the weight of that charge wasn't something he could do in his own might. Lately, he'd developed a lingering fear of future consequences his family would face because of their dealings with the Brotherhood over the years. Fear that had seeped into his heart like poison.

The potential of damage he couldn't repair haunted him every day to the point where he felt suffocated. He had to be strong for his wife and unborn, but also had to make Salma aware so she wouldn't be in the dark. However, even this decision and how much to tell her weighed heavily on him because once spoken aloud, it could never be unsaid or taken back.

Qasim knew that the first time he asked for forgiveness years ago and accepted salvation, he was absolved of his past. But sometimes the shame of his past actions caused the enemy to trick him into believing he wasn't worthy of a new beginning.

Moments later, Qasim turned off the shower and stepped out. Wrapping a towel around his waist, he walked over to the sink to handle his nightly skin routine. "Oh, also Lord help me temper my lady's attitude. You made her this way so..." His lips turned up at his silliness.

"What are you doing here?"

As he left the closet dressed in his pajama bottoms, Salma's groggy voice startled him. He walked over to the bed and pulled back the covers to get in. He leaned against the headboard and Salma straddled him.

"Last time I checked, I lived here." He grabbed her waist and stared into her eyes. "Apart from that, the people that make me whole are here."

"Are you still mad at me? I've told you this in the multiple texts you *ignored*, ... I'm so sorry for keeping the pregnancy from you. Even though I thought at the time it was right, it was wrong. I'm sorry."

He wasn't going down the rabbit hole to explain why he didn't respond to her texts. He was too tired to argue with her. His deep inhale released a sad sigh. "I was hurt. I'll probably still feel disappointment and anger at myself for mishandling the TOB situation." He threaded his fingers in her hair. "But none of that is on you. You're giving me another precious gift." He nipped her earlobe with his teeth. "As fine as I know you gonna be with my kid growing inside you, I might decide to keep you barefoot and pregnant."

Salma swatted his shoulder and laughed. That sound always had his heart swelling with pride and satisfaction. Qasim smirked. But he was only half joking. However, they had plenty of time to figure that out.

Salma ran her hand up and down his bare chest. She bent slightly to brush her lips against his in a soft kiss. "I love you, honey."

Qasim pulled her closer as his lips engulfed hers in a never-ending kiss that felt like it could last for all eternity. Then he whispered tenderly in her ear, "Not more than me. I love you too, my Star."

Before their embrace intensified, Salma suddenly pulled away.

His brow rose and she pecked his lips a few times. "I'm sorry. Oh gosh! I forgot to check on Yas." She tried to lift off him, but he held her tighter.

"Relax, your sister is on the second floor. I can't believe you were going to let her—"

"She said she had something to do with KJ—"

"Yeah, she said so, but I shut that down. After she was settled, he sent me a text thanking me for forcing her to stay." He kissed her neck. "Now, can I get back to what I was doing?"

He took her low moan as his go ahead then flipped her on her back. He kissed her stomach a couple of times.

"Hey, my Starlet, it's Daddy." Qasim looked up at Salma who had tears pooled in her eyes. He winked at her and continued talking to his unborn. "You easing up on your mama? I promise we'll talk more in the morning. But now I need you to go to sleep because I'm about to do some very nasty but godly things to your mama."

Salma gasped. "'Sim, don't talk to my baby like that."

"What? I need Starlet to know that even when she or he gets here, this is the time we need no interruptions."

Salma placed her hand over her eyes and chuckled. Qasim proceeded to push her nightshirt out of the way and plant kisses along her body. Her pants and moans gave him the added encouragement he needed to do exactly what he told his baby he would.

~

"Qasim Adesina, will you move out of the way?"

Qasim looked over his shoulder to see his mother with a bowl of peppersoup approaching the island in the kitchen. Salma, who stood in between his legs with her hands on his chest, peered over him and let out a sigh.

"Ooh, thank you so much, ma," Salma said, slightly pushing him out of the way.

"You're welcome, my dear. This should be soothing. I made sure there wasn't too much pepper in it."

Salma sat on the barstool and said a quick prayer before lifting some to her mouth. Qasim stared at her with a smile on his face. It had been three weeks since they made up and they'd been wrapped in their cocoon. Their routine was back on track. He got a kick out of pampering her every morning before he left for work, and loved coming home to meet her relaxed and waiting for him. There were some days that they both had to work late, but they tried to eat dinner together every evening.

His wife had canceled the idea of getting a dedicated workspace out of the house until sometime down the line. Despite her decision, he still went ahead and got an office designed for her in his Sim & Co building, about a fifteen-minute drive from his office.

"So, you're just going to keep moaning without offering me some?" Qasim teased.

Salma smiled up at him and he kissed her forehead. He was glad she was feeling better. She had been fine for the most part. That was the reason they were able to travel to Accra last weekend to hang out with Yasmine and Kojo for one of his artist's listening party.

Qasim's parents got back from London two days ago and invited them over for midweek dinner. His mother always made sure there were also some Moroccan foods Salma was familiar with. Halfway through the meal, she felt queasy. Qasim was on her heels when she darted to the guest bathroom. Salma only heaved for a few minutes before they returned to the table to meet curious eyes. After breaking the news of their pregnancy, Wednesday night dinner turned into a mini celebration.

Now dinner was done, and his mother, convinced Salma didn't have enough to eat, had the chef make some pepper soup.

"Don't you have something else you should be doing? Stop harassing my daughter," his mother said from the opposite side of the kitchen.

"Lemme go meet with Chief and Q in the study."

"Yeah, go before Q accuses me of being a big baby and I will have to fight him."

Qasim chuckled. "Not with my baby in you, you won't." His eyes landed on the soup. The reddish-brown liquid was filled with assorted meats. "Gimme some."

Salma held a spoonful of soup with some meat in it and lifted it to his mouth. Accepting the delicacy, he kissed her lips, and kissed his mother's forehead before he scurried out of the kitchen.

"Can they do this? This was not the deal!"

Qadir's voice reverberated through the room like a clap of thunder. Qasim rushed into the room, where he found his father sitting in a plush recliner and Qadir seething by the bookcase.

"*Kini n lọ lọwọ?* What's going on?" Qasim asked.

The air crackled with tension, a stark contrast from the laughter and banter that had filled the dining room moments ago. They had talked about church events, politics, and family plans for Christmas and the new addition, but now it felt like they were in a completely different world. As Qasim waited silently, his stomach soured as various worst-case scenarios played out in his head.

Qadir's eyes bored into his brother's with a sense of desperation, only to shift swiftly over to their father in search of approval to speak.

"Qasim, *wá joko nibi.* Come and sit down," his father commanded sharply.

Qasim dug his hands into his pockets, unmoving, and countered with a furrowed brow. "Pops, from the looks of things, whatever you have to say won't be made better by sitting. Q, *kini?*"

His father shifted closer to the edge of his chair and leaned forward intently towards him. "Alhaji Ribadu decided that the contract we have cannot expire at this time...

"What?! Explain how someone who just stepped into this role can change what has been in place for so long!" Qasim fumed. "How is that even possible?"

"'Sim, calm down!"

Rage bubbled up inside him as he shot back, "Don't tell me to calm down! You let me walk into this blind! Did you know something like this could happen?"

"I can't believe you'd ask me that," Qadir seethed.

"Why? You've kept something from me before..."

"*Ṣe o ya were*? You're outta line." A harshness crept into his voice as he continued, "I've allowed you to put this on me for years. I'm your big brother and I could handle it...but this ends today. On some level, you knew something was up...your fancy education abroad and all the luxuries you enjoyed before you joined the FC did not come from a farm! Just because you've turned over a new leaf doesn't mean the consequences go away—"

"I'm not naïve, but at the same time, I asked you if we were legit. You've been working with Pops since day one. *Mo beere lọwọ rẹ!* I asked you!"

"What? You were wallowing in self-pity from losing your career, and we were at war with the Aminus. You think I was going to let you keep being reckless and remain in London? No, I did what I had to do and brought you home by giving you the job!" Qadir bellowed. "When you decided you wanted to sever ties with TOB, I supported every move you wanted to make. I'm not to blame you allowed your anger with me, lead you to tamper with their accounts prematurely. But you got your wife back. So, get over it!"

Qasim cringed at his brother's words, knowing he was taking it all out on him even though he had no real part to play in this present mess. Qadir was right. He had been drowning himself in alcohol, neglecting security protocol, and staying late in clubs after his career ended – a period of self-pity where he'd lost all hope. But his brother gave him a chance to start anew, offering him a chance to work with the family and that reignited his purpose in life.

"Enough!" their father thundered, his voice echoing around the room. His brows furrowed in rage, daring them to disobey him. "That piece of trash decided he didn't want to go through the hassle of finding another route for their money. Something they should've done since this was coming."

They were no longer in the organization's fold, but that

didn't mean that their dad didn't have a pulse on what was going on. Some of the members were still his friends.

"What can we do now that we couldn't have done years ago?" Qasim asked desperately. He had a wife and child on the way, and he could not continue living a life of sin and praying at night for redemption. He just couldn't.

"I don't know, son," his father replied. "For now, we act accordingly until I figure something out."

Qasim turned to his brother with guilt in his heart. "Q, my bad." Then he faced his father. "I can't do it, Pops. I got a family and—"

"Your mother and I raised all of you while I was still a member. Don't you think I can protect the family?"

"The thing is... this is *my* family. I don't want us to ride in bullet-proof cars because we *have* to, but because we *choose* to."

"Your name is Adesina. You're my son. We'll always have to move around accordingly. Legit or not!" his father seethed.

Qasim scoffed.

Qadir walked up to him and placed a hand on his shoulder. "'Sim, give me a week before you make a final decision. One week." His gaze was steady and sincere. "We're family – blood and we'll forever be stronger together."

No one had to tell him whose son he was or whose blood ran through his veins. He was reminded every day he was the son of Chief Qavi Adesina. He'd been paying for the sins of his father even before he'd committed his own.

CHAPTER 18

I miss his smile and I want it back.

Three days later, Salma rode the elevator down to the ground floor. Stepping into the kitchen, she gave the house-keeper last-minute instructions. She made her way to the front of the house and opened the door. She saw Daniel putting the last piece of luggage in the car. Since they would be gone only for a few days, Jide would stay behind. Qasim was grumpy that they were leaving in the first place, but he had no say in the matter. This was her show.

The picture of him storming into the kitchen and grabbing her hand for them to leave his parents' house was etched in her memory. He was literally shaking with rage. She tried asking what was wrong and he begged her to give him space. That night, she catered to him like he had done her so many times. She couldn't understand why her Superman was so dejected as she gave him a massage and facial. Since he refused to speak, she put on the Christian R&B playlist she had compiled and allowed the music to float through the room. She then led him to the shower, and soon after, they had said their prayers and were in bed.

Sometime during the night, she heard him praying. Enveloping him in her arms, he must have felt the safe space she was trying to provide because he confided in her. Not about the specifics of every detail, but their talk ended with him telling her about the Brotherhood and the possibility of them relocating to Canada. She'd follow him anywhere, but she also knew he would never be happy. She wasn't sure if his stance was because of her, but she had to make him see reason. He had been walking around with a scowl on his face and she was tired of it.

"Honey, what are you doing?" Salma said, walking into Qasim's home office.

He lifted his eyes to her and the smile he gave didn't reach his eyes. "Working. Didn't I tell you we had to work on relocating?"

Salma took in a breath at his unusually brazen tone. "If we didn't love you, Starlet and I would kick your behind for talking to us like that."

He sighed. "Come here."

"No."

"Star baby, come on…," His voice was low and slow, delivering the warning intended.

She folded her arms and leaned on the door frame in defiance. "No."

Qasim leaned back in his chair and smiled at her challenge. "Salma Adesina, if I have to come get you, that sexy shorts set you have on will be ruined."

Salma rolled her eyes. The last time she refused his summons, he chased her around their kitchen until he caught her. Then he tickled her so much she peed on herself. Qasim joked about it all day until she threatened to stop talking to him. The thought of the floral print ZF shorts set she had on being messed up propelled her legs forward.

Qasim smirked and swiveled his chair so she was standing between his legs. He reached up and placed his hands around her waist and pulled her onto his lap.

Qasim slid his index finger along the V-shaped cut of the tank top she wore under her blazer. "I'm sorry, baby," he said, cradling

the back of her neck with one hand as he brought her close for a
kiss.

"'Sim, we're going to be late. Let's go."

"With all I told you, is this the right time to travel?"

She put her hands on either side of his face. "Yes. From what
you said, you promised Q a week. While you give him that, let me
spoil you. You do so much for me."

He sighed and met her gaze. "It's my job."

"That doesn't mean I can't express gratitude, reciprocate, or
reward you. It's the least I can do. So come on, let's go."

He raised his brow. "I'm the planner in this relationship, so do
I have to be concerned about where we are going?"

Salma shook her head. "Have you forgotten my day job?"

Qasim laughed. "No, and that's why you dislike doing it when
you don't have to."

"Well, I have to, and I want to. Come on, Qasim."

He cocked his head at her. "You're calling me Qasim...okay,
let's go. I sense your attitude."

"Good."

Qasim kissed her lips then her stomach before lifting her to
her feet. She was beginning her second trimester, and her spells of
nausea were now nonexistent.

~

While there were things money couldn't do, the
access and power it could provide wasn't some-
thing Salma thought of often, but at this moment she appreciated
it. Two days ago, she and her husband boarded a chartered jet to
Windhoek, Namibia. Once they were in the air, she sent Qadir a
text to let them know he had the time he requested. He'd left for
the US the day after the argument with Qasim.

She'd never appreciated her brother-in-law more than when
he showed the faith he had in her to use her influence and power
for the family's benefit. All he wanted was time. Salma was happy

to give it to him, relax her husband's nerves, and do her best to provide him with another perspective all at the same time.

After their seven-hour flight, they arrived at the Desert Quiver Camp. While there were plenty of activities to choose from, such as helicopter rides over the Namib desert, guided excursions to explore the ancient desert of Sossusvlei and its dunes, and nature drives, Salma did not book their trip for any of those things. She booked it so they could enjoy an unspoiled view of the Milky Way.

Although stargazing used to be her thing, Qasim had become equally or more passionate about it. The best part about everything was that in the absence of Wi-Fi, they were completely unplugged from their lives. So, after spending the last two days sleeping in, playing games, swimming in the exquisite pool or just talking in their luxury tent, they were spending their last night on a star bed.

Salma had watched a documentary about sleeping out under the African sky and wanted to try it with Qasim. On the rooftop of the lodge, there was a large bed with a variety of decorative pillows. To their side were their drinks. The only sounds that could be heard were the call of the creatures. She had wanted them to fall asleep out here then wake up to a beautiful sunrise. She had it all planned out in her head. However, while they were having dinner earlier, along with the cricket sounds, the whooping of hyenas and gentle rumbling of elephants, they heard the roar of a lion.

Qasim's eyes bugged at the sound. "Star baby, I see what you trying to do. And I adore you for it, but ain't no way we're sleeping out here."

She'd pouted but knew he was right. Although the staff tried to convince them that these animals were at a safe, far distance, last she checked, lions had some speed to them.

Currently, dinner was done, and they were having dessert. The stars were out in full force, twinkling and dancing in the night sky. While they ate, they looked up and discussed the

constellations they could see in the sky, their conversation punctu-
ated by the occasional cosmic flash from a shooting star. The
wonders of God's creations were simply beyond comprehension.

Qasim lifted a spoonful of malva pudding to her lips which
she accepted. Salma giggled at the memory from earlier.

"What's so funny?"

His warm breath tickled her neck, causing her to shudder
slightly at the sensation. Salma replied to his question, and they
shared a chuckle. He had situated himself behind her and leaned
against the pillows. She sat with her back to his chest while they
gazed at the stars twinkling in the night sky. His circular
motions over her stomach were soothing and calming. She
breathed deeply, allowing the feeling of joy to ripple through her
body.

"What's wrong, baby? I could feel your nervous energy all
through dinner," Qasim said.

"Are you happy?"

He thought for a moment before replying, "You know happiness is a function of circumstance...so yes, here with you and our
growing Starlet, away from the world, I'm happy. What I want is
genuine joy." A pause followed as they both basked in the rhythm
of their beating hearts before he continued speaking, "Because
pretty soon our circumstances will change. We'll be living in a
new city, new opportunities..."

"What makes you so sure your brother and father won't come
up with a solution?"

"One they couldn't come up with years ago?"

"But things change, honey. Have a little faith."

"How are you team my father suddenly? Did he say anything
to you?"

"No, he didn't. And I'm team you! Detaching yourself from
your family won't bring you joy. You guys are like a well-oiled
machine, each one of you inspiring the other with life and energy.
Your bond is so enviable, like my family. Sure, you bicker and
argue but when it comes down to it, even knucklehead Qamar

knows what's up. The Brotherhood found me in New York; why do you think they can't find us in Canada?"

"They can but I'll no longer have anything to do with the family business, so whatever beef they have, they take up with Q and Chief."

"You are your brother's keeper, honey. There's no way you'll leave Q to handle that alone. Especially knowing what you know now."

"So, you're saying I should continue to sin and ask forgiveness at night?" He sighed. "Baby, despite what we tell ourselves, Jesus's love is in His judgment, just as His judgment is in His love. I'm not trying to keep taking His grace for granted."

Salma rolled her eyes. "Don't put words in my mouth. That's not what I'm saying. I'm saying instead of running, help Q figure out a solution. You need your family, and they need you. Besides, I'm beginning to like amala. And I'll never be able to make it, so I need my mother-in-law."

Qasim threw his head back and cackled. Amala, known for its dark brown color, was a swallow food specific to the Yoruba people. The first day she saw the food that was eaten with three different colored soups on top of it, she frowned. However, the delicacy was growing on her.

"Honey, whether we leave or stay, we are still Adesinas. That means that someone who may not be associated with the Brotherhood could seek revenge for something that was done to them in the past. Can anything truly protect us in a foreign land?"

Salma decided to leave the conversation there. She knew her words would settle with her husband. She prayed that some of them would get through to him as well.

～

"Oh my gosh Zay, she is so stinking cute!"

Salma gushed at her new niece on the phone screen. Removing her fruit bowl from the fridge, she set it on the island

and went in search of a fork. She and Qasim had finished dinner not too long ago, but she wanted a snack.

Jamila DuBois-Arazi was a replica of Salma's big brother and had her mother's auburn curls. At two weeks old, she was perfect. She and Qasim had been on the jet back to Nigeria when Zaina went into labor. However, because their phones were still off, they didn't get the notifications until they were in the truck on the way home.

Just like he was with his wife, Mustafa was ultra protective when it came to his daughter. When Salma called the first time, Zaina's phone was off, so she called her brother. Big mistake. He rushed her off the phone claiming his wife and daughter were resting. He did make sure to send her pictures. However, Salma wanted to see her niece on video.

At that time, Salma accepted his excuse, but when Yasmine complained about not being able to speak to Zaina after three days as well, they both got on a call and threatened him with their physical presence. Mustafa always fussed that they hoarded his wife, so they knew that would do it, and it did.

"Say thank you, auntie," Zaina said, in a baby voice.

Zaina covered the breast the baby had been feeding on and placed her on the other one. Before her eyes returned to the screen, Salma picked up one of the oranges. She was resisting the urge to put a little red pepper on it. Qasim, who was in his office on a call, would have a fit if he came out and saw her. She knew it sounded nasty, but it tasted good to her.

Salma peered in closer and saw Zaina wince. "How do you feel?"

"Still a little sore," she whispered.

Salma frowned. "Why are you whispering?"

"Because if your brother hears that, he will start doing a whole lot."

Salma laughed. Zaina loved Mustafa's possessiveness until she wanted to do whatever she wanted to do, and he shut it down.

Salma always told her she couldn't have it both ways with an Arab.

"If you're feeling really bad Zay, I'll tell him myself."

"No! I'll be fine. I just had a baby. I'm supposed to be sore. He and my mother are going to drive me crazy."

Salma laughed again, but warned that she would check in on her in a couple of days.

"How is 'Sim?"

Salma chewed on an apple slice and waved her fork in the air. "Still mad I delayed our relocation by a week. But he'll be all right…"

Salma had been praying hard for Qadir or Chief to come up with a plan. She wanted the luxury of traveling whenever she wanted, not the forced relocation her husband was bent on. She didn't want him engaged in illegal activity either. She wanted more than anything for his pride in himself to outweigh his self-loathing. But instead, worry, regret and shame were what laced his features lately. Since they got back from Namibia, she had been praying Psalm 59 consistently, morning and night. Though she couldn't recite the whole Psalm by heart, verse one had become second nature while she went about her daily activities.

"Cut him some slack…"

Since the illegal past of her husband's family was something she kept to herself, she grunted and changed the topic. Moments later, Salma watched as Mustafa walked into the nursery. After they greeted one another, he placed a baby towel on his shoulder and picked the baby up to burp.

Soon after, Qasim joined her in the kitchen. He paused when he saw what she was eating. Picking up a fork, he took a mango slice. He nodded, satisfied she hadn't put pepper on it. He kissed her forehead before peering into the phone. Both couples talked for a few more minutes. As Salma disconnected the phone, the doorbell rang. Qasim looked at the security app on his phone and grunted.

"It's Chief." Pausing, he cupped her face. "You good?"

Salma nodded. Qasim rubbed her stomach, then kissed it, and brushed his lips against hers before leaving the kitchen. Salma finished off her fruit and washed the bowl. The chef had the kitchen spotless before he left, and Salma always wanted him to meet it the same way in the morning when he arrived. Taking a bottle of water, with her phone in her pocket, she put her Kindle under her arm and turned out the lights. As she made her way down the hallway, she met Qasim and his father, heading to his office.

"Good evening, Sir."

"*Iyawo wa*, how are you, my dear?"

Salma smiled at the name he called her. In two and a half months, she'd gone from Salma to Qasim's wife to *iyawo wa* which she was told meant *our wife* in Yoruba.

"I'm fine, Sir."

"And my legacy?"

"He's doing well." Salma rubbed her stomach.

At their last doctor's appointment, they found out that they were having a boy and Chief had been calling her unborn child his legacy since then. His excitement for his first grandchild was so immense that he celebrated the news by killing a goat—he had it slaughtered and butchered and sent chunks of meat to his closest friends. Salma couldn't help but dread what antics would follow when her little one actually arrived.

After he suggested yet again that she pause her job now so "she could rest," she gave him a strained smile and bid him good-night. She headed for the elevator to her bedroom, praying her father-in-law came with good news.

Salma felt like time was standing still as she glanced at the clock for what seemed like the zillionth time. She had been in her room for almost two hours, trying to distract herself with anything she could find, from taking a shower to scrolling through Instagram.

When Qadir arrived shortly after Chief, she was sure the meeting would wrap up soon, but she'd been wrong. Now, all she could do was wait and wonder. Her anxiety was at an all-time high. Salma gave up trying to silence her curiosity. She was going to stand by the landing in case she could hear anything.

As she reached for her robe, she heard the door opening. Qasim entered the room. His expression – unusually stoic – caused her heart to plummet into her stomach. Salma froze in place as Qasim sauntered over to her. With a passionate kiss, he enveloped her body with warmth and tenderness, but she couldn't tell if this was an "I need you" kiss or a "celebration" kiss as his tongue explored her mouth. The intensity of their embrace made it difficult for her to focus on deciphering his true motives.

Moments later, he grabbed her hand and pulled her to the bed. Sitting, he placed her on his lap. After leaning in the crook of her neck for a few minutes, he lifted his head and locked eyes with her. "Thank you, baby, for having faith even when I didn't."

"So, we're staying?"

"Yes. All these years, my dad refused to let anyone buy into the farm. I'm so blown away by what he did."

For the next several minutes, Qasim went on to tell her about the Brotherhood's desire to expand abroad. They couldn't because most of the places they wanted to enter were controlled by foreign cartels. One of these was La Mano Nera, or The Black Hand, in Italy. One of the former leaders of La Mano Nera was their grandfather's old friend from his days as a customs officer. Then, he saw the potential in the farm and wanted to buy in, but was denied. Now, years later, the same cartel was interested in Ilẹ Oloro's research and development, specifically precision agriculture in wineries.

Since the days of Qasim's great-grandfather, the family had sworn that there would be no foreign investors or partners. However, Qadir was able to broker a deal where he gave the legitimate side of La Mano Nera a ten percent buy-in, in exchange for protection, and for them to give the Brotherhood an audience for their proposal.

Salma frowned. "So, in essence the cartel bought the family's freedom from the Brotherhood in exchange for ten percent of the business?"

"A part of the business, yes. We'll be completely legit, except that we've gone against the wishes of our great-grandfather."

Salma detected a hint of regret. However, their great-grandfather's son got them into this, so he would be okay getting them out of it. Qasim explained why La Mano Nera wanted access to the research and development from Nigeria. The new leader wasn't a full-blooded Italian. His interest in the farm had been inherited from his own grandfather – their grandfather's friend. He wanted to reconnect with his ancestral heritage, and he was seeking to prove himself to the others in the organization by bringing in a hefty sum of profit from Nigeria, a land he'd admired for ages.

"And your dad is now okay with this?"

Qasim shrugged. "Yes. According to him, God has blessed him enough that he'll soon see his legacy. And he can't allow him to grow up outside of the family because of past mistakes."

"And Q is sure these folks are legit?"

"He brought over all the paperwork. I will go through every line myself." He kissed her neck. "But I can now breathe, baby."

"So can I. I'm so glad everything is over."

Qasim lay down in the bed and tucked her under his arm. They remained in palpable silence for a minute before he kissed her again. "I told you, you were my guiding star."

"I love you, honey," she said.

"Not more than me. I love you, my Star."

Salma closed her eyes and the past seven months played at a speedy rate inside her head. She absently traced the tattoo of her name on her husband's chest, grateful for another chance to fulfill the vows she made five years ago.

THE END

EPILOGUE

Three months later...

Qasim's eyes shifted from beneath the hood of his sweatshirt to Salma's restless legs. She folded her arms across her swollen breasts, and her gaze burned with fierce fury. The pilot had just announced that they were prepared for takeoff. Qasim laid his laptop down in the vacant seat beside him. The one his stubborn wife should be occupying, but, in her defiance, she decided to sit on the opposite side of the aircraft.

He knew her well enough to know that once the plane was airborne, she was going to make a run for it. Qasim looked toward the back room and made a mental calculation of how many strides he'd need to get to her. He planned to take full advantage of the two things that were working in his favor – at seven months pregnant, she was a lot slower, and he would always...always be faster.

Qasim continued to scroll idly through his phone until he felt her eyes on him. Looking up, he winked, only to be met with an eye roll. He sighed. This babymoon to Mauritius was supposed to get him out of the doghouse. But if Salma thought he would allow her frosty attitude to ruin their week away, she had another thing coming. He'd rather turn the plane around so she could sulk in one of the numerous rooms in their home.

The last twelve weeks, things had been great for them. They weren't void of disagreements or fights, but their bond was stronger than ever. Back when they first got together, he used to joke about her bratty behavior, but the reality of it was he lived to give her what her heart desired. Saying yes to his wife gave him joy. However, over the last couple of months, Salma has changed in certain ways...dare he say matured. Except for times like now when she was being stubborn for no reason.

Qasim jolted to his feet when he heard the click of his wife's seatbelt echo through the cabin. He'd been so lost in his reverie that he missed the pilot's announcement that they were safely in the sky. He held up a finger to stall the hostess who was coming his way before bounding down the aisle. In a few quick strides, he jammed his foot in the bedroom door, barely stopping it from closing.

Salma's eyes narrowed. "What Qasim? Don't you have a hidden camera in here or something? You can monitor me from out there."

Qasim shrugged, a smirk playing on his lips. "No, baby, you're with me, so no need."

"Oh, you think this is funny?" She tossed her duffle bag on the bed.

He shifted his feet and cleared his throat. "No, I don't. I think you're taking this to the extreme. But funny...no."

Salma rubbed her swollen stomach and dug into her bag, flinging one of his sweat suits on the bed. He was slowly losing his loungewear to her, but he wasn't complaining. In admiration, he watched her replace her dress with more comfortable clothing. When she was done, she twisted her hair into a bun, all the while murmuring some Arabic words. He knew she was probably cussing him out, but he would never apologize for doing everything he could to keep her safe. As she prepared to get into the bed, he hooked his hand around her waist. She resisted for a few moments before melting into him.

Qasim caressed her stomach before planting a kiss in the crook of her neck. Lifting her face with his index finger, he looked into her eyes. "If I had told you I had someone in Tweedes keeping an eye on you, would you have let him stay?"

She pouted and he couldn't resist stealing another kiss. This time her lips.

"No, but—"

"Ain't no buts, baby." He walked them to the bed. He sat and pulled her down to his lap. "There was no way I was going to walk this earth without having you covered by someone since I couldn't be there."

A week ago, Paul walked into Qasim's office when Salma was there to have lunch with him. The minutes that followed were not pretty. She lost her temper and only the threat of her having to answer to him if she stressed out the baby was able to calm her down.

"He was a good worker, but gosh...all this time Paul was working for you?" She shook her head. "Is his name even Paul?"

"Yes, baby. If you'd have let me explai—"

"Don't try to turn this around on me. I was easy on you."

Qasim laughed. "If by easy, you mean a week of silent treatment, then insisting my penance be taking you on this trip that I was against, then I guess you could say that."

Salma chuckled and shook her head.

The Adesina clan was fresh off a Christmas trip to South Africa – one Salma and his mother planned. His wife and his mother had become closer in the last couple of months. Something he was grateful for as it made his life easier. After Christmas, while the rest of the family headed back to Ibadan, the couple took a detour to Tweede Kans Cove for New Year's. While there, he told her of the house he bought them in Mauritius. His first time ever going to the island nation that served as a tax haven was when he was handling the Brotherhood's funds.

Salma was insistent on visiting, but he was against it. Even though his wife had been having an easy pregnancy, he didn't want to push it after all the traveling they had just done. Her doctor okayed it, but he was still skeptical. Salma had come around and they'd settled back into their routine. The baby nursery was done, and they were excited about their son's arrival.

Everything was good until Paul, who couldn't follow instructions, waltzed his way into Qasim's office last week. His not following the specific order of resuming as Shola's security detail in America was the reason they were now flying thirteen hours to their home in Mauritius.

"I've been kinda harsh, huh?" Salma asked.

"You think?"

"I'm sorry."

"And I'm sorry for not telling you about Paul since we've been back together." He kissed her lips. "But baby, he was the last thing on my mind."

She shrugged. "I'm getting my babymoon, so he did serve a greater purpose."

Qasim laughed and Salma joined in.

"We good now?"

"I guess?"

He scoffed. "Guess? Star, we're not out of Nigerian airspace yet. I'll turn this plane around..."

She rolled her eyes. "Okay, okay, we're good. I guess I should my man, my man, my man." She mimicked the TikTok trend where women bragged about their men. The first day she did it was when she got back home, and he had put all the furniture in the nursery together.

"You want something to eat before your nap?" he asked.

"I asked for Jollof rice and goat meat. Can you ask them to warm it up for me? With my fruit bowl."

Qasim stood and helped her into the bed. He kissed her forehead before handing over her Kindle. "Sure, hang tight." As he approached the door, Salma called out to him. He turned to face her.

"Thanks, honey. I love you. I know I give you a hard time, but I'm so grateful for you."

"Not more than me. I love you back, my Star." He waggled his brows. "Besides, I got the remedy for your crazy so…"

She shook her head. "Must you always be so nasty?"

He laughed and reached for the doorknob when Salma spoke again. "Honey, I know how I can forgive you completely."

He furrowed his brow. "Really? I thought you already did."

"Yeah, but I mean total clean slate…"

Qasim leaned against the doorframe and folded his arms across his chest. He knew exactly what she was about to say, and he had his "No" ready.

"If you tell me about the woman that Omar has been—"

"No."

"I didn't even finish," she whined.

"And the answer will still be no. Leave that man's business alone. When he's ready and if there's anything to tell, he will."

Salma rolled her eyes and picked up the remote to adjust the blinds and picked up her Kindle.

Qasim snickered, closed the door, and made his way to the front of the plane in search of the staff. Over the past several weeks, his relationship with Omar had been on the mend. Right before the holidays, his friend visited them in Ibadan. Omar had been to the house before, but this time he was there as his brother-in-law. Things were finally falling into place.

The second phase of the agritourism project was scheduled to kick off in six months. Business with the farm was running smoothly. His parents were healthy and so were his brothers. Most importantly, his wife and unborn son were with him. The La Mano Nera representative visited the farm before the holidays to get the initial requirements ironed out. The Brotherhood was no longer a factor for the Adesinas. Chief informed him and Qadir that the cartel was still reviewing the Brotherhood's proposal to do business in their territory. None of that concerned Qasim as their part of the deal was done.

Almost a year ago, he had asked God to restore what had been broken in his life and God did him one better. He gave him another chance to fulfill his vows.

GLOSSARY

<u>French/Arabic/Yoruba Translations</u>

Although Tweede Kans Cove is a fictional town, it is located in Morocco. Therefore, the culture of Morocco is threaded in the story. Moroccans speak Arabic and French mainly. However, with foreign influences, English is also spoken to some extent. The Adesinas are from the Yoruba ethnic group in Nigeria where the language is also Yoruba.

Below are translations (done to the best of my ability) of the languages I used in the story. I have this in the order in which they appear.

O tọ: You're right (Yoruba)

Ti gba: Agreed (Yoruba)

O fẹ sọ fun baba rẹ? You want me to tell your father? (Yoruba)

Bonjour, grand-mère: good morning, grandma (French)

Mon enfant, tu es en retard: You're late, my child (French)

"*Ẹ kú ìrọlẹ*: good evening (Yoruba. Normally used for early evening)

Iya mi: My mother (Yoruba)

Omo mi: My child (Yoruba)

Gele: headwrap (Yoruba)

Parle-moi, mon enfant: Talk to me, my child (French)

Dans cette vie ou dans la suivante, mon âme te trouvera toujours: In this life or the next, my soul will always find you. (French)

aikhti alsaghira: little sister (Arabic)

lam tukhbirih biedu: You haven't told him (Arabic)

Ẹni to bá ta ará ilé rẹ ni ọpọ̀, kò lè rí irú ẹni bẹẹ ra ni ọ̀wọ́n: One who sells his family for a measly amount, won't ever buy them for good value (Yoruba)

Ẹ kale: good evening (Yoruba. Used for late evening)

Kini n lọ lọwọ: What's going on (Yoruba)

wá joko nibi: Come sit here. (Yoruba)

Kini: What? (Yoruba)

Ṣe o ya were?: Are you mad? (Yoruba)

Mo beere lọwọ rẹ!: I asked you (Yoruba)

FINAL NOTE

Thank you for reading Salma & Qasim's story. Please consider leaving a review on the platform you bought the book from. I appreciate honest feedback. They really go a long way. The number of reviews a book receives improves how well it does in the algorithm.

If you liked this story, I trust you might like some of my other titles. But before we get to those, never miss a sale, new release announcements, or freebies. You can ensure that by joining my mailing list. I'd love to stay connected.

Next up in the DuBois-Arazi family is Omar DuBois-Arazi. Click here to preorder here.